A WINDOW TO LOVE

ANNETTE MORI

A Window to Love

Annette Mori

Affinity
Rainbow Publications

2019

A Window to Love
© 2019 by Annette Mori

Affinity E-Book Press NZ LTD
Canterbury, New Zealand

1st Edition

ISBN: 978-1-98-858813-1

Editor: CK King
Proof Editor: Alexis Smith
Cover Design: Irish Dragon Design
Production Design: Affinity Publication Services

ACKNOWLEDGMENTS

A huge thank you to all of my beta readers: Gail Dodge, Ali Spooner, Carrie Camp, Ameliah Faith, Dana Holmes, Elle Hyden, and Danna Micoletti, who made great suggestions to improve the initial draft. Thanks to KC Luck for her assistance with the blurb. Of course, once again, I have to acknowledge Erin O'Reilly, who is a constant support and encouragement to me. I am honored to call her a friend and to have her support me in my journey.

I would also like to express my gratitude to Affinity Rainbow Publications and the wonderful trio (JM Dragon, Erin O'Reilly, and Nancy Kaufman) who continue to provide feedback to tighten up manuscripts that need assistance and publish my unconventional work. My other family members who are also very supportive include my nephew, Aaron, and his wife, Chelsea, my older sister, and my father who struggles to read my books with one eye.

I always enjoy working with the beta editor, Nancy Kaufman, who is so skilled at finding plot holes. Thanks to CK King for her magic as the final editor. She is a joy to work with. I wrote this book during a dark time in my life and she helped me tease out some of the emotions to make the final version more worthy of reading. Inevitably, there are those pesky final errors that slip through, and I am thankful for the final proof editor, Alexis Smith, who catches those before the book goes to print. Thanks to Nancy Kaufman for the final cover. Nancy is also a promoter extraordinaire.

A huge thanks to all the other readers and fellow writers who have sent personal e-mails, written reviews, and posted nice things on Facebook (you know who you are). The Affinity authors are an especially supportive group and often share posts or send words of encouragement. Finally, my wife, Jody, continues her support even when it interferes with our time together on the weekends.

Dedication

To all those individuals who have endured major changes in their lives and come out the other side, when that window opened for them like it did for me.

As always, to my beautiful wife who continues to support me through it all.

TABLE OF CONTENTS

CHAPTER ONE

Mandie Carter jogged back to her office across from the main hospital. She hoped to send an email to the new union representative before her meeting with the CEO. The flame that needed dousing was small but required her special brand of fire extinguisher. The union rep kept inviting himself to department staff meetings, unannounced, and irritating the new CEO. Arlene had said enough was enough and expected Mandie to take care of it.

The morning was already filling up. She had only a sliver of time before the last-minute meeting. When the hospital's executive secretary had asked Mandie to meet with Arlene during the lunch hour, she'd said, "Of course." Arlene's schedule was always tight, as busy as Mandie's own, but she would push things around to accommodate her.

Meeting location is in your office. Arlene will be over in 5 minutes.

Mandie crinkled her forehead at the confusing text message. Normally, she had to shuttle herself to the main building when she met with Arlene. She slid into her office chair and began furiously typing.

She reminded the union rep of a clause in the contract which required him to give notice whenever he planned on visiting the hospital. His response was almost instantaneous.

> *I'll be at the plant engineering staff meeting today.*

Time to step up the response. Mandie copied the relevant contract clause, and highlighted the section where management had to agree to a visit for any reason other than the investigation of grievances.

> *There is no ongoing investigation, and the hospital does not agree to the disruption of a rep attending a staff meeting uninvited.*

The bell on the outside door tinkled. As Mandie was finishing her terse response, she wondered where her staff had gone. Although it was lunch time, they normally informed her when they left the office so she could cover and listen for the bell. She glanced at the bottom, right-hand corner of her computer and noted the time. Noon. It was probably Arlene.

She popped up and went to the door. Both Arlene and Liana, the Chief Nursing Officer, were in the waiting area. Tiny alarm bells were ringing in Mandie's head.

"I'll be right there. I need to finish the email to that union rep who's giving us fits."

"We'll wait in the conference room for you," Arlene said.

Liana had a strained look on her face. More alarm bells. Mandie wondered if the rep had also wreaked havoc on the nursing units. She sighed. *Where is my staff? The office feels like a tomb.*

At first, the new union rep had seemed reasonable, easy to work with. They had combined forces to resolve a sensitive situation in the business office, and she believed he would be a partner to face the difficult issues that often presented themselves in the workforce. *Wolf in sheep's clothing.* He had visited the hospital more in the last two weeks than the previous rep had in a year. Mandie had passed it off as his need to connect with the employees he represented. Now she wasn't so sure.

Finishing the last line of the email, she hit *Send.* She walked into the conference room eager, but at the same time dreading to learn the nature of the unexpected meeting. Arlene's hands were clasped in front of her, and she wore a grim expression. Liana wouldn't look Mandie in the eye. Mandie sat down across from Arlene and waited for her to begin.

"Last evening, I had a meeting and ran into Jillian Cochran," Arlene said.

Mandie rolled the name around in her mouth, but it didn't taste familiar. "Jillian Cochran?"

Arlene ignored the question. "Jillian expressed concern about my ability to work with her on the state committee. She informed me that the HR director told her the reason we did not choose her for the position was that I believed she might undermine me. Jillian now represents her new employer on the same state committee I currently chair." Arlene sat back in her seat, but her hands were still clasped together.

Mandie was still trying to place Jillian Cochran. Her brain cells hadn't kicked in yet, and her blank stare must have generated Liana's response.

"Jillian was our Business Development Director candidate," Liana added.

Mandie blinked. She had been on the other side of the table enough to recognize the trajectory of the conversation. Her pending termination was coming into focus.

"I can't have people in the community thinking that about me." Arlene pushed a piece of paper in front of Mandie, with an envelope clipped to the top. "We've prepared a generous severance package. After all, Washington is an 'at will' state. We didn't have to offer anything."

All the pieces of the puzzle clicked into place, and a bitter taste filled Mandie's mouth. Arlene was new to the organization; the board had appointed her as CEO less than a year ago. Over the past few months, Mandie's relationship with the CEO had deteriorated. Arlene had chosen not to believe Mandie without hearing her side. She was stunned, and at the same time, she was not. This was the perfect ruse to move Mandie out of her position on the senior leadership team.

Arlene was flexing her muscles. The hospital's impending affiliation with a large healthcare system was no longer on the table, and Arlene was free to pursue ultimate control of the ship. She'd already quashed casual-Friday jeans and attempted to implement random drug testing. Mandie had tried to help Arlene understand that none of the other hospitals in Washington State performed random testing. That was a major conflict to overcome with the unions.

Arlene pushed those facts aside and served them up as an example of Mandie's shortcomings. According to Arlene, Mandie didn't embrace change. Flying under the radar was the only way to survive, but that was hard. Aside from disagreeing with the CEO, she didn't want Arlene to step into a hornet's nest without warning.

Arlene insisted she wanted her team to provide input, yet gave the distinct impression the entire C-Suite's viewpoint needed to align with her way of thinking. Any diversity of opinions was seen as not "having her back." As Chief Human Resources Officer, Mandie was a key person in C-Suite, and expected to have Arlene's back. Mandie had bluntly informed Arlene that she would follow any of her directives. She was, after all, the boss. But if asked her opinion, Mandie would give an honest one and not try to guess what Arlene was hoping to hear. Mandie dreaded her meetings with Arlene.

An out and proud lesbian didn't exactly fly below the radar in Arlene's world. Mandie had brought Caroline to the hospital fundraiser, where Arlene's husband failed to hide his disgust. In a moment of pure insanity, Mandie had asked if her sexuality contributed to the strain in their relationship. Arlene turned crimson and flatly denied that Mandie being a lesbian had anything to do with their difficult conversations. Mandie wasn't convinced.

"I won't fight this," Mandie said. "In some ways, I suppose it's a relief. But you know I would not say what Jillian claims. I would never throw you under the bus. As I recall, Jillian's personnel file described her as having a vitriolic communication style. That is why we did not offer her the position. Liana, you were there when we met with her and had a candid conversation about our concerns. You know I wouldn't provide feedback that would compromise Arlene's reputation in the community."

"I confirmed with Jillian that it was the HR Director and not the CNO," Arlene broke in. "I've already asked Liana about this. She assures me, she did not tell Jillian that I was the reason she didn't get the job."

"So, you believe Jillian, whose personnel file is filled with written warnings. My own reputation is untarnished, yet you don't trust that I would not act so unprofessionally. I suppose that says it all and is the reason why I won't fight this," Mandie answered in defeat.

Mandie was tired. Tired of her job. Tired of her relationship with Arlene. Tired of the undercurrent of discrimination that hovered below the surface. Why would she wish to work for an organization that would treat their leaders in this manner? She'd lost her will to fight. The better option was to take the severance package and figure out a plan for her future…after she didn't feel so bruised and battered.

"The package is generous," Arlene defended. "We don't need to offer this, as Washington is an 'at will' state," she repeated.

"I'm well aware of that. I'll sign the paper right now." Mandie took the pen Liana offered her and scribbled her name.

"I'll help you remove at least some of your personal belongings, then we can arrange a time…." Liana said softly. Arlene pivoted out of her chair and scurried from the office.

She'd completed her unpleasant task and could leave Liana to finish.

"Thanks," Mandie mumbled, as she stood and walked into her office. "The databases, projects…" She looked at her desk, filled with folders, and shook her head. "Never mind, I'll just grab the pictures of my girlfriend and my bag. I'll get the rest later."

Liana grabbed a bag and started to help pull off the pictures from the metal filing cabinet.

"Liana, you know I would never say that."

"I know. I said it didn't sound like you. I believe you."

Mandie wouldn't let them have the satisfaction of seeing her cry. She grabbed the framed picture of her and Caroline that prominently sat on the credenza and tossed it in the bag. "Can we do the rest on Monday? After my staff leave, please."

"Sure. I'll meet you here," Liana answered.

†

Mandie looked down as she left the building, barely acknowledging Kim. John wouldn't meet her eyes. Mandie wondered what they'd said to her staff. Liana walked her out. Escorted out—like some criminal—to make sure she wouldn't steal a company pen. As soon as she crossed the parking lot, Mandie pulled out her cell phone and texted Caroline.

> Mandie: *I just got fired.*
> Caroline: *Did they give you a severance?*
> Mandie: *6 months*
> Caroline: *You should push for more.*

Mandie was done. Through with everything, including Caroline's well-meaning advice. She didn't respond. She drove home to her condo on the lake, still in relative shock. She'd worked steadily since the age of fifteen. No organization had ever fired her before. This was all new to her.

Her cats greeted her at the door and looked up in confusion. Why was their mommy home in the middle of the day?

Mandie made a beeline to her laptop, typed *Indeed.com* in the search bar, and began the laborious task of job hunting. An advertisement on the side of the screen caught her eye. *Stuck in a Rut…Come Get High with Us*. Washington State had recently made marijuana legal but this advertisement wasn't for wacky weed.

Something about the idea of skydiving tugged at her. She was sick and damn tired of playing it safe. Of being the good girl. Of not fighting back. Of not speaking up. The advertised special for the weekend was two hundred dollars. Jobless, she could ill afford the cost of a crazy activity she'd never once considered. Her phone pinged.

> Caroline: *Sorry about the job. I'll be home late, heading to the winery with friends.*

Mandie wasn't sure how she felt about the text from her girlfriend. Heading to the winery was becoming a frequent occurrence. Combined with Mandie's already shitty day, she was irritated. No, she was pissed. Maybe she didn't want to talk about the firing or be on the receiving end of Caroline's advice. Wasn't your girlfriend supposed to at least try to support you?

She ignored the text message and punched in the number for the skydiving place. Before sanity took over, she made arrangements for a dive on Saturday. Caroline wouldn't care one way or another. She often had plans on the weekends that didn't include Mandie. They had been drifting apart over the last year and needed to put their dying relationship to rest. End the misery. It was a habit, like work. Mandie had continued on, because everyone expected that of her. She giggled as she thought of Caroline coming into the condo. *You're fired. I found a new girlfriend who actually likes experiencing the great wines of the Northwest.*

†

Mandie's cell phone started to vibrate across the heavy wooden coffee table. She absently flipped it over, expecting to see Caroline's name. Her father's name blinked on the screen. Insistent. Unrelenting. She kept ignoring the buzz, as it intermittently pulsated on the hard surface. Mandie was just as relentless in her refusal to answer; no matter how many times he called. His calls in the middle of the day were never an emergency. It hadn't mattered how many times she'd reminded him she couldn't talk during work hours. He didn't know she'd been fired.

Ever since her mother's death, her father had felt the need to call all the time. Frank Sr. had mentioned, on more than one occasion, that all he had to live for these days was his children. Mandie felt guilty for not answering. The guilt wasn't enough to overcome the shame.

Her father had an inflated view of her job and the ultimate importance of her role in the organization. Coming clean and telling him she was fired could only be avoided by not answering his call. Lying to him was not an option. She'd already disappointed him by not having children. Frank Sr. would definitely not consider her furbabies an appropriate equivalent to grandchildren. The bitter chuckle bubbled from her throat and felt like bile filling her mouth.

Mandie scratched Xena's head as she cuddled up next to her on the couch. "If only you could answer Dad's call and redirect him so I don't have to confess."

"Meow," Gabrielle answered from her relaxed position at Mandie's feet.

"Oh, so you think you can push the answer button with your paw? I probably should have pursued another line of work. What good did it do me to become a boring administrator if that isn't any more stable than an artist? God forbid I would have pursued photography."

"Brrppp, meow," Xena answered.

"Hmm, I guess you won't be left out of the conversation, huh, Xena? Well, good for you. Now stop distracting me, you two, Mamma really needs to find a new job before Dad finds out his daughter is not the successful career woman he brags about to his friends."

CHAPTER TWO

Mandie had been on her computer for four hours straight, looking for executive positions that might match her skills. She didn't want to move, but that might be her only option. After emailing a recruiter, Mandie learned of an opportunity in Nebraska. Was she desperate enough to consider a position in the Midwest? When she heard Caroline's key in the door, she pushed up her glasses and stopped typing.

"Hey," Mandie greeted her girlfriend.

"I see you didn't waste any time. Find any good job prospects?"

"How'd you know what I was doing?"

"Oh please, like you wouldn't jump right on your laptop and start searching. You don't do idle." She held up a bottle of wine. "I'll pop the cork and you can have a glass with me."

"Why would I want to drink wine right now?"

"You can either drown your sorrows or celebrate a much-needed, forced vacation. You were starting to hate the job anyway. Serendipity, I say."

"You do know that finding a job grows exponentially more difficult when you don't have one, especially at my age, don't you? What if I never work again?"

"Drown your sorrows it is. At least you have a tidy nest egg. I think you should push for more severance. You know it's because your boss is a homophobic bitch." Caroline set the cork on the counter and reached for two wine glasses in the cabinet. "By the way, your dad called me. You should have answered his call. He said he tried like five times to reach you today. Persistent bastard, isn't he?"

"Hey, don't call my father a bastard." Mandie clenched her fists.

Caroline waved her hand in the air. "You know I didn't mean it like that, but I'm not going to be your shield. You need to call him."

Mandie sighed. "I know. It's just that his vision of a successful career woman is so deeply embedded into his perception of me. I can't really pop that little fantasy balloon of his. My mother started him on that path."

Caroline poured the wine and crinkled her brow. "Your mother?"

"Yeah, when I was younger and at that perfect age for marriage, my great aunt asked about my prospects for a husband."

"You're kidding, right?"

"Nope, Italian matriarchs never kid about that. She used sly comments about breaking the hearts of all those young men and asked why didn't I want to settle down."

"You don't look one bit like your mother. I still can't believe you're half Italian. Did you tell her you were breaking the hearts of all those young women instead?" Caroline joked.

"My mother quickly answered that I was a career woman and didn't need a husband to take care of me. My dad chimed in with something like, 'Mandie runs the hospital.' Obviously, that was a gross exaggeration. I think my mother thought it was the acceptable feminist thing to say. I knew she was embarrassed about my sexuality. It hurt when she pulled me aside to ask me not to say anything about being a lesbian. That was something she would never be proud about."

"I think your mom was okay with you being a lesbian. She was always gracious with me and didn't seem bothered by us being together. I get the sense your dad never cared about you being a lesbian either."

"Maybe, but he certainly gives me grief about not getting married and having kids. He used to remind me all the time that lesbians get married and have kids."

Caroline frowned. She brought over the wine and set a glass on the coffee table. She settled next to Mandie. "You don't want to get married, do you?"

Mandie choked out her answer. "No! Of course not. We haven't exactly followed the lesbian handbook. After five years, we aren't even living together."

"That's because you insisted on us both keeping our own places, just in case." Caroline lifted the glass of wine and took a generous sip.

"I did not. That was all you. You said something about the market not being right for either of us to sell." Not wanting to get into an argument, Mandie changed the subject. "I'm going skydiving tomorrow. How do you feel about Nebraska?"

"You're going skydiving in Nebraska? Are you out of your fucking mind?"

"No, the skydiving place is in Spokane. Nebraska has a Chief HR job, and the recruiter thinks I'd be a perfect fit."

"You know I can't move. I have a good job with the college. You'll find something else, or not. Retire early. Take up photography again. Your photos are good."

"Photography will not produce a six-figure income."

Caroline shrugged. "The Prophets are playing tonight at the bar. Let's go, okay?"

Friday night was usually date night, the one day a week neither would make plans with anyone else. They could invite other people, but they tried to spend the time with one another.

Mandie took a sip of wine. "Not really in the mood to go out."

"All right. Is it okay if I go? Robin and Lacey are going."

"I thought they broke up."

"They did, but you know lesbians, we remain friends no matter what. There are too few of us in these tiny towns not to."

Mandie decided to push down the little green monster and ignore the reason the couple had broken up. Robin was madly in love with Caroline.

As if the earlier comment about skydiving had just broken through, Caroline stopped mid sip. "Wait, are you really going to jump out of an airplane?" Her faced contorted in apparent disgust.

"Yeah, I didn't make a reservation for you, because I didn't think it would be your cup of tea. Was I wrong? I can go on the Internet and add you to the reservation."

"No, I don't want to go, and I think you're being a bit rash. Let this job thing settle and then you'll be rational again."

Mandie glared at Caroline. She wasn't looking for sympathy after her shitty day. But damn, Caroline didn't seem to register the full weight Mandie felt. Maybe skydiving was a crazy way to symbolically remove that weight, but she needed outrageous right now. Caroline the Naysayer wasn't helping. "I'm going. You and Robin can go wine tasting. It's what you always want to do anyway. I'd rather not spend hours at the winery."

"Fine. I can see you're in a mood. I'll just go and stay at my place tonight instead…" She let the words trail, gulped down her wine, and stalked out the door.

Mandie blinked at the retreating figure that was her girlfriend and wondered why it didn't bother her one bit that date night was a bust. *I almost wish Caroline and Robin would get together tonight.* The inertia that had taken root might loosen and force Mandie to do what she knew was inevitable.

Over the years, Mandie had become less enamored with alcohol as a central focus of their date nights. She wanted more variety. When did Caroline lose interest in cycling or attending a musical in Seattle? Had Mandie evolved and changed in one direction and Caroline in another? Maybe Caroline hadn't changed at all. Caroline had always enjoyed going to the bars or wineries, and so did Mandie, in the early years. Lately, kayaking and cycling had become a much more prominent part of her life. The world was huge, and

Mandie wanted to explore more than her tiny neck of the woods. Maybe she wanted to take dance lessons or a photography course. Lifelong learning was important to Mandie but not to Caroline. It was time to work on that bucket list. *Change is good, isn't it?*

Screw it. Mandie decided it was time to stop obsessing over Internet job boards. She jumped onto the social media sites where people often posted pictures and talked about their shared passions. She posted her latest photo, a fluke after glancing up from her computer and noticing the beautiful sunset over the lake. She knew it wasn't anything spectacular. Photography was merely a hobby for her.

Before Mandie realized, several hours had passed and it was almost time to settle in for the night. She wasn't sure if it was terror or excitement that kept her awake. She'd officially lost her mind when she made the reservation to jump from a plane. Fear had always crippled her anytime she climbed too high on a ladder. Now, she was twelve hours away from facing her fear of heights with the granddaddy of adventures. Fear of the jump settled into the lethargy of depression.

Lethargy. Now that was a great word. Right now, she couldn't muster enough emotion to feel scared or motivated by anything other than wasting her precious time on the ever-present social media suck. Did social media cause more depression?

When was the last time she'd been inspired by anything? She'd been like a robot lately. Up at four thirty, exercise for an hour, work at the office for ten hours, return home and scrounge around for dinner, read and retire for the evening. Rinse and repeat. The walls had closed in and she hadn't even noticed.

Would ignoring her father's calls come back to bite her? No way was she prepared to fess up. Total and utter devastation clung to her like cheap perfume that penetrated her pores and wouldn't wash off.

She shrugged, grabbed her tablet and started a new book. The pop-up messages dragged her back into social media; the temptation was too great. She bounced back and forth between the reading groups and the photography sites. Her head bobbed up when she heard the key in her door.

"Shit," Caroline giggled.

Mandie assumed she'd stumbled on the five-gallon water jug in the hallway. Caroline was drunk. Pushing the covers aside, Mandie got out of bed and greeted her girlfriend. "You're drunk."

"No, I'm not." A hiccup punctuated her declaration.

"You shouldn't drive after wine tasting. You know how all those small sips add up."

"What? Don't I get a kiss?" Caroline pushed her lips out.

"I thought you were staying at your place tonight?"

"I changed my mind. Women do it all the time." Caroline took an unsteady step toward Mandie. "You look sexy in your sleepy clothes with your hair all tousled." She planted a sloppy, wet kiss on Mandie.

"Come on, let's get you settled in bed. I'll bring you a bottle of water and some aspirin." Mandie sighed and pulled her girlfriend by the hand.

Caroline began pulling her clothes off and tossing them on the bedroom floor. "Come on, Mandie, get naked with me."

"Just get into bed, okay? I'll join you in a minute."

When Mandie returned to the bedroom with the water and aspirin, she heard the telltale sign that Caroline was out for the night. Her snoring joined the sound of the ceiling fan, creating what Mandie called gray noise. White noise, like soft music, helped her fall asleep. Gray noise polluted the air waves and kept her alert. At least the book she'd started was good. She left the water and aspirin on the night stand.

CHAPTER THREE

Gail rushed inside her house, looking for her keys. She was always scurrying around. There weren't enough hours in the day. Something had to give, and it had. Two months ago, Desiree finally had enough. A broken date on their anniversary was the final straw. The whole reason Gail needed to keep ungodly hours was her girlfriend's discriminating taste in clothes, food, and everything else. Des appreciated quality. They'd lived beyond their means for far too long, and Des left Gail up to her eyeballs in debt. She'd had to continue working all the time just to keep her house. She didn't even like the house. Like every other demand in her life, time was at a premium and hadn't allowed her to draw up plans for her own home.

She'd bought the land ten years ago with a dream of designing her own house and living a more authentic life. Des hadn't wanted to live out in the "boonies." Small town living wasn't her cup of tea.

A stack of unopened mail sat beside Gail's keys and her ringing cell phone. "Hey, yes, I know. I'm on my way. I'll be there in an hour. I promise."

Dale grunted his response, "This is important, Gail, and they aren't interested in talking with me. They want your special touch. Do you have the plans?"

"Don't worry. They're in my car. I think. I'll make sure. I'm leaving right now. Gotta go if you want me to be there on time—or close."

"Don't speed, that'll just delay your arrival. That cherry-red car is a beacon to the police, especially since you're on a first name basis with the cops."

"Funny." Gail ran into her garage and peered into the back seat. She sighed in relief that the cardboard tube with her plans lay right where she'd left them. She must have tossed them into her car the night before. Lately, she felt like everything was leaking out her ears. Keeping her schedule, a comprehensive to-do list, creative ideas, and any other important thought in her brain, was becoming increasingly impossible. She was so busy, she didn't know if she was coming or going.

Who was she kidding? Leaving this late in the morning almost guaranteed she would be stuck in traffic and late for her meeting. Her business partner wouldn't have to worry about her getting another speeding ticket. She'd be crawling along the highway. Forget a primo parking space that was only available to early birds. She added *find affordable office space that isn't smack dab in the middle of downtown Seattle* to her mental to-do list. Of course, there was the distinct possibility that thought would magically disappear.

Lately, they were making a lot of money—enough to afford the office and her mortgage. Maybe her life was finally turning a corner, and she could begin to ease up on her frenetic schedule.

†

Gail glanced at her watch. Not bad, only fifteen minutes late. Dale could cover by getting the clients settled with coffee and pastries. The bakery down the block was a selling point for the current location of their office.

Dale had insisted that having a downtown office would make them appear more reputable than working from home. She supposed it did help, but at what cost? In her humble opinion, the addition of a few high-end clients did not compensate for the hassle of commuting into work or the increase in office costs. When she'd added the cost of parking, it was almost a wash. The recent surge in business was tipping the scales in favor of downtown Seattle. She had to grudgingly admit that he might have been a tiny bit correct.

The parking lot three blocks from the office left her baby exposed to the elements. Her cherry-red, 1989 Porsche 944 had been a birthday present to herself when she turned forty. The fact that Desiree thought it was a stupid purchase made it all the more satisfying to drive after her girlfriend walked out, a tiny rebellion after capitulating to Des's every suggestion. She'd made her wishes known about what events they should attend, the type of clothes Gail should wear, the neighborhood they should live in, and a hundred other decisions about Gail's life.

Gail grabbed the tube of architectural drawings and repositioned her handbag over her shoulder. After locking her baby, she jogged down the street to the high-rise office building. Her long, brown curls flowed as she attempted to reduce the number of minutes she would be late to the meeting. She thanked whatever higher power was out there that it wasn't raining.

With her free hand, she pushed the button on the elevator that would take her to the fifth floor. Natural Dwellings was tucked between an accounting firm and a financial planner. Gail chuckled at the irony. Her modern, chrome-trimmed office was the exact opposite of the houses she designed. Her unique structures seamlessly incorporated a property's natural surroundings. Gail's office was cold and sterile, while her renderings were full of warmth and life. Yes, she needed a new office. Her professional space should demonstrate her vision for how the world could live in harmony, without cutting down every single tree in their industrial path.

Gail glanced at Dale, who sat in the small conference room with a forced smile on his face. She could tell he was pissed but would never let on while the clients sat patiently across from him at the laminated conference table. That was another item she'd not gotten around to—purchasing a solid wood table. They'd accepted the furniture that came with the office. Another selling point in Dale's mind but not hers.

She smiled sheepishly as she entered the glass-enclosed room. "Hi, hi, sorry I'm late. Seattle traffic…"

The young Microsoft executives smiled at her. "It's okay, we've only been here for twenty minutes. Besides, you're the only architect who is able to create exactly what we want for our house on the lake," the man answered.

"I drove out to the land you purchased. There are several sites to choose from that will weave in the designs I'm about to show you. We won't have to clear any of the trees, and each design has its pluses and minuses. I have three different plans to show you. If none of these appeal to you, I have ideas for other sites on your land that would also work." Gail pulled the cap off the tube and removed the documents.

"We also bought some land on the Columbia River Gorge, and we'd like you to design a house around the rocks," the young woman said.

Gail nodded absently, as she rolled out the blueprints. She looked at the top document. "Shit," she murmured. "Oh, I am so sorry. I must have grabbed the wrong plans this morning."

Dale glared at her. "Could the correct plans be in your car?" he asked through gritted teeth.

Gail shook her head. "I must have left them in my home office."

The man chuckled. "We should have arranged for the meeting there." He looked around the conference room. "No offense, but this office doesn't suit you. Why don't you work out of your home office?"

"That is a good question." Gail gave Dale a pointed look.

"How about we give you the address of the new piece of land we bought? After you've drawn up plans for that, we can set up a new meeting." The man and woman stood. "Can you accomplish that by next week? Hon, can you give her the address?"

The woman reached into her purse and pulled out a business card and pen. After scribbling on the back of the card, she handed it to Gail. "Here's the address."

Gail had several projects that still needed work. Since she'd screwed this meeting up, she felt like she had no choice but to accommodate their time frame. She noted Dale giving her the stink eye. "Sure, I'll have the plans ready by next Friday."

"Does this same time next Friday work for you?" the man asked.

Dale was the one who kept their calendars. He nodded. "Sure, that works great."

†

There was a small flaw in the drawing, other than being the wrong set of plans. Gail reached into her bag and pulled out a mechanical pencil. When Dale touched her shoulder, she jumped. "Don't say it. I know, I know. I screwed up, it's just—"

Dale sat down. "Gail, I'm worried about you. Those bags under your eyes could hold enough clothes for a year-long trip around the world. Look, you're a genius, and there's a certain amount of leeway given to people who have the kind of talent that you have. But lately…"

Gail pushed her hand through her hair. "I can't keep this pace up, but I also can't afford not to. With the recent uptick in business, I can just sustain this office, my house, and my maxed-out credit cards. The list is endless, Dale."

"If I could get away with murder, I'd strangle Des with my bare hands. I could look into breaking our lease. You're right. We have more than enough work and don't need this office. Your reputation is solid now. After landing this client and one more that I have lined up, I promise you'll never have to worry about money ever again."

Gail looked at Dale with unshed tears in her eyes. "I think I love you but not in that, 'I want to have sex with you,' way."

"Ewww, I don't have sex with women. All that squishy flesh. Give me a hard body any day of the week." Dale sat up and ran his hands over his chest and abdomen.

"Some women have hard bodies."

"Yeah, but they don't have hard—"

"La, la, la, la. Do not finish that sentence." Gail pushed the drawings in front of Dale. "Here, at least you can do your magic and transform these plans with your computer program. These are for the Murphy place."

"We need to wait on that. Go ahead and roll them back up. At least you remembered to bring them today. We meet with them this afternoon." He narrowed his eyes.

"We do?" Gail asked.

"Yeah, we do. If you would learn Revit, we could share files. Then you wouldn't get mixed up with which plans to grab on your way out the door."

"You know there isn't a computer program that exists that will show exactly how my designs work. Clients prefer to see my drawings. I know the builders need CAD, but even they need to see my drawings when they get to working around trees and rocks."

"Too bad there isn't a market for a computer program that would meet those needs, but you're one of a kind. There's no sense in me trying to develop one. You have an hour to finish tweaking those plans before we meet with a potential new client. He's an Amazon exec."

Gail smoothed out the plans and focused on a section that caught her eye. "Oh right, yeah. This little corner here needs a tiny adjustment."

Dale chuckled. "Have at it, but don't be too much of a perfectionist. You have sixty minutes, that's all. *Capisce?*"

Gail saluted. "Aye, Aye, *El Capitan.*"

"You just combined two completely different sayings." Dale pushed away from the table and stood.

"It's the way my brain works and what allows me to create the designs I construct. It's all about combos, Dale. I was never good at Garanimals. I always wanted to combine my bunnies with my elephants."

"I'll leave you to your creative genius. I'll be back," he said in a poor imitation of Arnold Schwarzenegger in *The Terminator*.

CHAPTER FOUR

The alarm from her cell phone roused Mandie from a night of restless sleep. She rubbed her eyes and turned toward the offending noise. Caroline was still dead to the world. Mandie had finally nudged her onto her side to stop the snoring. Caroline had mumbled a few words and turned over. Mandie had eventually fallen asleep around three in the morning. Six o'clock came quickly. For a groggy split second, she considered rolling back over and trying to get more sleep.

Screw it. Come on you chicken shit, if you don't follow through, you never will. Mandie climbed out of bed. She might be able to sleepwalk her way out of the plane before she realized what she was doing.

Xena and Gabrielle followed her into the kitchen and meowed. She proceeded to fill the teakettle with water, then placed it on the burner turned to high.

"Shhh. We don't want to wake up Sleeping Beauty."

"Meow, meow."

"Okay, okay. Mommy will get your treats in a minute. Just please be quiet."

"Meow, meow," the cats cried in stereo again.

"Shit." Mandie turned around and was face to face with Caroline's scowling glare.

"Why are you up so early?" Caroline was pinching the bridge of her nose.

"Airplane, crazy, jumping. Don't you remember? I signed up for an adventure today."

"I thought you were kidding."

"Nope, not kidding."

"Don't you think you should be…um…well not be throwing your money away, especially now?"

"You think I can't get another job." Mandie crossed her arms over her chest.

"Your prospects are limited if you plan on staying here. You might have to consider moving or something. It's not like you're some spring chicken. I don't like it any more than you, but age does matter."

"Well, aren't you a ray of sunshine."

"Listen, I've been meaning to talk to you anyway…" She rubbed her temple and looked down.

Mandie put up her hand. "Save it. I need coffee first."

Caroline sighed. "I'm not saying we should end things. You shouldn't let anything get in the way of taking an opportunity that comes your way. If it means you have to move, you should consider it. We can evaluate at the time whether a long-distance relationship will work for both of us."

"You don't ever listen, do you? Fine. We can get into this now before coffee. I suppose this little epiphany came to you last night while having wine with Robin and Lacey. You and Robin want what's best for me. Isn't that the spiel?" Mandie measured out the coffee and put the ground beans into the French press.

"We care about you."

"Right. So tell me, did Lacey also weigh in on this, or was it mostly a discussion between you and Robin?" Mandie hugged herself as if there was a chill in the air.

"Now you're being ridiculous and jealous. I thought you would appreciate not having to feel pressure from me to remain in this little backwater town."

"Skydiving I wasn't kidding about, but Nebraska I was. I love this little town and so do you. Moses Lake doesn't have that damp, west side fog that creeps into your bones. You're right about one thing. I will have to expand my search area. Getting a second place in this state will be an option. I'm not moving out of state."

"I think you should—"

The whistling of the teakettle created the perfect interruption. "Saved by the whistle." Mandie poured the hot water into the press, then set the timer to four minutes.

"You're not thinking clearly right now. Take time to settle before doing something rash like jumping out of a fucking plane. Come on, Mandie, you have to know that's crazy and expensive." Her volume increased with every word.

"My money, my decision. Two hundred dollars is a drop in the bucket compared to my monthly expenses. If I'm going to have money troubles, it won't be because I spent a couple hundred dollars on something."

"I can't talk to you when you're like this. Besides, my head is splitting." She waved her hand in the air, brushing away Mandie's words.

"Didn't you see the water and aspirin I left for you on the nightstand?"

"It hasn't quite kicked in yet."

"Well, if you wouldn't pound down like a hundred different samples," Mandie mumbled.

Caroline laughed. "I hardly think I would be standing right now if I'd tasted a hundred different wines. The winery doesn't even make that many varieties. And they aren't samples. That's Costco, not a winery. Wine tasting is a lot of fun. You should come with us. I meet all kinds of different people at the winery. I'll bet you could make a connection and find your next job at one of these events. Networking. That's what it's all about."

"No thanks. It borders on pretentious. Too bad I don't like beer. I'd fit into the beer tasting crowd more readily than connoisseurs of wine."

"Whatever. I'm heading back to bed. Go ahead and break every damn bone in your body. It would serve your stubborn ass right. No one can talk sense into you once you've made up your mind. Have at it. I'm done trying." Caroline walked back into the bedroom, shaking her head.

"Meow."

"Oh shit, sorry guys. I'll get your treats right now, before the grumpy goose comes back and yells at you."

"I heard that," Caroline yelled from the bedroom.

Mandie mouthed, *I heard that*, while shaking her head in a mocking gesture. She retrieved the bag of treats from the cabinet and pulled a plate out to dump them onto.

After setting the plate of treats on the floor for the cats, she pulled a spoon from the drawer. She began stirring the steeping coffee grinds in the glass container. A few seconds later the timer went off. She pushed down the press filter and finished making her morning jolt. Leaning against the counter, she let her foul mood wash over her. Life sucked sometimes. Maybe on the way to her crazy adventure she could take a few photos. Photography might not be a vocation, but it was a way to settle her nerves.

†

Mandie had plenty of time to consider her decision, as she drove the hour and a half to the hangar in Spokane. She'd stopped along the way and captured the stark beauty of the high desert. Not many people found this part of the state as appealing as the west side's lush greenery and mountains. Mandie insisted there was beauty everywhere. People just had to look for it.

The aluminum-sided warehouse loomed in front of her, the tiny plane parked outside an innocent bystander to her demise. The flurry of activity appeared disorganized, and she wondered if the group of twentysomething jumpers was a bad sign. *Pride goeth before a fall.* It was pride, pure and simple, that caused her to undo her seatbelt and keep moving toward the building. She needed to check in and get weighed.

The release forms weren't at all comforting. The serious-injury-or-death clause was clearly spelled out. Before Mandie booked the skydiving adventure, she had watched the video that went on and on about how many things could go wrong. She'd kept stopping and starting the video as she wrote down the words, *There is not, nor will there ever be, a*

31

perfect parachute system or packer, a perfect airplane or pilot, a perfect parachute center or instructor, or for that matter a perfect student. That was a whole lot of imperfection. The fact that the guy making the video looked a lot like one of the band members from ZZ Top, made the warnings more ominous.

Mandie clutched the handwritten caution tightly in her fist, but she couldn't bring herself to read it again. She might hightail it back to her car and drive away—two hundred dollars poorer and a permanent *chickenshit* tattooed on her forehead. She stuffed the paper in her pocket without glancing at it and walked toward the large building where all the people were bustling about.

What the hell was I thinking? Mandie ducked her head and stepped into the small plane. Attached to her tandem partner, she moved along the floor of the plane to reach the very back. There were no seats nor any seat belts. What would be the point? She was about to jump from a plane. Seat belts seemed contrary and unnecessary safety equipment.

When the plane reached the death-dive altitude, the experienced divers scooted along the floor like on some conveyor belt. *Butt dusting. That must be how they keep the plane clean.* She shook her head at her ridiculous thought. She felt the winds of death swirl inside the small space, whipping her ponytail around to sting her face. Buckled to her tandem partner, she wondered if the rank smell was her own nervous perspiration or his questionable hygiene. He was a scruffy twentysomething the skydiving unit insisted was the best, and she had accepted their assessment. Lately, her judgment had been far from rational. A droplet of sweat tickled between her breasts and traveled down the crevice inside her bra.

She glanced at her white-knuckled grip on the parachute strapped to her chest. There was absolutely nothing else to hold on to. No "oh crap" straps anywhere. Nothing for brand-new divers to hang on to when their life depended on remaining inside the tiny, tin, holding cell. Everyone else had already left the plane with maniacal grins plastered to their faces. She was officially in hell. She'd made the decision; she couldn't blame this on anyone else.

With a small tug on her shoulder straps, her scruffy partner yelled over the wind and loud motor of the plane. "We have to go now, Ms. Carter."

Mandie slammed her eyes shut and gave the thumbs up signal she'd been taught. She reluctantly let Scruffy Man push her along the floor of the plane and ultimately into a swan dive into the unknown. There was no pool of cool, crisp water to cushion their fall. She imagined his body connected to her like a turtle's shell. His hands gently moved to her arms, pulling them out so she could get the most from the dive. He was offering her the experience of flying through the air before the abrupt uplift when the parachute engaged. After a few seconds, she felt him fumbling around. That's when she knew.

Her tandem guide was frantically trying to move them closer to the copse of trees. What was the point? She would soon expire, strapped to a smelly turtle dude. Maybe the impact wouldn't hurt and she would instantly die. Mandie would have preferred dying in her sleep, cuddled up to a woman she'd spent the better part of her life with. She sighed. She'd never found her other half. The first branch hurt like a bitch.

CHAPTER FIVE

Why did I bother going to bed last night, or rather this morning? Gail had stayed up late to put the finishing touches on her drawings for Microsoft Couple. She couldn't remember their real names, despite the label on the edge of the drawing.

It had taken several weeks and countless flirtations, before Classy Lesbian with Beautiful Blue Eyes became Des. Dale had to remind Gail of the woman's name several times before it sunk in. Des was beautiful; there was no doubt about that. Nothing distinguished her from any other attractive woman Gail had lusted after. If she ever fell madly in love with someone, would their name stick? Maybe she'd hear a lyrical song in her head, like some ridiculous notion of love at first sight.

Gail picked up the tube from her kitchen table and popped the top to make sure the right drawings were all there. She floated her hand over the rich wood grain. Her mother had scoured antique shops to find the perfect graduation gift. Gail had happily dragged the early 1900s beast around ever since, along with her vintage oak drafting table.

Smiling, she thought about how lucky she was to have a mother who supported her passion for creating her own kind of art. Architecture was a stable, accepted profession, but Gail took a risk and deviated from the more traditional designs. It paid off in the long run. Dale was a huge part of the success. He took care of the more mundane affairs of running a business and allowed Gail to concentrate on being an eccentric artist.

Damn, she was missing the drawing she'd just worked on. She hurried into her office and rolled the final drawing into the tube with its sisters, snug as bugs in a rug. *Ew. Where does that saying come from?* She might have to Google that. Another time. Already running late again after she'd promised Dale she would be on time, she climbed into her Porsche and screeched out of the driveway. She glanced at her watch and sighed in relief. All she had to do was speed a tad. She'd get there in plenty of time.

†

Crap, crap, crap. Red and blue lights flashed in Gail's rear-view mirror. She pulled to the side of the road. She noted the blonde ponytail hanging down the police officer's back. Maybe it was her lucky day. *Please be a lesbian and subject to my blatant attempt at flirting.* The handsome woman approached her car. Gail rolled the window down and smiled broadly.

"License and registration, please."

"Good morning, Officer. Of course. Let me get those for you. Wow! It's so nice to see a female officer." Gail looked up and offered her sexiest smile before reaching into her glove compartment. She pulled out her registration and grabbed her license from her bag. She handed both to the patrolwoman. "Here you go. I'm so sorry. I was running late, but I didn't think I was going that fast. Maybe only five over."

"It was closer to fifteen, ma'am." The officer stood rigid, a foot from the car door.

Gail sighed and offered a sheepish smile. She couldn't get a read on the female officer behind her mirrored sunglasses. "I know being late is no excuse. You can save yourself the trouble. I don't merit another warning. I have a bad habit of speeding. This ticket is a fitting punishment. I also deserve to be late, yet again. You wouldn't happen to have any cotton I can use for earplugs when my business partner reads me the riot act? No one can beat a gay man for dramatics."

The officer glanced at the rainbow flag sticker on the windshield, and the corner of her mouth turned up. Gail almost pumped her fist in the air. Yes, this might turn out to be her lucky day.

"If you plan on driving this route every day, you might want to slow down. The next time, I will give you a ticket. I hope if I do run across you again it won't be on this highway. Perhaps at the WildRose on karaoke night?" She handed Gail her license and registration and treated her to a smile.

Gail smiled back. "If I ever get any time off from work, the WildRose is a perfect place to unwind. I'll definitely keep that in mind."

"I'm afraid your car is very distinctive and a beacon for police to pull over. Slow down, Ms. Forrester." She tipped her hat and walked away.

Gail eased onto the highway and wondered when she would ever be able to slow down long enough to visit the women's bar and restaurant. Hopefully, she'd run into the attractive cop again without getting a speeding ticket. If the officer introduced herself, would Gail remember her name? She really needed to work on that. It was rude not to remember someone's name, especially if you were cruising them.

Gail frowned. How important was this flaw? Maybe it was inconsequential. Maybe her inability to remember a person's name was an indication of a broader issue at play. Did the demise of her relationship with Des share elements with those of all her former lovers? Could this be the tip of the iceberg? If she couldn't be bothered to remember a person's name, could she put enough into a relationship to make it work through the good and bad times?

†

Gail knew she was risking another ticket by jaywalking. She giggled to herself about another sexy cop stopping her as she ran across the street. Her coat billowed all around her body, whipping furiously. The clomp of her flat heels on the pavement kept the beat for the howling wind. Sounds of traffic seemed far away.

The famous Seattle rain tickled her face. Clutching the drawings and her bag, she kept her head down to keep the rain out of her eyes. She didn't want her mascara to run. If she hurried, she might have time to fix herself up before the meeting.

Screeching brakes were clearly someone's last-second attempt to avoid an accident. The sound was too close to ignore. Sometimes small details caught her attention at the same time she ignored the big ones.
The black tires of the large metro bus were bald, a terrible combination with the slick roads. No matter how slow the 30,000-pound vehicle was traveling, it was going to hurt. A lot. Gail supposed Seattle's rabid enforcement of jaywalking laws was a good thing.

CHAPTER SIX

"Stay with me. Come on, stay with me, miss… We're losing her. Clear…"

Beep, beep, beep

"Can you hear me?"

Light shimmered, like a mirage on black pavement in the middle of a very hot summer day. Mandie looked around. To the right was a bright white light, and to the left a swirling kaleidoscope. The colorful tunnel appealed to her a lot more than the calming white light. She turned to her left. A light mist came up to her knees and hid her feet. Everything felt like a dream. Shapes were muted around the edges, as she made her way toward the rainbow eddy. She felt a presence to her right and called out to whoever was there.

"Hello?"

"I don't know which way to go," a woman responded.

"I like color." *What a ridiculous thing to say. But white light takes you to the other side of death.* That wasn't a place Mandie wanted to visit. She was far too young to die.

"Who are you?" the voice asked.

"Mandie."

"Mandie?" The voice was close now. "I don't know anyone named Mandie. How do I know we're going in the correct direction?"

"Seriously? Hasn't anyone ever told you that people see a white light right before they die? I'm not about to test that theory. Besides, it's a rainbow of color. Rainbows suit me." Mandie squinted in the direction of the voice.

The woman giggled. "Me too."

The strange woman popped into Mandie's line of vision like a ghost who'd walked through a wall. Maybe they were both ghosts and destined to haunt unsuspecting enemies together for all eternity. Mandie only knew of one person she'd like to haunt. Perhaps Arlene had also screwed this woman over.

"Hey, did you ever work for Arlene Nelson?" Mandie asked.

"What? No. I'm an architect. I have my own business. I don't work for anyone, unless you count my overbearing partner. I sort of work for him in a manner of speaking, because he keeps my schedule. I'm not so good at organizational skills. I'm Gail, by the way." Gail extended her hand.

Mandie accepted her delicate hand and got a good look at her face. Maybe she *was* dead and had somehow managed to sneak her way into heaven. Gail was definitely her type. A mop of curly brown hair topped a face with enormous chocolate-colored eyes. A classic Mediterranean beauty, except for two impish dimples set below those ridiculously high cheekbones. They gave the appearance that, any minute, she'd lead Mandie down a road that would get them both in trouble. Mandie had the urge to capture those plump, kissable lips.

"Um, hello," Mandie croaked.

"Do I have spinach in my teeth? I don't remember eating breakfast, much less something that would hide in the crevices. You're staring." The woman scratched her head. A few of the curly strands stuck out above the others.

"You're beautiful," Mandie blurted before she had a chance to censor herself.

The dimples deepened with Gail's smile. She cocked her head. "Right back atcha. I do hope we get to continue to hang out. At least I'll have some beauty to look at in the afterlife. Do you think there will be trees on the other side of that tunnel? I would miss trees. Mountains too. Oh, and rocks. Big, beautiful rock formations. I hope there are rocks."

Mandie laughed. "We might both be dead—ghosts destined to haunt my old boss—and you're hoping there are trees and rocks."

Gail shrugged. "I'm hoping we're heading to heaven. In my version of the blessed afterlife, there are trees and rocks."

"I guess I'm low maintenance. I already have everything I need for my version of heaven. Unless…you're not a lesbian or I could be considered a cheater after I'm dead."

"I don't know about your second question, but yup, I'm a lesbian. Vows always have something like 'til death do you part. I suppose that means you're free. Let's go with that interpretation." She nodded her head as if the matter was settled.

"You know, this could all be a dream, a figment of my overactive imagination."

"Wonderful. I've never been a part of someone's fantasy. What a rush," Gail answered.

"I seriously doubt that. I'm sure you've been in plenty of women's fantasies."

†

Gail decided she'd settle in and enjoy the dream for a little while longer. Mandie. How ironic that she could remember the gorgeous woman's name in her dream state. In real life, she'd likely name her Stunning Swede. She wasn't sure if Mandie was Swedish, but with her long blonde hair and pale blue eyes the color of a summer sky, she could be. She had the tiniest hint of crow's feet at the corners of her eyes and the beginnings of deep-set laugh lines. Neither of these marred her appearance. This woman would remain beautiful well into her sixties or longer. Gail guessed the woman was five foot nine or taller. The slender frame could wear any outfit and look good.

Gail might have to find a step stool in heaven, so when they kissed it wasn't uncomfortable. There were always ways to work around the height difference. She tended to gravitate toward women who were much taller than her petite five foot two. In bed, it never mattered. Whenever she kissed a taller woman on her doorstep, it helped to have her date remain on the lower step.

Mandie's hair was pulled back as if she'd been exercising. A hint of makeup accentuated her cheekbones and full, red lips. The black mascara and eyeliner made her eyes pop. Gail thought Mandie might have wanted to kiss her as much as Gail wanted to run her tongue over those beautiful lips.

Gail was convinced God didn't give two shits about lesbians and gays. Otherwise, why would he put Mandie and her together on their first day in this strange place? She was glad they'd gotten that little secret out of the way right from the start. Gail hadn't been in that tiny closet for twenty years or more, but most people didn't peg her for a lesbian. That's why she had a rainbow sticker on her car, wore a rainbow watchband, and flirted with women every chance she got. Her gaydar had pinged the minute Mandie blurted out she was beautiful. *Gaydar in heaven. Convenient.*

"So, Mandie, do you think there are others waiting to make a choice between color and white light?"

Mandie furrowed her brow. "Don't know. Maybe both are heaven, but we're attracted to the colors because that's where all the lesbians go."

Gail laughed. "Wow! That would be incredible if we had our own little slice of heaven. I don't mind being separatists. As long as the standard truly is separate but equal. Goodness knows it wasn't like that on earth."

The swirling colors seemed to brighten as the women approached. Gail thought of neon signs, and a small wave of fear washed over her.

"Are the colors blinking?" Mandie asked.

"I thought that was just me. I've never seen anything quite like it. Weird, huh? Will you think poorly of me if I tell you that I'm scared?"

"Not at all. Um…you can say no, but how about we hold hands and enter the tunnel together? It looks wide enough for both of us," Mandie suggested.

Gail took Mandie's offered hand and their fingers intertwined. "Thank you. Okay, let's do this."

The two women stepped inside the swirling neon tunnel of blinking colors and hesitated. They attempted to make sense of what lay in front of them. Someone had photoshopped Earth. Everything was a shade too bright. The colors were all wrong.

Royal-blue tree trunks stretched toward a sky of forest green. The dirt path was a rich yellow like the sun in a child's painting.

CHAPTER SEVEN

"You're late."

A short, stout woman with close-cropped gray hair was tapping her pen on a clipboard. "It says here that both of you played fast and loose with time schedules."

Mandie blinked at the woman and turned to Gail.

"Chop, chop, ladies. This way please. Orientation is about to begin. Mandie, you will need to pay special attention. If you end up staying here for a while, we'll need you to learn the orientation spiel. I understand you've done this sort of thing before."

Mandie realized she was still holding Gail's hand and was about to release her.

"Please don't let go." Gail squeezed Mandie's hand. "I still need the physical touch. I am totally freaking out in this place."

Mandie looked around. "Well, you got your wish." She pointed at the scenery all around them. "There's your trees, rocks, and mountains."

The gray-haired woman walked toward a large building, if it could be called that. They followed her into a solid version of the rainbow tunnel they'd just come through. Elbow joints took them to the right and then left in the enormous pipe. Every time they took a turn, the tunnel widened. Eventually, they were in a large hall. Splashes of color streaked the multicolored chairs, the raised stage, and the curved walls. Even the podium and microphone were kaleidoscopes of color.

Men and women milled about, looking as dazed as Mandie felt. The tall woman who stepped onto the stage even wore a multicolored robe. *Joseph and the Amazing Technicolor Dreamcoat. I loved that production.*

Tap, tap, tap.

"Welcome to Intermediate for Fluids," the woman's voice boomed inside the room. "Please select a seat, and I'll explain everything."

Mandie led Gail to the last row of seats and selected the bright, lime green and royal-blue chairs at the end of the row on the left. She was trying not to panic and to lend Gail the support she needed.

"Fluids?" Gail raised her eyebrow. "Does that mean what I think it means? Is it possible that's the term for anyone who is not strictly heterosexual? How politically correct and all-inclusive of them."

The woman narrowed her eyes at Gail. "This is not a joke, Ms. Forrester." She pointed down. "I want to inform you we do not exclude anyone who meets the definition of not heterosexual. We needed to find one word that would encompass everyone in this realm. Frankly, LBGTQQIAA doesn't work for us. Besides, y'all keep adding letters. How are we to keep up?"

Mandie felt the need to take the focus off Gail. *In for a penny, in for a pound.* She raised her hand. "How come we don't get our own Intermediate? You know Intermediate for Lesbians. I'm not being discriminatory here. I just think our own space might be nice."

The woman sighed. "It's been suggested. We're looking into it. For now, you'll have to be okay with Intermediate for Fluids. I'd rather we not continue talking politics. We have too much to cover and can't afford to get sidetracked. Can you please hold your questions until I finish?"

"You're supposed to be listening to Cornstalk, not challenging her," Gail whispered. Playfulness curled around the edges of her voice.

"Cornstalk?" Mandie pushed the word out of the corner of her mouth.

"I'm allowed to give her and Gray Hair nicknames, because neither properly introduced themselves. Besides, even if they revealed their names, I wouldn't remember them. Don't you think she looks like a cornstalk with that tuft of hair on top?"

Mandie giggled.

Cornstalk huffed and glared at Gray Hair. "See, I told you I wouldn't be any good at this."

"You're doing fine," Gray Hair answered. "We need someone who will be here for a while, and I'm afraid our choices are limited. Don't worry, you'll have a replacement very soon." Gray Hair looked directly at Mandie and winked.

Cornstalk cleared her throat. "My name is Harriet, not Cornstalk." She paused and let that sink in.

Gail leaned over. her warm breath touched Mandie's ear. "Yikes, I should have named her Bat Ears," she whispered so low Mandie doubted Harriet could hear her. The glare told a different story.

"Let me get out of the way that you aren't dead. Intermediate is a kind of holding zone. I won't lie to you. Some of you may end up in the great beyond, but a fair number of you will return to earth at some point. Most of you will be here only a short time. Others, like me, will reside in Intermediate for an extended period. If you reach under your seat, there is a piece of paper that gives the approximate time. Of course, we don't exactly know how long before final dispensation is determined. The approximates are ninety percent accurate within a 24-hour window of time."

Mumbling filled the room, as everyone began to reach under their seats. Mandie had a whole list of questions. How did they know who was going to sit where? Why did they use such a low-tech method of providing people with important information? Apparently, the times were unique to each person. She wanted to reach into her nonexistent bag to take notes. She wouldn't remember all these important questions when they were allowed time to ask them. Gail was reaching under her chair and had the envelope in her hand—a royal blue to match the chair.

"Anyone who has a time frame of greater than twenty-four hours will be provided lodgings. Since this is such a large group all at once, we're asking for volunteers willing to share their space with another person," Harriet continued. "Can I see a show of hands from those who are interested in helping out?"

Mandie looked around. No one was raising their hand. She hadn't opened her envelope to read how long she might be stuck in Intermediate. It didn't matter. She'd be thrilled to room with Gail. "We should volunteer. Nobody else is."

"Works for me," Gail answered cheerfully and raised her hand.

"Thank you, Ms. Forrester. I presume you agree, Ms. Carter?"

Mandie nodded and raised her hand with a huge smile on her face. Gail was already opening her notification. Mandie grabbed her own envelope from beneath her chair. She heard Gail say, "Oh, thank goodness, I'm only stuck here for seven days, give or take. How about you?"

"I don't know yet. Let me get this open." She flipped open the lime-green flap and gasped at the single sheet of paper. "Shit. I'm stuck here for 364 days. One day shy of a year. An entire year," she responded in exasperation.

Gail's hand shot in the air. "Hey, I have a question."

"Well, I'm not done with orientation yet. But go ahead, Ms. Forrester. I'm sure if I don't let you ask now, you'll interrupt this presentation with snide comments."

"What happens if we don't like the time frame listed? Can we either shorten or lengthen it?"

Harriet's mouth gaped open long before any words came out. "I…don't know. No one has ever asked that question before."

The good humor slipped off Gray Hair's reddening face. "Um…we'll get back to you on that." She nodded for Harriet to continue.

"Idleness is the devil's playground. Everyone will be assigned a job." Harriet pointed to Gray Hair. "Evelyn has your assignments. It's a little different here in Intermediate than down on earth."

"That's an understatement," Gail mumbled.

"You won't have need for food or water here, so…you know…um…no bathrooms to clean or meals to prepare."

"What's left if the scut work doesn't exist? Do we just go around and shine the rainbow?" Gail blurted out.

"Well that's a plus, bathrooms aren't a lot of fun to clean," Mandie added.

"Sometimes we get people who struggle with accepting their time here. We can make use of those individuals who have the ability to soothe the panicky types. Writers are especially needed. We don't have much technology, so we need people with excellent penmanship to transcribe everyone's stories."

A mousy woman on the other end of Mandie and Gail's row raised her hand. Harriet nodded to her. "I'm a writer," she offered.

"That's great. How long will you be here?" Harriet asked.

She looked down at her paper. "Ninety-six days."

"Good, good. Hopefully that will be enough time to pen an entire novel. Are there any editors in this group?" Harriet stood up straighter and was looking more confident on the stage.

A man and woman a dozen rows ahead raised their hands.

"Wonderful. We'll be able to add to the library. Books are a popular form of entertainment." Harriet smiled for the first time.

"I'm guessing that computers don't exist in this realm," Gail noted.

"That's correct." Harriet nodded.

"What about sports, games? I don't suppose you have any tennis courts? How about some low-tech bikes?"

"We put in a requisition for bikes, but we're still waiting," Evelyn answered.

Gail frowned. "Um…no offense, but on the way in here I noticed your dwellings all look the same."

Whispers in the audience grew to a low rumble. Mandie looked around, trying to understand what had generated the chatter.

"Maybe I could design something else for you and incorporate those colorful rocks and trees into the design. It's what I did, you know, down there." Gail pointed to the ground. "I'm not very familiar with the materials you use. If you allow me some extra time here, I'm sure I can figure it out and make it work."

Evelyn clapped her hands. "Initiative. I like that. We don't often get someone who is enterprising. People know this is a temporary situation and don't care about their surroundings. Renting versus buying. There's no investment." She sighed.

"Well then, you have more reason to advocate for me staying as long as Mandie," Gail said.

Mandie felt a flush of warmth. "You want to stay for a year?"

"Sure, I needed a vacation, and it seems pretty relaxed here. After going a hundred miles an hour, literally at times, I'm ready for a slower pace." Gail smiled.

CHAPTER EIGHT

Fascinating. A group of men and women in tie-dyed clothing materialized and began escorting the newbies to their tube dwellings. Gail noticed Gray Hair wasn't wearing tie-dye or a technicolor robe. Her striped shirt and pants made her look like a big rainbow flag. Gail giggled at the sight.

"What's with the different uniforms?" she asked.

"I suppose that's what it might look like to you as a brand-new Inter-flu. The clothing helps us differentiate between various jobs. The ones you see in some kind of tie-dyed garb are greeters. Besides, we don't choose the color scheme or other details—you do."

Gail thought that last comment was odd but held her thought while Gray Hair continued. "Usually, I don't show the new Inter-flus to their lodgings. I mostly organize the flow of work. I've taken a special interest in you, Gail."

"What makes me special?" Gail asked.

Gray Hair tapped her clipboard. "The cryptic report I received from Transition Messiah. I was directed to personally handle your acclimation to Intermediate. Mandie's too. Apparently, it's a rare occurrence when two connected souls arrive at the same time. Yes indeed, very rare."

"Can you be more specific with your explanation?" Mandie interjected.

"Well, you see, every single person in your orientation group entered into a coma today, just like you. Unfortunately, a fair number of them will go on to the great beyond. We don't tell the new Inter-flus that. It kind of freaks them out."

"Um, that kind of freaked me out," Gail added.

Gray Hair waved the concern away. "Oh, don't worry. It says right here—both of you have a sixty-five percent chance of returning to earth. Nothing is one hundred percent." She grinned. "To add even more to your specialness, neither one of you will have any permanent residuals from your experience upon your return."

"I hope that means, we'll both walk, talk, eat, and have sex again. Especially have sex again. I'd miss that." Gail sighed.

"Oh yes." Gray Hair frowned. "There are some trials on the horizon for you both. The ultimate outcome has not been decided."

"What trials?" Mandie asked. "I don't like the sound of that."

"I can't reveal more. I've already bent the rules…" She looked right and left. "I wonder if Transition Messiah knew you were going to ask that question. She might already be working on an answer."

"So, we'll get to know what trials lie ahead for us?" Gail asked.

"Oh no, not that question. The one you asked in orientation—about whether you can stay in Intermediate longer than what's already been decided."

"Who died and made this messiah person in charge of how long I get to stay?" Gail grumbled.

"Nobody died." Gray Hair scrunched up her face. "Transition Messiah was appointed to her position and given ultimate powers by Creator. She'll never leave this place. She's been here for nearly a millennium. I don't know the full story, but she was frozen in the ice. No one found her. Creator decided she was the perfect person for the job."

"Great. Another place where I don't have any say in my own future. Well, at least I'll have a new job. I suppose that's better than being unemployed," Mandie remarked.

"I want an audience with this transition person," Gail petitioned.

"I'll send a request, but she doesn't respond well to demands." The tiny crinkle in Gray Hair's forehead grew to a deep crease.

They stood in front of a large, psychedelic tube. Gail noted there wasn't exactly a door, more of an alcove that curved to the right and revealed a large open space accented by the jazzy purple of the bed's feather comforter. Gail grinned at the thought of sharing a bed with Mandie. Gray Hair pointed to a tunnel on the left. "There's a second bed through here."

Damn. That would have been too easy.

"We had a few of these built when the overcrowding began. We call them double dwellings."

"Is this it? A space to sleep is all these are?"

Gray Hair beamed. "Oh no. Come with me, and I'll show you the lounge area. I've made a note to ask Transition Messiah—TM—if we can procure a drafting table. No guarantees, you understand, but I like the idea of designing different dwellings. I've been here a long time, and the surroundings are kinda boring. It reminds me of those 1950s cookie-cutter neighborhoods. Most Inter-flus aren't as imaginative as you two."

"I don't suppose this lounge has a big-screen TV. This might be a good time to catch up on the episodes of *Orange Is the New Black* I haven't seen yet," Mandie joked.

The small group made another left at the elbow in the tunnel. Two chairs that looked suspiciously like beanbags and a low, square table were the only furnishings to adorn the large space.

"No, sorry. TM is adamantly opposed to any form of electronics. She believes people on earth have lost their ability to communicate with one another. She's a bit disgusted with cell phones, e-readers, tablets, television, and most other forms of electronics. She thinks those gadgets keep people from connecting on a deeper level. We do have live plays. Would either of you be interested in joining the theater troupe? We're fortunate to have a lot of guys who want to be involved but not many women."

Gail and Mandie both shook their heads.

"Oh well, it was worth a shot."

"Hey, what about that microphone in orientation? How come that was allowed?" Gail asked.

"She had to acquiesce to that minor exception. The Inter-flus assigned to run orientation were losing their voices when they strained their vocal cords to be heard all the way to the back of the large hall," Gray Hair answered.

Gail surveyed the room and plopped down on one of the beanbags. "Well, it isn't much, but this chair's cool. I haven't lounged in one of these since college. What's this square thing between the chairs for? It's not like we'll be having coffee in the morning. Damn, I'm going to miss food and coffee."

"The table is a writing surface. We've accumulated an impressive library of handwritten books over the years. I guarantee you've never read any of those stories." Gray Hair was beaming.

"So how do the lights work? I'm guessing these little dwellings aren't equipped with electrical outlets." Mandie eased into the other chair and wiggled her butt. "Oh, this is comfortable. I've never sat in a beanbag before, but I've always wanted one." She laid her head back.

"We decided not to leave that to…oh never mind. Don't worry. It will be light enough when you are reading and relaxing in the lounge. The minute you crawl into bed, the lighting dims so you can sleep."

Gail wiggled her eyebrows. "What if we don't want to sleep in the beds?"

Gray Hair blushed. "Um…sound cues help."

Mandie burst out in laughter. "So, if I cry out, 'yes, yes, right there, ooh I'm coming,' we get light, and if I start snoring, it goes dark?"

Gail grinned. "A vocal lover. Be still my heart. So, there aren't rules against, you know, people hooking up?"

"Nope, we gave up trying to control that a long time ago. Besides, Transition Messiah couldn't come up with one single reason why we should stop it. I'm not sure Creator agreed. TM threatened to resign. Shortly thereafter, they allowed us to branch off from the mainstream Intermediate. I didn't much like my time there. I was happy when we got to form Intermediate for Fluids." Gray Hair looked right and left again, then whispered. "I think TM is a lesbian. We might get our own intermediate space if she has her way."

"Have you seen her?" Mandie asked.

"Every once in a while, I get to speak to her." Gray Hair got a dreamy look. "She looks like an Amazon princess."

"Nice," Mandie and Gail said in unison.

"You can settle in. I'll be back to give you your assignments later, after I check on the other new Inter-flus."

†

Mandie turned her head toward Gail. "Were you joking earlier about the, you know, lights going off in the…?"

The corner of Gail's mouth lifted. "Yes and no. I wasn't joking when I said I'd be glad to be able to have sex again. I was dumped a few months ago, and I kinda miss that. I don't miss much else about being in a relationship. The last few months we were together weren't pleasant, but at least I got to have sex with someone rather than self-service all the time."

"Having a girlfriend doesn't always guarantee participating in sex on a regular basis. It hasn't been a whole lot of fun being in my relationship lately, and I don't get much sex to make it worthwhile."

"So why don't you end it?"

Mandie shrugged. "I don't know. I should. I'm guessing if this is real and not some vivid dream, I won't have to end it. Caroline would never hang around for an entire year. She's not the loyal type. So how come you were dumped?"

"Typical story. I work too much, and she felt like she wasn't a priority. I wasn't invested enough in the relationship. The terrible thing is, after she left, life only got worse. I couldn't afford to live alone and had to work twice as hard. So now, even if I wanted to jump back into the pool, I'd never be able to devote any time to dating, much less a real relationship. Even worse, I don't do casual. I'll probably never have sex again. Sorry, I didn't answer your question honestly. I *was* joking. Yet I wish I wasn't. Does that make any sense at all?" She crinkled her nose, and Mandie thought that was adorable.

"It does. So, gut reaction, is this a dream?"

"I don't think so. The last thing I remember is a big bus barreling in my direction. Being in a coma fits," Gail answered.

"I went skydiving, and the parachute malfunctioned. A coma does make sense. Although, I really thought I was dead. I mean, who survives a jump from a plane when the parachute doesn't work?"

"You went skydiving? Are you nuts?" Gail's eyes bugged out.

"I'd just lost my job. It seemed like something to do if I wanted to face all my fears. Kind of a bucket list to combat my insecurities—which were plentiful. I figured if I could jump out of a plane and survive, then I could endure being unemployed for however long it would take to get a new job. I guess things didn't work out for me. Now I'll never get a new job. Being out of the work force for a year or more is career suicide."

"Even if you're in a coma?"

"Especially if I've been in a coma. Don't believe all that bullshit about nondiscrimination. It's hard to pinpoint discrimination against lesbians, persons of color, more mature people, or persons with a disability. If I wake up, I'll likely hit three of the four. *No* job for me." Mandie did her best to sound like the Soup Nazi.

Gail chuckled. "Seinfeld?"

"Yeah. I loved that skit. So dang funny. Only in New York City would customers suffer that abuse to get tasty soup."

"So then, what'll you do when you wake up?"

Mandie shrugged. "Good question. Maybe I'll be able to live on Social Security and my retirement nest egg. With Caroline out of the picture, I suspect my bills will reduce considerably."

"You're assuming you'll have lingering physical issues after you wake up."

"How could I not? After a year? At a minimum, I'll need to restore all my muscles and learn to walk, talk, and even poop again."

"Maybe we can appeal to Transition Messiah, and she'll allow me to stay a little longer and at the same time consider reducing your time here. Gray Hair did say we were special. Although I don't know what that means," Gail offered.

"Evelyn."

"Huh?"

"Her name is Evelyn," Mandie answered.

"Oh, sorry. I've never been able to remember names, so I give everyone nicknames." Her half smile was sheepish, yet Mandie still thought she looked adorable.

"What's mine?" Mandie asked.

"I know your name."

"Prove it," Mandie challenged.

"It's Mandie." Her wide smile was triumphant.

"And what nickname did you give me?"

Gail blushed. "Um, Stunning Swede."

"Aha, I knew it. I'm not that special after all." Mandie cocked her head. "Well, I think I'll call you Chocolate Decadence. Since that's a mouthful, I'm reducing it to CD for short."

Gail laughed. "Okay, I deserve that. But I did remember your name. That definitely makes you special. My business partner, Dale, had to remind me several times what my last girlfriend's name was. When we started dating, I kept calling her Classy Lesbian with Beautiful Blue Eyes. Now that was a mouthful. I could have shortened it to CLWBB and pronounced it club. She did hit my finances with a club."

"I only have a positive association with CD. I still hate iTunes for making compact discs obsolete. I'm not giving up my CD player, nor my collection of discs."

"And here I thought you were the kind of person to embrace new experiences. Skydiving, remember that?" Gail grinned.

"I don't think I need to remind you that new experience landed me in Intermediate, one step short of purgatory." Mandie groaned, as she remembered her impetuous decision to jump from a plane.

"I'd like to think it's providence. How else would we have met? I'm glad that bus mowed me down."

"Sure, easy for you to say. You'll only be here a week before you move on."

"But to where?" Gail shuddered. "The notion of death has always freaked me out."

"Me too." Mandie stood and held out her hand. "I think a distraction is in order. Shall we check out that rainbow forest? I'll bet a hike on those paths will be just what the doctor ordered."

Gail took her hand and emerged from the chair. "I haven't had the luxury of a hike in the woods in a very long time. I'd like that. Do you think we're allowed?"

Mandie shrugged. "Don't know. I'm going to think of this like the first day of classes or work, when they usually go pretty easy on you. We'll sneak out."

"I'm thinking Gray Hair—"

"Evelyn, I just told you her name like two minutes ago."

"Okay, Evelyn. She probably has a special way of keeping track of her charges. It's likely somewhere on that magical clipboard of hers."

Mandie was thrilled when Gail didn't let go of her hand as they walked through the tunnels of their temporary lodging.

CHAPTER NINE

The fluorescent-yellow, dirt path that led Mandie and Gail through the rainbow forest was an easy hike. The gentle slope crested near a rock formation more breathtaking than Gail had ever seen. The waterfall created another perfect rainbow, as it flowed over the brightly colored rocks.

"Do you think they patterned Intermediate for Fluids after *What Dreams May Come*? It seems as likely an explanation as anything else," Gail said.

Mandie laughed. "I seriously doubt it. Remember, Transition Messiah doesn't like technology."

"Oh yeah, I forgot about that." Gail continued to take in the sights and sounds all around her.

"I did love the interpretation of heaven he conjured up in that movie." Mandie's forehead crinkled. "Not that I want to dwell on death or anything, but if I do…you know…go to the other side, I'll have nothing to show for the life I lived. I didn't add a single thing to the good of the universe. It won't matter if I live or die." Mandie shrugged. "You're some kind of architect, right?"

"Yeah. Nature's Dwellings was my business."

"Are you for real? I've read about you. My God, you're famous. I wish I could have afforded your services," Mandie stated wistfully. "Your life matters—you left behind a legacy. There was absolutely no purpose for my life."

"Don't say that."

"It's true. I'm just one of the millions of people who were born to grow up and work forty or fifty years, then die leaving nothing behind but money and trinkets for their heirs. I didn't even have any kids. What's the point?"

"I don't believe that for a second. Haven't you ever read about how everything is interconnected? My favorite Christmas movie is *It's A Wonderful Life*. I'd bet one of my designs you've had a major impact on people's lives but just can't trace it back. By the way, where did you live? I know for a fact that people outside the state of Washington have no idea who I am."

"I lived on the east side of the state in Moses Lake."

"Oh, you live close to Cave B. I respect Tom Kundig's work. He's the architect who designed the structures. I like how he used the natural rocks on the land and mirrored the cliff tops across the gorge in his design for the inn and Cliffehouses. I wonder if we would have ever crossed paths? We should make a pact."

"What kind of pact?" Mandie asked.

"No matter what happens here in Intermediate, we vow to find one another when we return. Even if I go back earlier than you." Gail sought Mandie's eyes. Could the strength of her conviction be felt in that gaze? Gail knew this wasn't just another flirtation. She hadn't even felt this certain about Des.

Maybe this experience had changed her, or perhaps it was Mandie. She was worth the effort.

"I don't know. I wouldn't want you to seek me out, only to have a ringside view of my body shriveling up as pools of drool collect on the pillow."

"I can't really explain why this is so important. I simply know it is. You're different from my ex, in a good way. Des wore her beauty on the outside and surrounded herself in elegance. With my money, I might add. You are exquisite inside and out. There's something radiating from you that I can't ignore no matter what. I wouldn't focus all my energies on work. Besides, I'll bet you're cute when you drool."

"Are you flirting with me?"

"Uh huh, and I am going to track you down. You can count on that." Gail abruptly stopped walking and forced Mandie to see her resolve. This was so much greater than finally remembering a woman's name she was crushing on.

A white owl swooped across their path. The large bird was the first colorless thing they'd seen, living or inanimate. Mandie gasped. "Shit. One or both of us are not going to return to earth. A white owl crossing your path means death."

Gail stepped on a flat stone to bring her closer to eye level. She swiftly pulled Mandie into an embrace, engaging her in a passionate, toe-curling lip lock. She captured Mandie's lips and gently probed inside, increasing the pressure as she intensified the kiss. She grinned when she pulled back. "Nonsense. I looked up the meaning once, when it happened to me on a hike. Do you know what I found out?"

Mandie shook her head.

"This one site I came upon said I needed to pay attention to what happened immediately after the sighting. If it was something good that was a positive omen of delightful things to come. I just tipped the odds in our favor. Unless…"

"Unless what?"

"Unless the kiss wasn't welcome." Gail grinned.

Mandie touched her lips. "Unwelcome wouldn't exactly be the way I would describe that kiss. I'd say it fell into the wow category."

"Perfect. Then it's settled. Let's go find Gray Hair and demand that audience with Transition Messiah." Gail jumped off the rock, grabbing Mandie's hand and pulling her forward.

"Evelyn," Mandie exclaimed. "How is it you remember Transition Messiah, but can't remember Evelyn over Gray Hair?"

"Good question. Let me ponder that a bit, Mandible."

"Oh, now you can only sort of remember my name. I think I prefer Stunning Swede."

Gail laughed. "Mandible fits. For some reason, I get the impression you're strong, and the mandible is the strongest bone in a person's face. You have a particularly lovely face. Also, I sense you're the kind of person who won't let something go, you know, like a dog with a bone. Mandible, yes that's your new name."

"Okay, whatever, CD. Maybe I should call you GFW for Gale Force Wind. Blowing everyone over and sweeping them off their feet. Do you think I would be considered a cheater now? I do still have a girlfriend on earth."

"How about what happens in Intermediate, stays in Intermediate?"

"Not helping. That would be like saying I could cheat on her if I went to Las Vegas."

"Good point. Okay, I'm sorry. That was a bad thing to do. I won't do it again." Gail was disappointed, but she had to respect Mandie's values, even if it sounded like her girlfriend wasn't the type to hang around in the bad times.

"I wish there was some way to determine if I still have a girlfriend. Do you think Evelyn has that little piece of information on her ever-present clipboard?"

"That'll be my very first question to her."

†

Mandie wondered if she was skirting the edge. She continued to hold hands with Gail, as they strolled on the path. She rationalized the importance of human connection while they contemplated the real possibility one or both of them would not return to earth. This should be an exception to the no cheating rule. Evelyn had said the odds were in their favor. Mandie didn't think that was true. Not too many people recovered from a coma after an entire year of oblivion. A longer coma might increase her chances of passing to the other side.

"Gail, why do you want to stay longer?"

Gail squinted and turned her head in Mandie's direction. "I don't know. I can't explain that any more than why I'm not freaking out. It sort of feels like destiny or something. It's like I'm supposed to stay here with you, and it's all been predetermined. If we don't follow the plan, bad things will happen. The minute you offered me your hand; it was like a flash of clarity."

"Well, I believe in free will. It makes me uncomfortable to think I don't have any control over my future. I have to admit I feel a tug that has nothing to do with how adorable you are." Mandie reached over and placed a finger on one of Gail's dimples. "I've always been a sucker for dimples."

"I'm not saying we have zero influence over what happens to us. Just watch as I try to manipulate the time frame of my little vacation here. I definitely could use more than a week of downtime."

The sound of footsteps on the dirt path interrupted the women, and Mandie saw Evelyn hurrying in their direction.

She was breathing heavily when she approached. "Oh, I am so glad I found you. She'll meet with you, but you only have five minutes. Do you know how lucky you are? My goodness, the whole time I've been here, she's only met with one other couple. It took them forty years…very sad situation."

"Holy shit, they were here for forty years?" Gail asked.

Evelyn shook her head. "No, no. There's no time to tell you the story. I'm not supposed to anyway. Come on, you have to hurry. I'll take you there myself."

Mandie didn't need to hear the story. Likely, the other couple destined to reconnect had taken forty years to do so. That did not appeal to her at all. In forty years, she'd be eighty-one, much too old to enjoy a new love.

Evelyn jogged down the path, and Mandie let go of Gail's hand to follow. Gail began to lag behind, so Mandie slowed down.

"Damn, she's fast. I need to get back into my exercise routine," Gail exclaimed.

"It might have something to do with your tiny stature. We both have longer strides."

Mandie smiled at the memory of Gail climbing on the rock before kissing her.

"No short jokes, please."

"I wouldn't dream of it."

"Oh my…" Mandie gasped. The tunnel before them was at least fifty times larger than the dwelling they'd been assigned.

†

Gail looked around the room. *Is this place their great hall? Maybe it's named something fancier, like the antechamber.* "So, what is this place?"

"It's called, the antechamber. She likes large spaces. After being frozen in a cube of ice, she's a bit claustrophobic. I don't blame her. She's like seven feet tall," Evelyn whispered.

"Really?" Mandie asked.

"Enough idle chatter." An impossibly tall woman materialized as if she'd rearranged her molecules and moved through the enormous walls of the tunnel. "I am Transition Messiah. State your request, please."

Gail didn't detect any warmth or humor from the larger-than-life messiah. *At least she said please.* Manners on earth were at an all-time low. *Would it kill people to say please and thank you?*

"Um, I'm Gail, and this is Mandible, uh, I mean Mandie. We'd like to change the time lines so they match—maybe somewhere in the middle. Ideally, if you can see your way to shortening Mandie's to seven days like mine, that would be perfect."

"Why?" Transition Messiah asked.

"Even though we're not dating or anything, I've kind of got a rule about, you know, leaving with the person you came with. We walked into Intermediate together; we should pop back—or whatever you do to reenter earth—together." Gail tried to stand straighter hoping to convey an air of confidence.

A tiny corner of TM's lip turned up. "What makes you think either or both of you will return to earth?"

Gail shrugged. "Gray Hair told us we have a sixty-five percent chance. That's better than average odds."

TM quirked her eyebrow, and Gray Hair looked at the ground.

"Besides, I get the sense we were destined to meet."

"Not good enough. Mandie, why do you believe I should alter the time lines? You do not believe in destiny. What are you willing to sacrifice to achieve this outcome?"

"S...s...acrifice? Wh...what do people offer up?" Mandie stuttered.

"Your memory of this place. If I grant your request, neither of you will be able to share anything about this near-death experience. Not even seeing the white light. No book tours or talk shows. I hear it can be quite lucrative to those who return to earth."

"We won't know each other. Even if we meet, it'll be like we're meeting a stranger," Gail said.

"That is correct."

"Aw crap. Why you got to make this so damn difficult? It's like *Made in Heaven*, lesbian style. I don't believe you aren't peering into the movie theaters or people's TV sets. Admit it, you get your best ideas from American movies," Mandie challenged.

TM threw back her head and laughed. "Everyone's experience is tainted by their own notions of life, death, heaven, purgatory, and all those other purely human concepts. Don't blame me for your projections. The only thing I control is the technology limitation. Don't even get me started on those little devices you all insist on carrying around with you down there."

"Nice try, but I don't buy it. We wouldn't have the same hallucinations," Gail argued.

"Ah, but that's what makes you so special, Gail. Your notions of this place have synced perfectly with this other soul. Although, I do find it quite interesting the level of control you have given to Mandie. Perhaps it is because you are so much shorter than her."

Gail began to protest when Transition Messiah held up her hand. "I'm not sure why Creator gave you the ability to influence each other's experiences, but who am I to question fate? The only thing that does not line up is the time line. Only I can help with that. Your time is up. Do you both accept this sacrifice?"

"You said the word fate, not me. I'll take that as a positive sign. I accept," Gail said.

Mandie turned to Gail. "I knew you were special. I'm going to figure out a way to remember. I accept."

"Very well, you have thirty days together in Intermediate. Use the time wisely." TM waved her hand, and a heavy fog grew around her. She seemed to disappear in the colorful mist.

"Wow!" Gray Hair exclaimed.

"Well, it appears as though you're a figment of my imagination." A wry smile formed on Gail's face.

"I resent that comment. I certainly am not. Although your visual surroundings are unique to you, everything else is quite real. I've been here for twenty years. I should know."

"Right, like that bit about us not remembering each other and having to search out our soul mate. Please," Gail said.

"Oh no, that's for real, too. It happened at least once before that I know of, and it took…crap you're making me reveal stuff I'm not supposed to again. I can tell you that you don't control everything you see. TM has some influence, especially with foundational structures and lighting. Oh, and the no-technology rule."

Gail grabbed Gray Hair's arm. "So, no food, how about alcohol? Can I get you a drink or two?" She winked at Mandie.

Mandie skidded to a halt and turned around toward the lingering rainbow mist. "Hey, come back. I have one more question to ask."

Gray Hair shook her head. "Sorry, her schedule is limited. You had your time."

Mandie slumped. "I don't suppose you have more information about us on that clipboard of yours."

"I might," Gray Hair hedged.

"Can you tell me if my girlfriend intends to hang around while I'm temporarily indisposed? Did she even spend much time at the hospital?"

Gray Hair frowned. "Oh, she was there all right. Robin was right beside Caroline to console her during her *difficult time*."

"It says all that on your clipboard? And was that sarcasm I heard?" Mandie asked.

Gray Hair grinned. "The orb is a good substitute for television, very entertaining. A lot like the daytime soap operas I used to like when I was, you know, down there. Is Susan Lucci still on?"

Gail laughed. "Afraid not. And you know what really pissed me off? They canceled the show and didn't tie up one single story. Left us all hanging. They were going to do some Internet thingy, but that didn't work either. Same thing with *The L Word*. I really, really, hate that."

"You watched the soaps?" Mandie asked.

"Yeah, I'm a very good multitasker. I can watch TV and design houses."

"Can we get back to the original question?" Mandie asked.

"Transition Messiah doesn't like it when we all hover around the orb, but sometimes it helps us transition people back to earth. We uh, prepare them for their return. I guess telling you will help with reentry if that's what happens to you. Caroline doesn't hang around long. After hearing your prognosis, she cries on Robin's shoulder and, uh…do you want the details?" Gray Hair had the good sense to hesitate before giving Mandie all the gory particulars.

"No, I don't need the details. You said if I return. Doesn't your clipboard tell you who returns and who doesn't?"

"No, it doesn't work like that. I've already told you the odds. That's all the information we receive. Although, it says right here" —Gray Hair pointed to the clipboard that almost seemed like an extension of her hand— "you two will want to go back to…never mind. We try to make either option sound appealing so the person can decide without bias. Sometimes what happens here in Intermediate influences the outcome."

"Are you saying we have a choice?" Gail asked.

"Sort of. Free will and all that has an influence on the final outcome. When a soul wants to return, no amount of alternative information will sway them to consider moving on."

"There wasn't a lot of free will happening when my parachute malfunctioned."

"True, but there was a considerable amount of free will that went into your decision to make the jump." Her statement was matter of fact, but the small tug on the corner of her lips displayed her good humor.

"Good point," Mandie answered.

"So, let me summarize," Gail interrupted. "One, Mandie here is single again. Two, we get to choose whether we move on to the other side or return to earth. Three, we have thirty days together to get to know one another. Finally, if we return, we won't remember our time here or one another. What do you know about the other side? Is there really a heaven and a hell? Would we remember each other if we both wound up in heaven?" Gail did not like thinking about this possibility and could feel a sense of panic starting to creep in.

"Sorry, I don't have the answers to those questions. Everything is on a need-to-know basis here, and I don't need to know the answers," Gray Hair responded.

"What about those, what do you call them, uh, transition counselors? Do they know?" Mandie asked.

Gray Hair shrugged. "I've been assigned as your transition counselor, and no, we don't receive that level of detail."

"Hey, what happens if we waive our right to some perfunctory meeting designed to theoretically exercise our free will?" Gail asked.

"You want to waive your right to meet privately with a transition counselor? If you do that you won't be able to explore your individual destiny."

Mandie and Gail nodded in unison.

"No wonder it says you two are special," Gray Hair studied her clipboard again.

Gail inched closer to Gray Hair, discretely stretching her neck. Gray Hair clutched the secret documents close against her chest.

"You are naughty," Gray Hair said.

Gail winked. "You have no idea how naughty I am. But seriously, is there anything else on that magic clipboard of yours that you can share?"

"No, sorry. You two have weaseled out of me more information than I am technically allowed to share. I cannot offer any more."

"Fine." Mandie crossed her arms over her chest and pouted. Gail thought that was cute—even for a grown woman.

†

Evelyn and Harriet hovered around the orb with their eyes glued to the moving images. Evelyn had managed to zoom in on Caroline and Robin again. She wanted to prepare herself in case Mandie asked for more details.

"Hey, you're hogging the view," Harriet said.

"Why that little…" Evelyn declared.

"I told you she was cheating on Mandie. I won the bet, so you have to make sure Mandie takes over orientation for me. You know I only agreed under duress. Are you gonna tell her?"

"Shhh, let's watch a little more." Evelyn was seething.

Caroline and Robin were at a small table in an intimate winery on the Columbia River Gorge. They looked quite cozy.

"Don't you feel the least bit guilty? I thought you were going to tell her about us on Friday," Robin asked.

"She'd just lost her job. I didn't think I should kick her while she was down."

"Now you'll be labeled an insensitive, uncaring bitch who won't stick by her side while she's at her most vulnerable," Robin said.

"She may never wake up. People will understand that I was so distressed about Mandie. They'll see we became a couple only after we leaned on each other for support. It's the perfect way to ease our friends into our relationship. They'll understand."

"I'm not so sure about that. Her dad was giving you the eye. I don't think he likes you very much. Neither does her sister."

"Oh, who cares about them? They both live thousands of miles away." Caroline grabbed Robin's hand. "Come on, can't we enjoy our evening without thinking about those unpleasant things? I can't help it if I fell in love with you. Mandie became very boring. She never wanted to go out or do anything. She had to know we weren't going to last."

"Maybe, but I still think it doesn't look good. I wish you had told her six months ago when we started seeing one another."

"Well hindsight is a bitch."

Evelyn tsked. The only bitch she saw in this messy scenario was Mandie's ex-girlfriend.

CHAPTER TEN

Mandie wondered why she didn't feel much pain after learning Caroline would not be by her side when she returned to earth. She'd already decided. She wouldn't give up. She would convince Gail that returning was the right decision. She'd find a way to turn everything around in her life, get a new job, lose that last five pounds. Last but not least, she would find Gail. The five pounds might happen while she laid in the hospital bed for thirty days. She was already ahead of the game. Cold reality hit when she thought about trying to get her atrophied body back into shape.

When she was younger, she'd broken her leg. When the cast came off, she asked the doctor, "What the hell happened?" Her mother chastised her swearing with "the look." To add insult to injury, the bad leg had eight weeks of unshaven hair.

Mandie had thought her emaciated leg would never match the other one. She might as well join the circus as a freak show attraction. *Come see the lopsided girl. She can only walk in circles. It's a wonder she can even walk—just take a look at her legs.*

With a lot of hard work, she had eventually rebuilt the muscles in her right leg. That was a long time ago. Building muscles in her forties would be a lot harder than in her teens.

They'd returned to their own rainbow tunnel and the comfortable beanbag chairs. The next day, they would receive their work assignments. Mandie wondered if hers would be altered, because Gail had negotiated a shorter timeframe. Something was bugging Mandie. Something Transition Messiah had said.

Why would a famed architect perceive the afterlife with such simplistic structures? Something wasn't adding up. Was Transition Messiah lying?

"Gail, something is not right about what TM said." Mandie turned her head to Gail.

"These houses, right?"

"Yeah, how'd you know what I was thinking?"

"I don't know. The one part I do believe is that we are somehow in sync with one another. Our experience in this realm is a shared experience. Maybe this is completely your version of the afterlife, not mine. You were supposed to be here longer than me. I didn't see the swirling tunnel of color until you pointed it out. You said it was a rainbow of color, then I saw it. TM did say I'd given you the control."

"Really? Wow that's freaky. Why wouldn't you have a lot more influence on the buildings? I mean, that is your specialty, even if you gave most of the control of the illusions over to me." Mandie waggled her eyebrows. "I wonder what other situations will warrant my special brand of dominance?"

"Good thing you didn't make a short joke. I'm going to ignore the sexual innuendo for now. I do think that is a very good question we should explore, later.

"Why tunnels of color for every damn building? That's just, oh, I don't know, kinda weird. Don't get me wrong. I like the rainbow forest and all the bright colors, just not a fan of the circular structures. I like variety, angles, and things that curve around nature seamlessly," Gail said.

"What's wrong with circles? They're soft, like the curves of a woman. I don't particularly like things that jut out with harsh edges. A tunnel is like a protective cocoon. It wraps around you. It's subtle and warm."

"I wonder why they said they would let me design new houses. Isn't it all a figment of our imaginations anyway? Besides, I was only supposed to be here seven days. That's barely enough time to create a design worthy of Intermediate."

"Another good question. Maybe they want to provide us with a purpose, rather than allowing us to aimlessly wander in Intermediate. Without direction, I would definitely travel down the freak-out tunnel."

"So, you think it's all a ruse to keep us sane? Once again, the timelines don't add up. I don't think seven days would cause a freak-out."

Mandie shrugged. "It's as good a theory as any. You got a better idea?"

"Maybe there was a mix-up with the paperwork. After all, there's only one demigoddess, the rest are all humans in a sort of waiting pattern. What if I'm the one who was supposed to be stuck here for nearly a year?"

"Does it matter? I'd like to deal with a more pressing issue. Let's see if we can find a loophole or something in the no-memories rule. Evelyn knows more than she's sharing. If it's true she's been here twenty years, we need to pump her for all the information we can get out of her," Mandie stated.

"Okay, let's change the rules a bit. I can't believe your version of heaven or this intermediate place doesn't involve food and drink, especially alcohol. I'd kill for a hard cider. Maybe alcohol would have an effect on Gray Hair. You know, loosen those lips a bit more."

"Caroline put a lot of emphasis on wine. It really isn't my thing…"

"Oh. Is she an alcoholic or something?"

Mandie shrugged. "Maybe. I don't know."

"Okay, I get the alcohol part, but food, come on. A nice pasta dish and some apple pie. Ooh…I'll take some lobster please."

Mandie laughed. "Okay, I'll see what I can do. A candlelit dinner for two."

"Now you're talking."

"I am very pragmatic, I suppose. My idea of heaven means no food and drink required—no weight-loss issues— no bathrooms. Who wants to clean bathrooms in heaven?"

"Do you think it works the same as on earth? Just because we have a nice quiet dinner, doesn't mean our bodies have to purge what we eat. Back on earth, we've probably got catheters in us or something, while we're both in la-la land."

"Good point. Do you have any idea how I conjure this dinner for two?"

"How'd you come up with those weird tunnels? Maybe meditate or something. Do some kind of mantra. Just keep repeating lobster dinner with Dutch apple pie." Gail rubbed her belly. "By the way, you can keep these beanbag chairs.

They're super comfortable. Takes me back to my youth." Gail stretched her small body.

"The beanbags were all you. Remember, you're influencing this whole illusion. So, do I say this mantra out loud or silently? Maybe I should close my eyes for the full meditative effect." Mandie was taking the whole thing very seriously. A romantic, candlelit dinner with Gail sounded perfect. Gail could have her lobster. A nice eight-ounce rib eye, medium rare definitely activated Mandie's taste buds.

"Silence, I think, and sure, close your eyes. It couldn't hurt."

"I know I have to do the heavy lifting here, but could you maybe lend a hand?" Mandie poked Gail's beanbag with her toe.

Gail closed her eyes too. "Um, something is happening…oh, wow," Gail exclaimed.

Mandie opened her eyes. Her mouth gaped open, as she surveyed her handiwork.

The room was dim. The curved walls had faded from view. A single candle flickered in the center of a small, round table. Elegant perfection. Fine china and crystal rested on a white table cloth. The soft glow of a full moon reflected off the shiny surface of two silver domes that covered the plates. The table and two chairs sat outdoors, on a smooth, paved deck. Twinkling stars added the final piece of magic.

She looked down at her slinky, royal-blue dress and four-inch heels. *Nice choice.* She looked at Gail, and her breath hitched in delight. The low-cut, black number with slits up the sides molded to every delicious curve. She, too, was wearing high heels, and a quick glance at her calves was almost enough to make Mandie expel the dinner scene and go straight to the bedroom.

"I guess it worked. Score one for our imagination. I do believe these four-inch heels are all you. I would never dream that up for myself," Mandie said.

"You look amazing. Can we please keep the heels, even if they aren't your style?" Gail begged.

"I suppose I can endure them for you. It's amazing how in sync our fantasies are."

"Shall we?" Mandie pointed to the table and chairs. "I suspect there is lobster under one plate and a nice juicy rib eye under the other. If you pick the wrong seat, we can swap. *Bon appétit.*"

✝

Gail laughed when she lifted the lid and found the bloody piece of meat staring at her. "Perfection is overrated. There had to be something in this beautiful ambiance to correct. That's what makes life, or rather the between life, interesting."

Mandie looked under the lid of the silver dome in front of her, then offered her plate to Gail. "Besides the mix-up of the meals, do you think this is perfect?" Mandie asked.

"Uber-perfect."

"Considering perfect is sometimes an adjective, I wonder if uber-perfect is overkill."

"No, definitely not. There has to be a description for something that is beyond perfection. Unless…"

"Unless what?" Mandie asked.

"Do you consider this a date? If not, I'll drop the uber and downgrade to mediocre."

"Wow! That is quite a jump from uber-perfect to mediocre. I don't think my ego can take that drastic of a downgrade."

Gail simulated a malevolent laugh and wiggled her fingers together in front of her face. "Ah, my evil plan is working. You don't have a girlfriend anymore, so that means the path is wide open for me to drive through. Just so you know, I kinda have a lead foot. It gets me in trouble all the time."

"I'll bet it does." Mandie smiled.

"Wait. Before I confirm the uber-perfect rating, where's my Dutch apple pie?"

Mandie chuckled. "Patience. Wait until we've finished our dinner. You want the pie warm, don't you?"

"You forgot, didn't you?"

"Yeah, I did. I know I'm new at conjuring, but if I was able to dream up this" —Mandie waved her hand over the table— "a couple of slices of pie will be a snap. Besides, I thought this was a combined effort? How come I have to be the one to keep doing the heavy lifting?"

"Hey, don't blame me. I'll bet that magic clipboard says everything is predetermined. Besides, I like the idea of you driving for tonight's adventure."

"Nothing is 100 percent predetermined," Mandie corrected. "But I'll gladly take the reins."

"Great, I want a big piece to make up for your oversight of the most important part of a good meal. Besides, I get the feeling we can eat anything we damn well please here. It'll never affect our hips. I say we eat and drink our way through the next thirty days."

"There might be one other thing we could do to pass the time." Mandie lifted her hooded eyes to Gail, and God that look was so sexy.

"Are you flirting with me? Was that a veiled suggestion of a good old-fashioned roll in the hay? Because you know it's been awhile for me. Getting me all riled up for nothing would be mean."

Mandie laughed. "Eat your lobster. We'll talk about the possibilities after dinner. I thought you were leaving everything up to me tonight?"

"Done. I can make an exception to my no-sex-on-the-first-date rule…"

†

A quiver of excitement tingled Mandie's mind at the prospect that this was a bona fide date with Gail. There was also a small twinge of guilt. Should she be happy about landing in Intermediate and forcing the breakup with Caroline? She wasn't naive enough to deny the inevitable path, based on the last couple of months. The signs had been there. Maybe it wasn't a bad thing that her skydiving accident tipped the scales.

The tender steak had melted in her mouth, and the last bite of warm pie was sublime. If she'd eaten the same amount of food on earth, she would be groaning with discomfort. Even after forty years, she hadn't learned to slow down and savor a meal—to push away the plate before she felt bloated and sick.

She leaned back in her chair, looking up at the sky. *Now what?* She flashed to a memory of watching classic movies and imagining herself leading the dance with Vivien Leigh under the stars. Mandie stood and offered her hand to Gail.

The table and chairs disappeared when Gail accepted her hand. Mandie hoped she had the power to summon a sensual tango. When the music started, Gail looked at her with such raw passion, that Mandie threw back her head and laughed. She instinctively led Gail to the center of the patio. She considered why she had taken Gail's right hand with her own right, instead of the more common and comfortable left hand clasped to right. She let her arm trail behind her as they made their way across the stone deck.

Mandie raised their hands together and spun Gail around. She pulled her close with a strong motion, using their clasped hands that rested against Gail's stomach. Moving ever so slightly, she rocked Gail from behind. Her free hand stroked Gail's left shoulder, exhaling warm breath against her neck. Mandie let her lips slide across Gail's skin, while her hand moved from shoulder to breast to Gail's quivering stomach. Mandie used the tips of her fingers and palm of her hand to brush over Gail's behind, as she pivoted to face Gail. She led Gail into a side step, then confidently performed the *sacada,* bringing their bodies close again. Pushing their intertwined hands out, Mandie found the rhythm of the music and began an accomplished rendition of the tango.

At the end of the dance, Mandie seized the opportunity and ensnared Gail's inviting lips with her own. She plunged her tongue inside in a completely different version of the tango. Letting the kiss come to an end, she kept her hold of Gail.

"Oh, holy hell, that was…indescribably hot. Where did you learn to tango?" Gail breathlessly asked.

"My illusion, my rules. I guess I decided Intermediate Mandie would be all smooth and debonair."

"After we return to earth, we're signing up for dance lessons. The first one I want to learn is the tango. When I'm motivated, I can learn anything. Trust me…I am very motivated."

Mandie frowned. "We still don't know how to find one another."

"I don't care what Transition Messiah said, I could never forget you or this night." Gail brushed her hand against Mandie's cheek.

"The night's still young, and I plan on leaving an indelible mark on you." Mandie clasped the hand that had lovingly stroked her. She kissed the palm, then nipped playfully at the fingers.

"Does that include biting? Little love bites work for me," Gail added.

"Good to know." Mandie blinked, and a round, king-sized bed took shape, ten feet away. Red silk sheets peeked out from under the bedspread.

"What is it with you and round things? It looks like we're in a bordello," Gail said.

"I know, I know. I guess my raging hormones have taken over." Mandie closed her eyes. "Okay, give me a second here. I'll adjust the scene." She squinted one eye open. "Um that is, if…um…you're on the same page."

"Oh, I'm definitely on the same page, but not in red silk sheets on a cheesy, round bed."

"Perhaps a bit of assistance here…" Mandie slammed her eyes shut again. When she opened them, the bed was square. Cream-colored sheets were topped by a moss-colored bedspread. "Better?"

"Oh yes, I'm getting the knack of influencing your illusions. I definitely prefer the more natural colors."

"Please, please, please, let there be an impossibly long zipper on that slinky, black dress of yours," Mandie declared.

"Ditto," Gail replied.

†

Forget architecture, she'd take up writing. Who else would think up this stuff? *If this is all part of an elaborate fantasy, what would be the harm in letting this scene play out?* Sometimes Gail's sex dreams were realistic enough to cause a physical reaction. She'd wake up the next morning with dampness that wasn't there the night before.

Her emotions and intellect were at war, and it felt like tiny little spears were flying all around her. Everything about this whole experience pointed to the implausible. She'd told the "fictional" Mandie that she wasn't the type of person to have one-night stands. That was true.

This didn't feel like a casual affair. Something about what was happening felt real, more real than a dream. All this mental wrangling took place in the blink of an eye, because Mandie did not waste time tugging on the zipper. Gail felt the separation of the individual teeth on the zipper, as the dress parted like the red sea in agonizingly slow motion. She could almost hear the individual clicks that obliged the air to caress her back. Gail did not have the same level of patience when she reached for the back of Mandie's gown.

"Um…"

Gail saw an irresistible hesitancy in Mandie's eyes, an unspoken question. Gail grinned. She suspected Mandie wanted to try something completely outside her comfort zone. "Don't be afraid to suggest something. I'm very open to trying new things. Considering you have the ability to dream up any host of special toys or accessories, you aren't in any way tied to convention."

"I'm a bit of an amateur photographer. I always wanted to see what it would be like to take photos as a sort of, I don't know, a form of foreplay. I saw myself directing a partner in naked poses, while I lined up the shots. It sounds weird, doesn't it? Oh my God, I have a camera fetish. Well, not exactly a camera fetish, more like an oddball kind of voyeurism. Forget I even suggested it."

"Not so fast. I'll do it, but I want you to continue to undress me like you've been doing. I can't even describe how hot that is. I'm warming to the idea of you making love to me with your camera." The irony was not lost on Gail, as she remembered her staunch refusal to ever have her photo taken. She'd told Dale she was selling her architectural designs, not herself. She remembered his insistence that her good looks wouldn't hurt sales. "*Like it or not, attractive people tend to do better in the business world. A mug shot in a magazine feature will sell more than an image of the product or service.*"

She knew Mandie's photos would never make it to the outside world, yet the idea was naughty and risqué. Gail grinned. *Why the hell not?*

Mandie nudged the expensive black material forward, carefully removing the dress. She caressed each shoulder, until the gown lay in a pool at Gail's feet. Gail marveled at how sexy she felt in a matching pair of lace undies and bra. Black, of course, to match the dress. Mandie took a few seconds and stared. Gail felt adored. She couldn't get over the feeling that Mandie looked at her as if she were a newly discovered treasure that only she had the tools to uncover.

Mandie took painstaking care, as she removed Gail's undergarments. In the same excruciatingly unhurried manner as with the dress, a feathery caress removed her bra, then her thong. Mandie's own dress still hung open in the back.

"Will you do me a favor?" Gail asked.

Mandie cocked her head. "What?"

"When you take my picture, will you do it nude?"

"Okay." Mandie slipped off her dress. Wearing only her underwear and stilettos, she reached for the bra's clasp.

"Wait. I have an addendum. That's an architectural term for a change or correction in a plan. You look scrumptious right now. Stay like that." Gail kicked off her shoes, sending them flying to the right of the bed. "So, where would you like me?"

"Get on the bed, and I'll position you," Mandie ordered.

Gail pulled the covers down and eased onto the bed. A sudden burst of cool air surged into the small space and flowed over Gail's body, eliciting an immediate reaction. Her nipples erupted into two tiny points. Pulling the sheet partially over her body, she sought a small measure of warmth, but soon found the air around her had lost that temporary chill.

Gail was too distracted by Mandie's enraptured blue eyes and the sound of the first click of the shutter to consider why TM allowed a camera into Intermediate. She felt her lips form the hint of a smile accompanied by something intangible. Mandie took that moment to capture her expression.

Mandie gently removed the covers. She arranged Gail in an asymmetrical pose. One arm was stretched upward toward the headboard, while her other arm and hand were provocatively resting on her thigh. Gail's finger hovered mere inches from her triangle of curly, brown hair. Mandie tucked one leg under the other.

"Can you turn so you're barely on your side?" Mandie stepped back. Her scrutiny reminded Gail of an artist surveying her masterpiece. Mandie raised the camera to her eye. Gail heard the rapid clicking sound, and her own level of excitement ratcheted to the engineered sky. She marveled at the view revealing thousands of tiny points of light.

Gail had the best of both worlds. She could sleep outside in the open air, face to the stars, and didn't have to bother with the elements or flying insects that would disturb her peace and quiet. Even though Mandie was definitely in the driver's seat, Gail wondered if she had unconsciously added this small detail to the evening's ambiance.

"Move your hand between your thighs and part your lips for me, but keep the other arm stretched upward. I promise I won't take a close up, but oh my God, that is so…I don't even have the words. Glorious, sexy perfection. Can you stroke yourself?"

"I can, but I prefer your fingers or tongue."

"Imagine the camera lens is reaching those places inside no one can ever get to."

Gail groaned. "Okay." She started to stroke herself. She could almost feel Mandie's narrow, reverent focus. The camera clicked away. Gail thought she would never again be able to hear the release of a shutter without a very physical response.

"Sit up now and tuck your legs under your ass. Tilt your head back and cross your arms over your chest, touching the top of each breast. You can stroke your breast if you wish."

"Ugh, you are officially killing me now," Gail exclaimed. She didn't think she had ever been so ready for someone to make actual physical contact with her. The shutter on the camera continued its rapid-fire clicks.

"Look at me now. You are dying of thirst. You need to wet your dry, chapped lips," Mandie suggested. She moved fluidly, capturing Gail's nude body from multiple angles. Gail was near frenzy. The noise from the quick shutter stopped. Mandie let the camera fall to her chest.

"I'm done taking pictures. I don't think I'll last one more second with this much distance between us. How'd you like my idea of foreplay?"

"Lose the camera and get that sexy body of yours over here. I'll show you how much I enjoyed it. I never thought I'd envision a camera as a sex toy."

Mandie lifted the camera over her head and gently set it to the side. She kicked off her shoes, then descended on the bed and straddled Gail. She began to layer kisses up and down Gail's torso. Gail took the opportunity to unclasp her bra. She caressed Mandie's smooth skin, before removing the bra completely and tossing it over the side of the bed.

Mandie gently pushed her down on the bed and lay on top of her. While Mandie was slowly grinding, Gail tugged at the silk underwear. Mandie must have got the message. She rolled over and removed the last piece of clothing, leaving the two women naked and ready. Both instinctively turned to their sides and wrapped their limbs around one another. They found a position that allowed them to simultaneously enter the other's now dripping centers. Arching their bodies together, they were both more than ready. After only a few deep penetrations they cried out in unison. The wave of emotion and pleasure overran their heightened state of arousal, as the tremors matched their beating hearts.

"Oh, God, yes," Mandie cried out.

This time, the blinding, white light Gail saw before her was a welcome sight. "Holy mother of God. That was intense. I wish someone had captured that moment on film." Gail surmised she'd had her first out-of-body, sexual experience.

"Hmmm, next time I'll have to set up a tripod and a delayed timer," Mandie quipped.

CHAPTER ELEVEN

Time was elusive in Intermediate. Night and day did not seem to exist, except as one created it. Mandie's experience with Gail had been more freeing than any other in her life. Something had always held her back from exploring what she considered the more fringe elements of her hidden desires. After an extended period of time when she and Gail had gotten very creative with their lovemaking, they'd yawned and fallen asleep.

When Mandie first opened her eyes, the only thing that existed was the woman slumbering peacefully next to her in the king-sized bed. Mandie became aware there was a kind of nothingness all around them. She abruptly sat up. Wide-eyed, she looked around, trying desperately to capture something else besides the bed floating in midair.

Gail stirred next to her. "What? What's wrong?"

"Nothing. There's nothing here," Mandie screeched.

"Huh? You're not making any sense. If it's nothing, why do you sound so panicked?" Gail stretched and sat up. A full night's sleep had tangled her hair. One side was mashed against her head, the other poofed around her face with wisps sticking out in various angles. The sight of something as normal as a woman with bedhead caused Mandie to burst out in laughter.

"You're laughing at my hair, aren't you? That's not very nice, but at least you don't look as though Hannibal Lector just walked into the bedroom."

"I'm not sure this" —Mandie pointed to the space around them— "can be considered a bedroom."

"Wow, it's like we're floating in midair. That's kinda cool, like making love on a cloud or something. Oooh, can we try that? You know, lose the bed and replace it with something white and fluffy? Maybe we can get a little light too—simulate daylight in the same way you created that wonderful nighttime with the stars and moon. You can add a little color if you want by putting a rainbow at the end of the cloud. This kind of dull gray look doesn't match my mood."

"I'll get right on that," Mandie answered sarcastically.

Gail lost her smile and touched Mandie's arm. "Hey, I'm sorry. You were really freaked out, huh?"

"This nothingness is disturbing and lonely. If you weren't here with me, I can't even imagine how frightening it would be. How do you think the others are coping? I got the feeling we aren't very typical. I'll bet most people arrive here alone."

"Maybe that's why they have people like Gray Hair to help with the transition."

"Evelyn," Mandie chastised.

"Right, Evelyn." Gail put both index fingers to her temple. "Evelyn, Evelyn, Evelyn, Evelyn, Evelyn—"

"What are you doing?"

"It's how I learn someone's name. I have to repeat it like ten times before it'll sink in. She has answers we need, so I wouldn't want to offend her by letting it slip that I call her Gray Hair. Shit, now I've forgotten again. That recency effect is occurring."

"Evelyn." Mandie chuckled. "I'll say her name with you. Ten times, right?"

Gail grinned.

"Evelyn, Evelyn, Evelyn, Evelyn, Evelyn, Evelyn, Evelyn, Evelyn, Evelyn, Evelyn," they both chanted.

"Thanks, Mandie. I've got it now. So, can you make things a little brighter? Then we can go search for Evelyn." Gail looked down at her naked body. "Oh, and some clothes would be nice. Something comfortable. Not that you didn't look smoking hot in that little royal-blue number—and I always wanted to rock a sexy, black dress—but some jeans and a t-shirt would work for today."

Mandie quirked her eyebrow.

Gail lifted her shoulders. "I've grown accustomed to you taking the lead."

"Okay, you asked for it." Mandie closed her eyes and created a picture of Gail in a pair of jeans and a tight t-shirt. She decided her own clothes should give a bit more room to move around in. She thought of a sunny day and luscious foliage around a sparkling, blue lake. She opened her eyes at the sound of laughter.

"Nice, but did you have to make this shirt so tight?"

"I like the shirt, but very well I'll give you one that's a size bigger." Mandie blinked. The bed disappeared, and Gail was standing on the path with her arms in the air, twisting her torso.

"Much better. I feel like I can breathe now." She held out her hand. "I notice you gave yourself roomier clothes."

"Next time, be a little more specific with your request, or offer to take the wheel." Mandie smirked.

"Hmmm, I guess I am reassessing. Maybe I no longer like the fact that you have all the control over the ambiance. It seems like it's a lot easier for you than me. Although, I have to admit that most of the time you are spot on with a perfect illusion. I suppose I can live with you occasionally going off the rails." Gail grinned.

"You have more influence than you think, it's just that we sync a lot more and it's less noticeable. Another mystery we'll have to wiggle out of Evelyn."

"You called." Evelyn appeared a short distance away on the path. "By the way, you don't have to chant my name. I heard you the first time, but I didn't think you'd appreciate me popping in while you were still naked."

Mandie spun around. "You, uh, heard us?"

"Oh, don't get your britches in a cluster. I don't pay much attention until I sense my charge or charges are ready to have me assist. Although, I do have a new interest in photography." She held up her hand and laughed. "I stopped overseeing when I heard the word foreplay. I have a great respect for privacy, but it did sound quite intriguing."

Gail narrowed her eyes. "So, what else have you been listening in on?"

"Well, um, you were kinda right. I made a little mistake with the paperwork. Gail, you were the one who was supposed to be here for 364 days, not Mandie. Oops, my bad. TM doesn't know about that little blip, and I'd greatly appreciate you not blabbing. Thankfully, she had her hands full with another little problem. She hasn't been paying attention to you two," Evelyn answered.

Mandie looked at Gail, who grinned. "We'll keep quiet, but only if you tell us how we can find each other after our little stint here in Intermediate," Mandie boldly declared.

"Oh, no, no, no, no. I can't. That's blackmail," she huffed.

"All right, how about a little hint, something to up our odds?" Gail cajoled.

"Well, since Transition Messiah already made an exception and altered the timelines, there must be a reason she wants you two to stay in sync. I don't suppose she would be too upset if I gave you a little hint on how to beat the odds. I could allow a tiny part of Intermediate to sneak through. One physical memento, perhaps."

"That's the ticket, Evelyn. We sure appreciate any help you can slide our way," Mandie said.

"A photograph, that's all you're getting from me. Mum's the word, please."

Mandie glanced over at Gail, who gave her the thumbs up. Apparently, she'd caught the clue. Mandie had a pretty good guess.

Something niggled just outside her consciousness. Mandie tried to remember an important detail, but the illusive thought slipped away as fast as it had surfaced.

"Okay, but we reserve the right to obtain further assistance from you. Besides, you're our transition counselor. Aren't you here to make our time in Intermediate less stressful?"

"Yes, I am. The first order of business is to get you settled into your new roles. It helps pass the time."

"I can think of better ways to pass the time," Gail grumbled.

"Thirty days of nonstop sex?" Evelyn asked.

"It's not a completely asinine idea," Gail defended.

"I'm sure you've realized you cannot escape fatigue in Intermediate. If you return to earth, you will need some energy to continue to heal. We can't let you resume your lives in a weakened state, no matter how pleasurable the sex was that created that less-than-ideal condition."

"Please, don't tell me we can't be intimate again," Mandie lamented.

"I'm not saying that. I'm just warning you everything must be kept in balance, same as on earth. So, no pigging out on food either."

"Suddenly all the advantages of this experience have flown out that imaginary window. Damn. Even in predeath we can't do as we please. That sucks," Gail added.

"How come these so-called assignments don't run the risk of causing fatigue?" Mandie asked.

"Balance. Most people need something to occupy their time. Work provides purpose. Now, before you go down the road of occupying your time in a sexual frenzy, you should know that has never worked out well. We used to allow that…let's just say there were dire consequences. It wasn't even two days before they were back here in Intermediate, and the majority went on to the great beyond. We learned our lesson. The greatest chance of returning to earth and staying there for an extended period of time, rests in providing some purpose"—Evelyn raised an eyebrow— "without you fixating on one activity."

"Fine, okay. What are our assignments?" Gail asked.

"Well, I suppose you now know that designing new dwellings isn't needed. We need talent acquisition experts, because we have a shortage of people who can help calm the newbies and give our daily orientation spiel. You weren't very nice to Harriet the other day. She didn't particularly want to do the orientation speech. After her disastrous experience yesterday, she's refused to fill that role."

"Oops, my bad. Hey, was the shortage of dwellings for people to stay, a ruse as well?" Gail asked.

"Clever girl. Yes, I told Harriet to say that in orientation, knowing you two would volunteer," Evelyn answered.

"Why?" Mandie asked.

"Because you're meant to go through this experience together. We've already been through this. So, Mandie, can you take over orientation?"

"I suppose. Do you have a script I can use? Oh, and do I need to be briefed about any special situations like ours? I must say, I'm not all that comfortable playing fast and loose with the facts. Why can't you be upfront with people when you greet them?"

"Hmmm, transparency. I'll take that up with Transition Messiah. I simply follow orders and what appears on my clipboard. Although, as you already know, my eyes aren't what they used to be. That's how I got the two of you mixed up."

"Haven't you had any optometrists show up?" Mandie asked.

"In my humble opinion, Transition Messiah needs to get over her issues and get with the times. Maybe she can come to a compromise. She can ban technology designed solely for entertainment purposes, but allow other more useful tools to help people settle more comfortably."

"Now Gail, don't jump to conclusions. She does allow some things. It's okay, I get by. I'll watch out for an optometrist in the future. Maybe one will have a good enough imagination to visualize a new pair for me without fancy exam equipment."

Gail snapped her fingers. "That's it." She paused a finger over her lips and shook her head. Mandie wondered what had flashed through Gail's thoughts. "What can I do?" was all Gail asked.

"You seem to have a plethora of ideas about how to improve Intermediate. Why don't you begin writing those thoughts down to present to Transition Messiah?"

"Well, it won't be as fun as designing houses, but okay. There's something else I've been curious about. It seems like time is somewhat elusive here and tied to a person's imagination. How do we know when it's night and when it's day?"

"Don't worry, you both are on track regarding time. Most people have an internal clock that helps to mold their view of Intermediate. That's why Mandie created a night scene last evening and the reason for the daylight you see right now. One day has already passed. You have twenty-nine days left of your time here." Evelyn handed Mandie the top sheet of paper on her clipboard. "Here's the basic script for orientation today. You have approximately one hour to prepare."

"What? I can't do this with only one hour of prep time." Mandie glanced at the paper.

"Sure you can. You wing it all the time. That's what it says on the background information I have right here." Evelyn pointed to her clipboard.

"Are you sure that's the correct info and you haven't mixed up Gail and me again?" Mandie asked.

Evelyn glared. "I would have expected that poke from Gail, but not you, Mandie. One little mistake, and you have to keep bringing that up."

"Just checking."

Evelyn squinted at her clipboard. "Yes, I have it right here. You're good at winging it."

Gail grabbed for the clipboard. "Let me see that."

"Oh, no, no, no. That isn't allowed."

"Come on, you don't want there to be another mistake that Transition Messiah will find out about, do you?" Gail reasoned.

Evelyn seemed to consider the argument. "Okay, but only a quick look."

†

Gail could not believe her good fortune. She'd been able to get Evelyn to agree to a quick peek at the elusive and very revealing clipboard. She scanned the words.

> *Soul mates with a 50/50 chance of finding one another again on earth.*

Damn, I don't like those odds. There was also a warning that Evelyn should not help the couple. Under skills, Gail confirmed Mandie did possess the ability to adapt to new situations and was a gifted public speaker. She smiled and was eager to see Mandie in action. Her eyes zeroed in on something she hoped she could use later.

If reconnection occurs, it will be at a gallery display of Mandie's photographs. The fates are in charge of whether this will occur or not. Do not interject any assistance in this.

Evelyn grabbed back her clipboard. "Okay that's enough time. Did you confirm I've assessed her talents accurately?"

"Yes. Mandie, according to the clipboard you adapt well to new situations and are a talented public speaker. Go get 'em," Gail answered.

Gail began to strategize how she would find Mandie once they returned to earth. By God, she was not ready to go to the great beyond now that she'd found her soul mate. Evelyn's earlier hint about a photo was not a coincidence. Gail had an idea. She would take a photo back with her and include a message on the back to make it easy to find the photographer. She wondered if any of the photos taken the other night would somehow make their way onto photo paper. Would she want to take one of those pictures with her and inscribe the message on the back? It might work. She'd have to get Mandie to produce the photo. Gail hoped tucking it in the pocket of a pair of pants would allow the picture to travel to a different realm. No harm, no foul for trying.

Evelyn gave Gail the stink eye. "You've got that look in your eyes like you're up to something. My nephew used to adopt that same expression right before jumping off the roof with his cape—pretending to be Superman."

Gail ignored the accusation. "Better get me a pen and paper so I can start writing those ideas down. Mandie, I'll mosey back to our place and get comfy on one of the beanbags. See you back there in a few hours. Oh hey, can you imagine us some sushi for lunch?"

"If you have specific little fishes in mind, you might want to start thinking about them. Oh shoot. Sorry, I forgot breakfast, and more importantly coffee, this morning," Mandie replied.

"It's okay. I only drink coffee for the effect anyway. I don't feel that caffeine withdrawal here. I'm good." Gail leaned in and gently pecked Mandie on the lips. Mandie rewarded her with a brilliant smile. Gail enjoyed watching the spring in her step as she walked away with Evelyn.

CHAPTER TWELVE

Mandie looked down at the rather boring script. She wished she had the ability to tap into her usual tricks during orientation with new employees. She loved to inject short video clips and tell stories. Adults had the attention span of a gnat. They were worse than children, especially now as they remained tethered to their smartphones. At least she wouldn't have to give her spiel about phubbing. She'd come across an amusing video about people snubbing others with their phones, and the new concept of phubbing was born. She thought that was a rather clever word for what most people did in restaurants, training sessions, and sometimes even in bed.

Maybe Transition Messiah was on to something. No technology meant people had to communicate with one another. Face to face, without the annoying gadget glued to their palm. At least she hadn't banned cameras. They'd been around since the 1800's, so Mandie suspected Transition

Messiah didn't consider a camera modern technology. Mandie frowned. The semiautomatic SLR she'd handled the other night wasn't one of the first ever used, but it wasn't a state-of-the-art digital camera either. Mandie preferred a camera that let her do all the work. That's where the magic happened. She preferred to choose the aperture and use the manual focus. Oh well. Best not to look a gift horse in the mouth.

"No videos," Mandie mumbled to herself as she stood on the stage. She'd altered the scene and turned the auditorium setting into something more intimate. Several round tables and chairs were interspersed within the large room. She liked the rainbow tunnel, so that stayed. This tableau fit her notion of what new inductee orientation should look like. She continued to talk to herself, "Well if I can't use videos, my fall back is stories. People can relate to personal experiences." She'd talk about her own first day.

The men and women who shuffled into the room looked shell-shocked. She wondered if she'd worn that same expression on her first day. She wanted to soothe their nerves.

"Welcome, everyone. Just so you know, I only arrived yesterday, and I must say I had one of the best days of my life. So, relax and enjoy the ride."

A quiet murmur filled the room, as people looked at one another. They were sitting at tables making connections with their new anchors to this unknown experience. Mandie had seen this before, but mostly when natural disasters hit. Humans needed to establish bonds, and strangers became good friends in mere minutes.

Mandie expertly wove in the script she needed to cover, along with her own take on the experience. She genuinely believed everyone who made it to Intermediate had a rare opportunity to reset their lives. A wake-up call to live life to the fullest and look for those special moments that could change everything. Gail was her special moment.

By the time she finished her job, Mandie could feel the energy in the room change from frenetic anxiety to a leisurely float on the river. Most of the men and women shuffled out with smiles on their faces.

"I knew you'd be a natural. It's too bad we'll only have your expert touch for twenty-nine more days." Evelyn shrugged. "Easy come, easy go."

A lifetime of polite manners kicked in. "Do you want to join us for lunch?" Mandie crossed her fingers behind her back, hoping Evelyn would decline.

"No, that's okay. There are a few of the new arrivals I need to follow up on. You did a great job. These newbies aren't as worrisome as you or Gail, but I do need to make sure they don't venture into troublesome territory."

"Worrisome?"

"Yes, I'm quite sure you both are bound and determined to get me into a great deal of trouble. But you know, the two of you are kinda special, and I've been here a long time. What TM doesn't know won't change my status." Evelyn started laughing. "Can't say won't kill me, because you know, we're in Intermediate."

"So, will you toss more assistance our way? I really want to reconnect with Gail when we return to earth. I've never felt such a strong pull toward anyone."

"I might see fit to not noticing a few things." Evelyn winked.

There was something about that statement that got Mandie thinking. Perhaps Evelyn did know about the camera and was choosing not to confront them. Mandie wasn't a hugger, but she pulled the older woman into her arms and gave her an overzealous hug. "You're the best."

†

Gail stared up at the nonexistent ceiling. She wasn't sure if it was her wandering thoughts of Mandie and their incredible evening or the lack of ambiance in the room that was causing her unease. It wasn't the physical nothingness that unnerved her, but rather the void she felt. Something important was missing. She didn't freak out to the same level as Mandie, but the missing details bothered her. The void seemed to parallel her life as an abject reminder of what she didn't possess—substance. She'd have to be more specific with Mandie regarding how to create a calming space that would generate ideas for Intermediate. Mentally shrugging, she settled in and waited for Mandie to return.

That's it! I need Mandie and whatever magic occurs when we're together. Their shared experience created the special sync resulting in those unusual multicolored surroundings. Gail's designs might be her legacy, but surely Mandie's presence in the lives of her family and friends would leave a huge hole when she did cross over. Hopefully, that would not happen in the next twenty-nine days.

Chewing on her pen, Gail stared at the page where she'd scribbled exactly two ideas.

Offer cocktails upon arrival.

Add pets.

She thought it would be nice to have a big fluffy cat to cuddle with, but others might prefer dogs, bunnies or ugh, an iguana. She'd have to ask Mandie if she had any pets and what she preferred. That could be a deal breaker. She'd heard of lesbian couples who couldn't agree on cats versus dogs. Gail hadn't gotten around to getting a new kitten when hers passed away after eighteen long years. Jasmine had been her most constant companion.

Dogs were far too much maintenance. Her dad had a hunting dog who incessantly licked his balls. Disgusting. She supposed cats and dogs both licked their butts. Cats simply had exceptional hygiene. Dogs would roll in all things stinky and dig in litter boxes for cat poop. Neither of those activities warranted any rationalizations for their behavior.

Shit, now I'm procrastinating with thoughts of cats versus dogs. Gail needed a new plan to occupy her time in Intermediate. This idea-generation gig wasn't working for her. *Mandie had better come back soon and save me from myself.* As if she had projected her thoughts, she heard her soft melodious voice.

"Hey you," Mandie greeted. "What brilliance have you come up with?"

"Thank God, you're here. You have to save me from my own ineptness. It appears as though I have but one talent—designing houses around nature. Unless…" Gail wiggled her eyebrows. "Do you think Evelyn would consider assigning me as your personal sex slave?"

"Let me see the list. It can't be that bad." Mandie plucked the list from Gail's hands, then her face scrunched up.

"See, I told you. Pathetic."

"No, not pathetic. Those are good. You should clarify the cocktails don't have to contain alcohol. There are some recovering alcoholics in the new arrivals," Mandie offered.

"Oh, good thinking. Hey, I could do some sample house designs to help people envision their dwellings. What do you think about that?"

"Excellent idea. Who knows? You might be able to provide a legacy both on earth and in Intermediate. Probably in the great beyond, too, when we eventually go there. I hope that won't be in twenty-nine days."

"It won't." Gail lifted herself out of the beanbag and reached for Mandie, grabbing her hand and pulling her on top. "I've always wanted to make out on a beanbag chair. What do you think? Want to send me back in time to my youth and college days? I feel twenty years younger already."

Mandie giggled, as she shifted her body to a comfortable position on Gail's lap.

Gail wrapped her arms around Mandie and started with a nibble on her bottom lip. She sucked lightly, before exploring with her tongue, then heightening the pressure and need. She was breathing heavily when she ended the steamy kiss. "You taste like summer."

"What does summer taste like?" Mandie asked.

"Sweet, refreshing, hot, exciting, and bright all rolled up into one sensation. As kids we used to stay up late and play outside until dark. I could never get enough of summer, like I'm sure I could never get enough of you."

A slow, sexy smile formed on Mandie's lips. "That's about the sweetest, most poetic thing anyone has ever said to me."

"You must have dated a whole series of losers then."

"Maybe I did. You know what I remember about summer?" Mandie asked.

"No, tell me."

"We used to stay up late and catch lightning bugs. We put them in little jars with holes in them. A see-through cage. I remember one night, when my brother crushed several so he could put their lights on his body. I cried all night long and wouldn't talk to him for a week. Another time we kept them in the jar for most of the night. My father told us we held them captive too long and they died, their bright lights were extinguished forever. I was an overly sensitive child and cried myself to sleep again that night. I never trapped another lightning bug again, and you know what?"

"No, what?"

"They continued to fly around me, rather than my mean old brother."

"I never put fireflies in a jar. I liked having them illuminate the night with their dancing lights swirling all around me." Gail twirled her hand in the air. "I would imagine they were little fairies sent to show me the way home."

"You're like those lightning bugs. No one should ever try to hold you in a tiny glass prison, simply admiring your beauty. You'd die a little every day and lose your bright light. I always look for someone like those lightning bugs—a person who wants to fly around in my orbit and stay because they're as fascinated by me as I am by them."

"Now who's being poetic?" Gail asked.

"I haven't found anyone like that yet. I don't live where I see lightning bugs anymore. I miss them. Growing up is overrated."

"Don't be so sure about that. There are definitely some advantages to engaging in very adult activities. My light got infinitely brighter the moment I met you. There will be plenty enough light from both of us to show us the way. I'll be your lightning bug anytime you miss them."

Mandie kissed the tip of Gail's nose. "I will find you."

"Can we have sushi now?"

CHAPTER THIRTEEN

Intermediate was a comfortable place for Mandie and Gail. They settled into a routine and the days slipped by effortlessly. When Mandie wasn't spending time with the new orientees, she was taking photos of Gail and everything around them. Their combined imaginations created spectacular photos. The creations were enough outside the realm of possibility to punctuate their experience as something unique and otherworldly.

One night, in the midst of some rather passionate lovemaking, Gail whispered her concern about how Mandie was allowed to have a camera amidst the no-tech rule. She worried that, if they talked of this openly, Evelyn would find out and her idea to take a photo back wouldn't work.

The tips of her fingers danced across Mandie's stomach. "Why do you think they allow you to have a camera here? Even if it isn't digital, it's still kinda considered technology."

"I don't know. Photography has been around for a very long time." Mandie lowered her voice. "I think Evelyn knows and is choosing not to notice."

"Really?" Gail's eyebrow shot up.

"Yeah, I think she really wants us to succeed. Maybe TM does as well. I'll bet TM has a soft spot for Evelyn. In turn, Evelyn has a certain affection for us. She pretends to be all, 'oh no I can't break the rules,' but I get the sense she loves doing it."

"Wow, okay. I have definitely underestimated her. Good thing I learned her name. She's deserving of that honor." Gail grinned when Mandie playfully smacked her.

†

Two days remained of their time. Gail wasn't sure how to convert the canisters of film to pictures, or if it was even possible to take a piece of physical evidence back with them. Evelyn had said a photograph was the key. There had to be a reason for that. The days had flown by, and Gail had forgotten to talk with Mandie about her idea. She wanted to sneak a photo of the two of them into the pocket of the pants she was wearing when she first arrived in Intermediate. She supposed she could slip a piece of paper with Mandie's phone number in her pocket. That could work too.

The silky sheet on the bed only partially covered Mandie's naked torso. One foot was peeking out the side. Gail propped her head on her hand and continued to watch Mandie sleeping peacefully beside her. Except for the bed they were lying in, a blank canvas surrounded them. The nothingness didn't unsettle her anymore, especially when Mandie lay next to her. Mandie seemed to have adjusted to

113

the blank state but would occasionally still have a panicked reaction when she first woke up.

Gail hadn't needed anything besides her drafting table, the beanbag chairs, a dinette set, and the king-sized, feather bed. That definitely got the most action. All those things she owned back on earth suddenly felt pretentious and unnecessary. Maybe Transition Messiah had the right idea. Simplicity.

She felt the covers skim across her bare thighs and knew her lover stirred beside her.

"Mmph," Mandie yawned and stretched, reaching over to make contact. She moved her hand along Gail's body, reconnecting them. "You were watching me sleep. The least you could do is wipe away the drool that escapes from the corner of my mouth."

Gail laughed. "We only have a couple of days to figure out how to take a photo back with us. I was thinking if you can somehow produce a photo from that camera of yours, I could stuff it in my pants pocket. Do you remember what I was wearing when I arrived?"

"Mmmhmm. A nice pair of black pants that hugged your body. Not too loose and not too tight. They were particularly good at showing off that fine ass of yours. Photography has been a hobby for as long as I can remember, but I don't know how to develop film. I don't know a single thing about making prints. There are specific chemicals and a whole complicated process. I always wanted to learn, but never quite got around to it."

"I know Evelyn wouldn't have tossed out that hint unless there was something to it. What about the thing I read on her clipboard? I think professional photography is part of your future. Evelyn wants to help. I can almost smell and taste her desire to assist us."

"What about me stuffing the film in my shorts pocket? I won't be able to resist having it developed even if I can't remember taking the photos. I'll be particularly curious, because lately I've only used my digital camera. I don't even know why. I guess I let Caroline talk me into getting it, because she would fuss whenever I took too much time setting up a photo."

"That won't tell you the identity of the person in the photos."

Mandie frowned. "True. Okay, how do we up the odds?"

"If you can take back the film, I should be able to put a note in my pocket to find you and then let nature take its course. What's your phone number? Oh, and I'd better write down your last name. Can you get that camera to take a picture of both of us together?"

"I think so."

Gail felt like a huge meal sat undigested in her stomach. She knew they were depending on everything working out, and that was an unlikely scenario. "Our reconnection on earth doesn't have very good odds, does it?"

"Gail, the way I feel about you, I promise I will find you. I won't know why I have this unexplainable obsession, but it will be all the fuel I need to ensure success."

"Yeah, I guess life can't be that cruel, can it?"

"It can. Remember Evelyn letting it slip about that couple who took forty years to find each other again?" Mandie shuddered.

"That's not going to happen to us. Can we add some daylight and warm summer skies now? I've had enough of nothingness."

Mandie cupped Gail's face with her hand and kissed her. "I'm going to miss not having to worry about morning breath. That is a huge perk of living in Intermediate. Maybe you should have asked Transition Messiah to lengthen the time instead of reduce it."

"Ah hindsight, that evil, elusive creator always foils my bright ideas." Gail touched the tip of Mandie's nose with her index finger and sat up in bed.

"I wonder what time of day we're supposed to return to earth. I'm not going to entertain the notion of moving on. That is unacceptable to me. I hope it's after we fully wake up. You know, later in the day. I want to be as prepared as possible to begin my search for you, and a clear head always helps."

"Good point, I'll ask Evelyn about it when I give her my latest blueprints. These are particularly good. I'll have to try to remember these ideas for houses on earth. I doubt I'll have room enough in my pockets to stuff the drawings. The bulge would be noticeable."

"Ooh bulge, that reminds me…" Mandie began.

"No, no, no. Don't start anything you can't finish. I'm guessing it's close to orientation time. This might be your last day to wow the newbies."

"Wow the newbies? I don't do that."

"Yes, you do. You have a way of interacting with people when you're not overanalyzing everything. I'll bet they regret shortening our time here. I suspect, what's her name, Cornstalk, is shitting her pants right now at the prospect of getting back up there to take over for you."

Mandie laughed again. "Harriet. Her name is Harriet. At least you learned Evelyn's name. All right. I'm getting up now. Today, I think I'll brew us some coffee."

†

Evelyn ran toward Mandie. With fast puffing breaths, her speech came out in fits and starts. "She's found out. Where are your canisters of film? Hurry, I need them. Quick before she catches us."

"Whoa. Slow down. What are you talking about?" Mandie asked.

"Um, you can't take them with you, unless I do something I'm not supposed to."

"They're back at the house."

"Can't you imagine them in your hands?"

"I suppose I can try to do that, but what about Gail's note?"

"Gail's note?" Evelyn frowned.

"She was going to jot down a message with my phone number. I suppose if you have to do something to make it work, you need to do the same thing to her note."

Evelyn looked like a cartoon character; her eyes shifted left to right, as if to subtly check her surroundings. "Hurry, get all of it, and I'll see what I can do."

"Thanks Evelyn, you're the best."

"I have to warn you; Transition Messiah is furious. I don't know what she's planning on doing."

"Understood. You know I have to find her. I promised, and I never break a promise."

Evelyn patted Mandie's arm. "I know, dear, and you two are the real deal. The first I've seen the entire time I've been here. So, I'll take whatever punishment they dole out to me. How bad can it be? I've already been in Intermediate for twenty years. So what if she tacks on more time? I don't have anyone to return to on earth. I like it here. I have a purpose, especially if I get to help in these situations. You two are like the daughters I never had."

Mandie grabbed the older woman and squeezed her for the second time. She had a special affection for this relative stranger who was willing to dangle over a cliff for them.

†

Gail was putting the finishing touches on her latest design. She particularly liked how the waterfall seemed to jut right out of the wall with the logs butted up against the rock. Startled by the sensation of someone approaching, she bit her tongue. Dale had told her he could always see a tiny pink end protrude from her mouth when she concentrated on a project.

"Did you write the note yet?" The question erupted from Mandie's mouth, attached to a gust of air.

"No, why?"

"Hurry. Write it. Evelyn has to do some mumbo jumbo thing so you can transport it with you to earth when we return."

A pad of paper materialized, and Gail used her mechanical pencil to write,

Imperative! Go find Mandie.

"Shit, I don't remember your last name." Gail looked up, then diverted her eyes.

"Carter. And crap, I can't think of my own phone number. Why can't I remember it?"

Evelyn slumped. "Transition Messiah. She's flexing her considerable muscles. That will have to be enough."

"I'm adding in Moses Lake, Washington. That should help." Gail scribbled Mandie's last name and Moses Lake, Washington, then held the paper up in the air and shook it. "Take that you mean old witch."

"God, Gail, don't antagonize her, or she'll toss another road block in your direction," Evelyn warned.

"Oh, right. Sorry," Gail mumbled.

Evelyn grabbed the paper. "The film canisters, hurry before she acts again."

Mandie ran toward the makeshift bedroom and returned with her camera and one small roll of film. She thrust the camera at Evelyn. "Can you please take our picture, together?"

"I'm not a photographer," Evelyn squealed.

"Just point and click." Mandie hurried to stand next to Gail, who wrapped her arm around Mandie's waist. Mandie draped her arm around Gail's shoulder.

"Say squeeze." Evelyn fumbled with the camera.

"It's the silver button on top," Mandie clarified.

"Right, right, I remember now. I'll take a few in case the first one doesn't turn out."

The shutter clicked four times. Gail heard the whizzing sound of the motor, as the end of the film wound itself into the cylinder inside the camera.

Mandie grabbed the camera and popped open the back, as she pulled out the final record of their time in Intermediate. Gail hoped this would work. She wanted a permanent record to help jump start their memories.

"Here." Mandie thrust the green and blue cylinders containing the precious photos into Evelyn's hand. Evelyn squeezed her eyes shut so tightly that the prominent crow's feet popped out like a protruding vein. She was mumbling something Gail couldn't quite hear; it sounded like gibberish. Gail giggled, as she got a mental picture of a person talking in tongues at one of the tent revivals.

"Shhh, don't disturb her. I want this to work," Mandie chastised.

"Sorry. It's just she looks kinda, oh, I don't know, possessed."

"I don't give two shits if the devil himself is possessing her, as long as it works."

"Good point."

The mumbling stopped. Evelyn handed the paper to Gail and the film to Mandie. "Gotta go now and take my punishment. Oh, by the way, she was so pissed she's sending you back" —Evelyn turned her arm and glanced at an imaginary watch— "in five minutes, tops."

"Clothes, Mandie. Put us back in our arrival clothes, hurry." Gail looked down and had just enough time to shove the paper in the back pocket of her black pants. A queasy feeling became nothingness.

CHAPTER FOURTEEN

That antiseptic smell unique to hospitals tickled the hairs inside Mandie's nose. She would recognize that odor anywhere. Having worked in healthcare for almost twenty years, it was both comforting and repulsive.

Mandie worked hard to pry open her eyes, but it felt like someone had superglued them. When she did manage to muster up whatever solvent loosened them, the stabbing light forced them shut again. She'd registered someone sitting a foot away.

She felt the rough hand attached to her own and fought to rally the fortitude she knew was required to face the knifelike pain on her second attempt.

Blinking against the agony, she croaked, "Bright light."

"Pumpkin?" The familiar voice identified Frank Sr. before his bulking frame took shape.

"Dad?" Her voice came out in a gravely whisper. "Please…turn down the light." She closed her eyes again and felt instantly relieved.

"Nurse, nurse…" Mandie heard the heavy tread of his shoes on the hard surface of the floors. "She's awake," he yelled from a distance.

Soon, a cool hand touched her arm. "Welcome back, Mandie. Let me dim the lights for you."

"Thanks," she responded, as she tried to get her synapses to fire again. The voice sounded familiar. She was probably at her former hospital. She figured she'd worked closely with this nurse.

As if the nurse could hear her thoughts, she answered, "It's Bethany. I'll get the doctor. Don't try to talk too much, okay? The lights are dim now."

Mandie nodded. This time, there was no excruciating dagger to her sensitive eyes. She heard the surprisingly soft shuffle of her dad's feet as he approached.

"I'm gonna purge for a few moments, okay? First, that ex-girlfriend of yours is a real piece of work. I wish I were part of the Italian mob. I'd put a hit out on her. Second, what in the Sam Hill made you think jumping out of a fucking airplane was a good idea? And third, I wanted to give that half-wit CEO a piece of my mind, but then I worried about the kind of care you would get. As it turns out, all the nurses were on your side, and a few of them advocated for you staying right here. Aw, pumpkin, those beautiful blue eyes of yours are the most welcome sight I've ever seen. I never gave up on you. I knew you'd pull out of this."

Mandie half laughed, half coughed. "Italian? You're…far from…that eth…nicity, Dad. Mom…would have killed you…for stereo…typing. So…Caroline is my ex, eh?"

"Oh, sorry. I hate to break that news to you, but she stopped visiting soon after the accident. The bitch had the nerve to tell me the news so I could relay it to you if you woke up."

"It's okay, Dad. We were done…before I had…the bright idea…jumping out…of a plane. How long?"

"Twenty-nine days, nine hours and fifty minutes."

"No seconds?"

"Actually, I had to extrapolate the minutes based on when the skydiving place said you made the jump. They were quick to show me the release you signed."

"Tandem partner?" Mandie's throat was raw. She was grateful to see she wasn't on a ventilator and didn't have a nasogastric tube. *They must have been feeding me intravenously.*

"He did. Somehow, he got you two in the vicinity of the only vegetation in a five-mile radius. The partially opened chute snagged on the blessed copse of trees."

"Xena? Gabrielle?" Mandie asked.

"They're fine. They follow me around the condo. I might be feeding them too many treats. They're getting a little chunky."

"Dad!"

"Sorry, but they're so cute."

"Okay, never mind that. Dad, something important happened… while I was out of it. Just beyond my comprehension. All I know is… that it could be… life changing for me. I don't want… to be an HR exec…anymore."

"That's okay, baby girl, you can always live with your dear old dad."

"Nice try, Dad. I remember…a generous severance… gives me time and space…evaluate my options. Maybe…I'll consider…opening a photography studio."

"Aw honey, that's not very lucrative. You gotta depend on customers to keep you afloat. At least working for hospitals is secure."

"Not with…what's happening…in healthcare. Can we…talk about this later?"

Mandie breathed a sigh of relief when the hospitalist strode into the room. He was one of her favorites, and she was glad he was on rotation at the right time. She wasn't relishing getting into it with her dad over her lack of employment. The humility gene did not come from him. He wouldn't understand her feelings of insecurity or shame.

"Hello, Mandie. It's very nice to see you've made your way back to us. I know your eyes are a little sensitive right now, but I need to shine a light in them, okay?"

"Sure…because the last time…I opened them…to bright lights…the tiny knives…didn't hurt enough." Mandie braced herself for the discomfort.

Dr. Sardin laughed. "I see the flying lesson didn't alter your sense of humor."

"Nor yours," Mandie sardonically replied.

Dr. Sardin shined a small penlight in Mandie's eyes. "Can you please follow the light for me, using only your eyes? No head movements for now. Good, good." He lifted her hand. "I know I'm not really your type, Mandie. You'd probably like one of those cute nurses to do this test." He laughed at his own lame joke. "Please squeeze my hand as hard as you can."

"Are any of them…single? I no longer work here…and find myself…suddenly unattached."

"Good, your strength is about where I expected it to be, but it's there. And yes, I heard. Hospital grapevine."

"Great. I love…being the central…topic of conversation." Mandie shut her eyes to hold back her tears.

"Oh, don't worry, they lost interest in that a mere twenty-four hours after your ex left the dirty deed for your father to relay. What do they call that? A dear Jane, or a queer Jane?"

Ironically, his insensitivity and attempt at humor was working to keep the tears at bay. "Funny. No, I think…they call that…clueless."

"I call that shittiness," Frank interjected.

"Now you'll be all the rage again, with your miraculous awakening," Dr. Sardin said.

"When can I…go home?" Mandie asked.

"I'd like to run more tests, starting with an MRI. Then we'll see. You know you have some serious physical therapy in your future. Got to get those arms and legs back to their previous state. Unfortunately, muscle loss happens more quickly than muscle gain. You have a long road ahead of you. It's a miracle you only suffered a few broken ribs and a very serious concussion. Damndest thing I've ever seen. Your jumping partner wasn't as lucky. He took a greater brunt of the fall."

"My pumpkin is tough. She'll be running marathons in no time."

"No…I won't, Dad." Mandie shook her head and opened her eyes to meet her dad's.

"Why not? That doesn't sound like you, honey. Where's that indomitable spirit?"

"I've never…run a marathon…in my life. No intention…of putting myself…through that… agony. I'll settle…for a brisk…three-mile walk."

"Oh, okay, but I still don't like this new version. You seem a little down, pumpkin."

"Dad!" Mandie smacked her head against the pillow in exasperation. "I've had a major accident…that landed me…in a coma…for thirty days. My girlfriend left…and I was…fired from my job. I don't think…pulling out the bubbly…is called for. I can't imagine…anything else…happening to me." Mandie was beyond caring what her dad thought of involuntary separation and the humiliation attached to the termination. He'd just have to get used to the idea. Not only did Mandie not run the hospital, she didn't want to be a part of any administrative team. That part of her life was over. Good riddance.

"Caroline took your cats and said she's not giving them back. She figures it's better if she has custody," Frank revealed without taking a breath.

"I thought you said…they were following you…around…and getting fat?"

"They were, until that bitch came by two weeks ago." Her dad patted her hand.

Mandie groaned. "Can my life…be any more…fucked up?"

"They say that once you hit bottom, there's nowhere else but up from there."

"Thanks…Mr. Sunshine…but I'll just wallow…for a few more moments…if you don't mind. Alone, please. I appreciate…you being here…Dad…but I need time…to absorb everything."

"I'll head to the cafeteria and get myself a cup of coffee, while the doctor continues to evaluate you." Frank walked out with a cheerful bounce in his step.

†

The steady beeping was starting to annoy Gail. That didn't sound like her alarm clock. *Who stuffed my mouth with cotton balls?* She didn't remember going on a bender. She hadn't done something like that for a long time. Maybe she'd met up with that sexy cop and somehow had forgotten the whole night. *Crap, I hope I didn't do anything embarrassing.*

Pain. A very unpleasant feeling was radiating up her arm and down her leg. Nope, too much sex would definitely not feel like this. Gail's brain was beginning to string together rational thoughts. She recalled how bus meets person never ends positively. She hesitated a few more seconds, before attempting to open her eyes and scan the damage. She was sure it would be considerable. That bus was huge, and her body was small.

The sting from the tiny pinch on her hand added insult to injury. "Unnnh. Do you mind? Stop messing…with my hand?" she croaked.

"Oh, Ms. Forrester. You're awake. That's marvelous. Let me get the doctor and call your friend," the pleasant voice responded. "Are you in pain?"

"You mean…does it feel like…I was hit by a bus? Yes." Gail responded in irritation. "How many bones…did I manage…to break?"

"Oh, that's so good you remember what happened. I'll let the doctor tell you everything, but I'll push some more morphine. That should help."

The nurse left. The beeping continued to punctuate the quiet in the room. At least she wasn't surrounded by nothingness. *Where did that thought come from?* Instinctively, she knew that opening her eyes wasn't going to be pleasant. She blinked and was thankful the room was dim. The low light seemed to allow her eyes to adjust more rapidly.

As she surmised, her leg and arm were in a cast. She couldn't see what was on her head, but she definitely felt something foreign.

A tall, thin man in a white coat entered the room and smiled at her. "I won the pool."

"What?" Gail asked.

"Oh, I bet my colleagues that today would be the day you would wake up."

"You're kidding, right?" Gail glared at the man. "Hey, can I get…a little water? It feels like…I drank my weight in alcohol."

The man chuckled. "Yeah, I wanted to lighten things up before I give you the bad news." He grabbed the big yellow water container and brought the straw to her lips. "Slowly, Ms. Forrester," he warned.

Gail sucked gently on the straw, until the dry sensation dissipated. "Thanks. Okay…lay it on me…doc."

"It's a terrible idea to go dancing with a bus. You suffered a compound fracture of your femur. That's the big bone in your leg."

"I know…what the femur is," Gail answered testily. If she hadn't felt so weak, she would have punched the man in the throat for being so condescending to her.

"You also had a compound fracture in your radius. The first surgery fixed both bones, but there were complications. That's why you're experiencing pain. You've had four additional surgeries, and we think you're on the mend now."

"So, the bad news?"

"These are serious injuries that will take quite a bit of time to recover from. The additional surgeries increased the recovery time. I understand you're an architect. Your fine motor movements of your right hand might be affected by the break. It will take a considerable amount of time and work to achieve full movement. Perhaps there are adaptive computer drafting programs that can help get you back to work more quickly."

Gail groaned. "Not…with the kind of houses…I design."

"Do you have someone who can help you, or should I order home care?"

"Any chance…you can send…a hot, single lesbian…my way?" Although the words came out of her mouth, the offhanded joke sounded all wrong. She wasn't looking for someone. Did she already have a girlfriend she couldn't remember due to the trauma? The twinge of guilt she'd just experienced was unexpected, different.

"You're an incorrigible flirt. I'm hot and single and signed up as your personal nursemaid," Dale interrupted.

"How'd you manage…to sneak in, Dale? Are we…bankrupt yet?" She remembered the accident and Dale, so it didn't make sense that there was a forgotten girlfriend.

"No. You've been holding out on me, partner. Good thing you gave me a key to your house. I found the motherlode. You have a whole room full of designs. It was like Christmas morning. I hope you don't mind, I pawed through your stacks of tubes and found a few I thought fit some potential clients and made the sales all by myself. I assured the clients you'd be back to work in no time," Dale explained.

"How long…have I been holed up…in this hotel?"

"Just shy of thirty days," the doctor answered.

"I'm not…letting you…give me a…sponge bath, Dale."

"Ew, I don't want to see your naked body." Dale's shoulders lifted and his body followed suit with a visible shiver.

"Doc, how much…can I do…on my own?" Gail asked.

"The first couple of weeks, you need to take it easy and be cautious. Not only do you have to contend with broken bones, but after laying in the bed for so long, your extremities have atrophied. It will be a difficult transition to doing things on your own. Arranging home care in addition to your friend helping out is the way to go."

A persistent thought kept knocking on Gail's brain, until she opened the door and expelled it. "Where are my pants?"

Dale and the doctor both frowned.

"Gail, are you okay? You were sounding so lucid until now," Dale said.

"I know…it sounds weird…but there's something…important…about my pants," Gail insisted.

"Hon, they had to cut them off. It was a trauma situation. I'll buy you a new pair."

"There's something…a memory…I can't reach. I think…it has the power…to change my life. What if…there was…something important…in the pocket? I vaguely remember…getting stopped…by a sexy cop. I could have written…her number down…and stuffed it…in my pants. She could be…the one." Gail felt her agitation increase. She tried to sit up, felt a twinge and lay back down. She heard the increased beeps in one of the offending monitors.

Dale patted her uninjured hand. "Don't get all worked up. I'll ask the nurses. If there was something important, we'll find it."

"Before they toss any clothes, the nurses always check the pockets," the doctor offered.

Gail settled with the belief everything would work out. She wished she could turn a dial and focus her woolly thoughts. She had a vision of a camera. *Unusual, I've never had any interest in photography before.* Some kind of déjà vu hovered around her fuzzy edges. "Can you go…check now? I want to see…whatever…was in my pockets."

"I'm on it," Dale reassured her.

†

Mandie felt bad for how she'd treated her father. She was being a grumpy goose, and she knew he was only trying to help. Although, this new injection of confidence to say what she really thought was a tiny bit exhilarating. Not doing exactly what was expected of her could be fun. She'd have to try that out some more. Even though it generated a reaction from her dad, the world did not come to a screeching halt.

Her continued push against what was expected would have to take a back seat to recovery, with the exception of one tiny act of rebellion. First order of business when they allowed her to go home was to get her cats back. She wasn't planning on being nice and tactful when she confronted her ex. *Caroline isn't even a cat person. It's just a ploy to impress Robin, who's never met a cat she didn't fawn over.*

The transporter had rolled her into the MRI and was trying to get her to relax. The large tube reminded Mandie of something. She was trying hard to remember, and he mistook her roaming eyes and tense face for panic. She tried to explain she wasn't claustrophobic. He ignored her protests, and she could hear his fervent whispers to the tech.

"Hey, Mandie," the tech greeted her. "Do you need a sedative? Or we can go find your dad."

"No, Randy," Mandie answered too quickly. "Please don't get my dad. He'll hover or spew his own brand of positive inspirational sayings. I'm good. A little music and a blindfold should work fine."

"Country, rap, or easy listening?"

"What? No elevator music? I'll take anything but rap or country." Concentrating on jokes might help the persistent anxiety she was feeling that had nothing to do with having an MRI.

"Hey, I wanted to say that was a pretty shitty thing they did to you. You'll be missed by a lot of us."

"Thanks, Randy. I sure am glad you're my tech. Any way to speed up the results so I can get out of here? It's a bit awkward. I know you guys are the best, and you've given me great care. It's just that…" If her broken body would have allowed, she would have shifted on the uncomfortable platform, away from the well-meaning, sympathetic looks. Nothing would make the intense amount of embarrassment subside. Everything was converging all at once to make this a profoundly uncomfortable experience. There was no way in hell she wanted to return to healthcare administration, no matter how great the position was.

"Hey, say no more. Sorry I brought it up. Okay, let's get you settled and do this thing." Randy positioned Mandie on the platform leading into the tube and handed her a mask. "Let me turn on the music."

She heard his footsteps, then Adele's voice came through loud and clear. "Nice. I do like a side of Adele with my MRI."

"Okay, are you ready?"

"Yup."

Randy pushed a button on the side of the machine. Mandie advanced inside the tube as if she were produce moving along on a grocery store conveyor belt. The faint thumping sound of the machine came through, despite the music. She felt like she was inside a washing machine. Somehow, the MRI would make her clean again, like a brand-new page she could write on and redirect her life. *Rap would have done a better job of masking the sound.* Perhaps she would suggest classic rock as another alternative.

After they rolled her back into the room and got her settled, her dad ambled in and sat heavily in the chair. She braced herself for whatever news he was trying to muster the courage to get out. Whenever he wouldn't look her in the eye and squirmed in his chair like he had to pee, she knew something was up.

"Okay, spill it. What else can I look forward to?"

"Now don't get mad, pumpkin, but I kinda moved into your condo."

"What do you mean kinda? Either you did or you didn't. That's like saying I'm sorta pregnant."

"Okay, I did. After your accident, and when you didn't wake up after three days, I called your brother. Frank Jr. took care of everything."

"Please tell me you didn't have that imbecile sell your house in Florida."

"He got me a good price, and I've been paying your bills so you don't lose your condo."

"Dad, I'm not destitute. The hospital gave me a generous severance."

"Yeah, about that…"

"Oh no, what did you do?"

"I got you a better deal, pumpkin, but I wasn't sure how long you'd be unemployed. When that bitch girlfriend of yours left, I figured you needed a roommate who could pay the bills. You know, just in case…"

"There are so many things in what you just said, I don't even know where to start. You know Caroline did not live with me, right? I don't need a new roommate." Mandie sighed. "Better deal?"

"Well that was one thing Caroline and I agreed on. That CEO totally screwed you. When I got here, I paid attention to the chatter at the nurse's station. They were saying things about being glad they were part of a union so that some homophobe couldn't fire them for no good reason. They were sure their CEO, who 'had a big old stick up her ass,' didn't like how you were out and proud. Then they said you should have gone to the board."

"Stick up her ass? Dad!" Her jaw hurt from grinding her teeth for the last hour.

"Hey, those were their words, not mine. I figured, as long as I was hanging out here, waiting for you to recover, I would pay her a little visit. When I mentioned going to the board, she offered more severance. I thought you would be happy about that."

Mandie sighed. "You hate Washington, Dad. The last time you visited, you bitched about the weather the whole time."

"That was when you lived on the west side. It rains all the time over there."

"No, it doesn't. Never mind. I'm not getting into this argument with you. I'll wait to remind you when the sun is shining in Florida, without humidity. The winters here get below twenty. You'll hate it soon enough. Then what'll you do?"

"I'll buy a new house in Florida, but only after my little pumpkin is settled. You could always move with me to sunny Florida and get a job there."

"No thanks, I like it here."

"You don't have to decide yet. Let's get you all squared away. Physical therapy and a girlfriend first. Then we can look for a new job worthy of your considerable talents."

"Do not, I repeat, do not go around interviewing any of the nurses for that new girlfriend position. I can get my own dates. Thank you very much."

"Oh, I know, you have the whole package, especially with respect to lesbians. There's much less competition, if you know what I mean. Not too many beauty queens out there that are lesbians."

Mandie groaned. "Oh my God, kill me now. I'm going right back out there to jump from another plane and hope this time, it does the trick. You do know that is the rudest most idiotic thing you've ever said."

"Just saying, not too many Portia de Rossis out there. You must rank right up there in the unbelievable catch territory. I bet if Ellen had met you before Portia, you'd be the one married to her now."

"Let's skip the girlfriend part and explore this whole roommate thing. Please tell me you haven't completely destroyed my condo? How much stuff did you move in?"

"Just my fishing gear and a few mementos. You need another junk drawer though. Oh, by the way, the staff here emptied your pockets and found two rolls of film. I tossed them in one of the drawers, but like I said, it was pretty full.

When I pushed it shut, I might have crushed one or both of them."

Mandie didn't remember taking her camera or film to the skydiving place. They had their own photographers and explicitly forbade cameras. She pushed this from her already crowded mind. Whatever was on the film was unimportant. "Do me a favor, please. Have a housecleaning service come and disinfect my place before I settle back in. Oh, and if any of your fishing gear is inside the house versus the deck, it better be gone as well."

"You got it, pumpkin. We're going to have so much fun living together." He rubbed his hands with glee.

"This is only temporary, until I'm strong enough to insist you move back to Florida." She pierced him with her fiercest look.

"Deal."

†

Dale was whistling when he entered the room, and Gail narrowed her eyes. She'd been stewing for twenty minutes, waiting for him to return. "What the hell took you so long?" She zeroed in on a piece of paper he held gingerly with his middle finger and thumb. The paper looked like it had been through a war zone, complete with red splotches.

"There was a very nice nurse who helped me. I wasn't going to be rude and cut off the conversation," Dale answered.

"Let me guess, he was male, attractive, and single?"

"Oh yes, he's scrumptious."

"Dale, I've been waiting for whatever you have in your hand that looks like you'd rather have your teeth pulled than hold it. Gimme please." Gail held out her uninjured hand.

"I'm not sure why they kept this because, ew, it has blood all over it." Dale dropped the paper in Gail's good hand and stepped away as if it were radioactive.

She struggled to smooth the paper with one hand and remove most of the wrinkles. She sensed the note was important, but it didn't make sense to her. Blood covered many of the words. She shivered, knowing the blood was hers. The note shook in her trembling hands. The only words she could make out were…*Imperative…Mandi…Lake*

"Dale, do you know anyone named Mandie?"

Dale's face scrunched up. "I don't think so. Why?"

"I can only make out three words, and Mandie is one of them. You know how I am with names. I thought you might know who this Mandie person is. I get the feeling she was important to me."

"Not that you tell me everything about your private life, but I'd remember if you started dating someone that was special."

"I remember being stopped by this sexy cop before that stupid bus hit me. Maybe her name is Mandie. Shit. I should ask the doc if memory loss is typical." Gail crumpled up the paper and lobbed it at Dale who let it hit his chest and fall to the floor.

"What'd ya do that for?" He brushed his clothes and made a face.

"I'm a little at a disadvantage here, and that garbage can under the sink is beyond my basketball capabilities at the moment. Surely you can pinch the paper again and toss it in the can. Maybe I'll remember later on. Right now, it's useless."

Dale bowed. "Yes, my queen. Let me hop right to it and do your bidding."

"Sorry, I'm frustrated and that felt pretty good. I've always wanted to smash a glass against a fireplace, but that wasn't exactly at my disposal. The next best thing was throwing the paper at you."

"Fine, I'll be your little whipping boy, for now."

Gail managed a small smile for her friend. "Good, now go chat up that hunky nurse, and see if he can con the doc into releasing me soon."

"Ooh, I can do that."

CHAPTER FIFTEEN

Mandie wasn't interested in letting the grass grow under her feet as she regained the use of her muscles. She asked the physical therapist what exercises she could start while waiting for the doctor to discharge her and jump-started her recovery with a routine of isometric calisthenics. Her dad was all too eager to push her around in a wheelchair, but she was having none of that. She needed to get herself moving about as soon as possible, and send her father packing.

Two days after awakening, Mandie attempted to make it to the bathroom on her own. Epic fail. Her father rushed to help, after she'd stumbled and fallen on the floor.

"Now pumpkin, you gotta crawl before walking and walk before running," he crooned.

Mandie growled at him. "It you take one more step, I swear I'm going to bite your hand."

"Can I at least get the nurse?"

"Fine," she said. The doc had informed her recovery would be a minimum of a month, just to get around a little bit. Mandie thought by then she would surely kill her father. She loved him, but he could be so irritating.

Her favorite nurse came striding into the room and assessed the situation. "Now, Mandie, you know we have the housekeepers for that job. You don't have to scrub the floor with your butt. They hate it when the patients take away their job. The union will definitely have something to say about that."

"Hardy, har, har. I want to go to the damn bathroom on my own. Is that too much to ask?"

"Yes. I swear, if you make our patient falls go up, I'll tell the doc you need an enema because we can't get your bowels working."

Her dad snickered.

"Don't laugh at her, it'll make my job harder. The independent ones are the worst."

"Yeah, Dad. Laugh again. When you get close, I'll poke your eyes so Nurse Ratchet here will have to attend to you instead of setting her sights on chastising me."

"Do you ever want to get out of here? Keep it up, and I'll tell the doc I don't think you're ready to be on your own, even with a caregiver." The nurse lifted her back onto the bed. "Sorry, Mandie, but I'm afraid it's the bed pan for you, until you gain a little more strength in your arms and legs."

After she settled back in the bed, Mandie looked up and mumbled, "Just great. I thought this day couldn't get any worse."

"Hello, Mandie. I wanted to come by and wish you a speedy recovery." Arlene, the CEO, wore a tight smile that didn't reach her eyes.

Liana, the CNO, sent an apologetic look in Mandie's direction. "I was about to do my patient rounds this morning, and Arlene wanted to join me. How has your care been so far?"

Mandie opened her mouth to complain, then realized she would be misdirecting her anger at someone that didn't deserve it. "The nurses and Dr. Sardin have been outstanding. Thank you for asking. You should move on to the other patients. I know how busy both of you are."

The muscles on Liana's face relaxed, and she looked relieved. "I'll check back with you later, okay?"

Mandie nodded and accepted Liana was trying to do her job as best she could. When they left, Mandie sent the nurse a pleading look. "Please, can you do anything to get me released early?"

"I'll see what I can do, but no more gymnastics. Don't get your hopes up, Mandie. I'd want to see you move around better before we discharge you to home. You could transfer to a rehab facility," she stated.

"I can't believe I'm going to admit this. I'd rather go home and let my dad hover than go to an old folks' home. I'm in my early forties, not eighties."

"You need to settle your behind in that bed then, because I don't think Sardin will let you leave here until he's satisfied with your progress. A couple more days won't kill you." The nurse pivoted and left the room.

"Easy for her to say." Mandie's physical discomfort was minor in comparison to how uncomfortable she was interacting with the staff at the hospital that had fired her. The helpless, out of control feeling was amplified by that tiny fact.

†

Dale's efforts with the nurse hadn't resulted in the desired outcome for Gail. She was stuck in the hospital for at least a few more days. The nurse was being cagey about when they would discharge her.

Gail had a deep mistrust of hospitals. She'd heard the news reports about how often human error caused harm. Sometimes people died in hospitals as a result of those errors. Her thoughts zeroed in on the doc's hint at complications. She needled the nurse, who finally admitted Gail had gotten an infection after the surgery.

Her partner was flitting around again, probably flirting with the nurse. Gail's eyes traveled to the trash can like a heat-seeking missile. The intense level of anxiety over the wadded-up ball of paper she herself had thrown at Dale was perplexing. She was the one who had directed him to toss it into the garbage can.

Gail pounced the minute the nurse came into the room. "I need that note in the trash can," she cried out as if her life depended on retrieving the blood-soaked paper.

The nurse tilted her head. "Sorry?"

"There was a note in my pants pocket and um…I might have been a bit rash, crumpling it up and tossing it away. I need it back, please," Gail rushed to explain.

The monitor started a double time version of a hospital song and seemed to concern the nurse. Gail's eyes darted between the garbage can and the noisy machine with wires sprouting out like vines. She wondered if this was what a panic attack felt like.

"I'll get the note, don't worry. I don't think housekeeping has emptied the garbage yet today," she said.

The machine's song settled into the pre-Alvin and the Chipmunks version as Gail relaxed. The slight shake of the nurse's head revealed how crazy Gail must have sounded. Grabbing gloves from the dispenser, the nurse snapped them on and plucked the note from the can. She gently laid it on the wheeled, bedside table. A grimace punctuated her distaste for the task.

Gail wondered if the nurse's reaction had more to do with something retrieved from the trash or the liberal amount of blood evident on the crumpled piece of paper. If the origin of her reaction was the blood, the nurse was definitely in the wrong occupation.

"Thanks." Touching the paper, Gail felt like the nurse had slathered a wound with soothing balm. She attempted to unravel the wad and smooth out the creases.

A tiny, sympathetic smile appeared with the nurse's subtle nodding. She helped Gail with her gloved hands. Gail wondered if that was the face she showed to the cray-cray patients when she wanted them to settle down and behave. No matter, Gail had her message, and she wasn't about to lose it again.

Dale bounced into the room and spotted the bloody note. "What the hell? Didn't I toss that disgusting thing in the can?"

"Any luck on operation Hunka Hunka Burning Love?" She mused that he was so easily distracted, and that was a very good thing. She wasn't ready to place her motivations under a microscope for either of them to sift through.

"Ooh, he is so dreamy—unfortunately straight as an arrow—without a single question. I thought the younger generation was supposed to be a lot more fluid." Dale sighed. "At least he didn't punch me."

The bells on the monitor sped up again. Fluid. That word jabbed at Gail's unconscious mind with an immediate prick.

The nurse frowned. "I need to report this to the doctor. I don't like how your heartbeat has been so erratic."

"Aw, you're worried about little old me," Dale said.

Gail took a few deep breaths. The heart monitor returned to the previous slow, steady beeping that seemed to make the nurse happy. "I hate that word fluid. I'm a lesbian. You're a gay man. End of discussion. I don't have a single question about my sexuality, and I'm not fluid with who I sleep with."

"You are a fuddy-duddy. I've met more potential partners in the last few years thanks to this new, adventurous generation. Please don't rain on my parade. Maybe he'll think more on the subject, and I'll take another run at it tomorrow." Dale grinned.

"I'd rather stick with my generation and someone who is 100 percent lesbian," Gail answered.

"I think you're limiting your options, but it's not like you ever have any time to date anyway. Maybe this whole accident thingy will rearrange your priorities. Honestly, part of me hopes it won't. I'm a selfish bastard, and your obsession with work is good for business. But the friend part of me wishes you would find a distraction. I want you to be happy."

"Ick, I don't like this mushy side of you. Can you please go back to being that selfish bastard? Too much change and the corresponding anxiety makes that thing beep double time. Then the poor nurse gets that unattractive frowny face. Besides, I want out of here. If the doc thinks my heart is erratic, he'll keep me locked up forever."

The nurse touched Gail's arm. "I would prefer to show you a more attractive face, so yes, please avoid getting worked up. That would make me feel a whole lot better. I'm still going to confer with the doctor about this. Push the button if you need anything," she said before exiting the room.

Dale winked at Gail. "She's cute. Did you notice how she didn't even blink at our discussion? Maybe it's that nurse causing your erratic heartbeat. I definitely get the questioning vibe from her."

"Didn't you hear a word I said? No to twentysomethings and no to anyone questioning their sexuality. I might amend my view to include bisexuals, but that's as far as I go."

"Too bad that accident didn't rescramble your inflexibility when it comes to matters of the heart."

†

The big day had arrived. The doctors agreed to discharge Mandie from the hospital, and she informed her dad they were making a pit stop on the way home. She'd roll her wheelchair over Caroline's toes and fracture every last one of them if she had to. She planned to take back her furbabies through whatever means were at her disposal. Including a runaway wheelchair.

As the car rolled up to Robin's house, Mandie's dad snuck a glance in her direction. "Are you sure about this, pumpkin? We can always come back after you've had a chance to heal a little more."

Mandie growled. "She's not keeping my Xena and Gabrielle. She doesn't even like cats. I'm not letting Robin be their stepmommy."

"Okay, okay. Let me get the wheelchair." Her dad scooted around the back and popped the hatch. He unfolded the chair, and Mandie pushed his hand away. She transferred herself to the chair without assistance.

Fueled by anger and frustration, she made it to the door and pounded with a closed fist. The dull thud against the wood door made her father cringe. Caroline and Robin were probably sitting down to dinner, sharing an expensive bottle of wine. That image didn't bother her as much as the picture in her head of her furbabies curled up on one of Robin's chairs. She didn't want them to feel cozy and loved in some other woman's home.

The door opened, and Caroline's shocked expression told the whole story. "Mandie, um, what are you doing here? I would have visited more, but…"

"But…you were too busy fucking Robin and stealing my babies. Don't worry, I got the memo about us breaking up. Don't care about that. I do want my cats back, and I'm prepared to do almost anything to get them. I nearly died, so I've got nothing more to lose."

"Hon?" Robin appeared in the doorway. "Oh, uh, Mandie. You look a lot better."

"She wants her cats," Caroline stated.

"Oh." Robin frowned. "Well, of course. Um, we were caring for them for you while you recovered."

"I thought you said we should keep them?" Caroline asked.

"I'm sorry, Mandie. I thought you might not recover enough to want the responsibility. Honestly, I was thinking of what was best for Xena and Gabrielle."

The anger dissipated and the only thing left to do was acknowledge their backhanded kindness. "Thanks, Robin. I know you love cats, and I'm sure you took good care of them. But I really need them…" Mandie choked up then composed herself. "Can I just get you to bring Xena and Gabrielle to us, then we'll leave you alone."

"Of course." Robin looked away in embarrassment. She wouldn't meet Mandie's eyes when she asked, "Um, do you want to come in? Maybe have a glass of wine or something?"

Mandie shook her head. She couldn't muster the words to politely refuse. Every bone in her body was screaming to get her cats and escape to the safety of her condo, even if she had to share it with her dad. The luxury of solitude remained firmly out of her grasp.

"I'll get them," Caroline stated.

"I can help." Robin scurried back inside, leaving Mandie and her dad awkwardly waiting on the porch.

He cleared his throat. "Nicely done, pumpkin."

"Thanks for letting me handle this, Dad. I guess this closure was a necessary evil."

Caroline and Robin brought out the cats, and Mandie settled them in the chair with her. She let her father push the wheelchair and assist her into the car. Mandie cradled a loudly purring Xena. When she was comfortable in the passenger seat, he placed Gabrielle in her lap next to Xena. Things were starting to right themselves in Mandie's world.

CHAPTER SIXTEEN

"Fuckity, fuck, fuck," Gail screamed in frustration. It was bad enough to have her entire right side encased in plaster. Now she was experiencing an excruciatingly slow return of the muscles on her left side. Two weeks had passed already since the doctor discharged her from the hospital after copious amounts of begging. They did not have an answer for the erratic heart rate, despite several unnecessary tests. She wondered if they'd ordered them to pad the bill. She had good insurance.

"Hey, don't be so hard on yourself. You were out of commission for nearly a month. It's going to take time for your body to repair." The cheery physical therapist tried to encourage Gail.

"Easy for you to say, with your buff arms waving in my direction, mocking me at every turn."

The therapist laughed. "We'll start more intensive therapy next week, after your casts come off. Hopefully, we can get you moving around much better, but don't expect miracles. You're still going to be very stiff and won't return to your pre-accident state for several months, maybe even a year or more."

"Great, just great."

"I would recommend investing in a home gym or joining a health club. You can hire a personal trainer who will help set you up."

"Isn't that what you're supposed to do?" Gail grumbled in irritation.

"I'm only responsible for getting you to the point of independent functioning. Beyond that, you're on your own. PT visits are limited these days, and you don't want to squander them on frivolous workouts."

"I need the fine motor skills back in my hand. I'm an architect for shit's sake. Who can I get to help me work on that?"

The therapist frowned. "I'm not a hand specialist…"

The hulking man undoubtedly lifted weights every chance he got. "Yeah, I figured your specialty is sports medicine, but I'm not about to enter a women's body builder competition. Do you think I could squander my remaining PT sessions with a hand specialist?"

He slapped his hand to his chest. "I am so wounded. I thought this was the beginning of a beautiful relationship."

"You do know I'm a lesbian, but my partner Dale…well…you are just his type."

The therapist laughed. "I'll get Lorraine to take over. She's a Certified Hand Therapist, one of the best in the state. You're doing a lot better than you think. I've shown you all the best exercises, so you should progress without my assistance. Now stop slacking and get back to those isometrics, then we'll move you to the machines."

"Torture chamber," she mumbled, but already she was beginning to lose her earlier agitation.

"I heard that. You know, that torture chamber will get you back to where you'd like to be." He pointed to her leg before glancing up at the heavyset man who was breathing too hard. "I'll be back in a sec."

After the therapist walked away, Gail pulled out the crumpled note from her pocket. Using the plaster on her arm to hold the paper down on her casted leg, she smoothed it out with her other hand.

The splotches of blood mocked her in more ways than one. The reminder she'd been in a terrible accident was secondary to the hidden words. She knew the message held the key to something too critical to her happiness for her to ignore. Gail couldn't bear to have the note anywhere but in her pocket at all times. The frustration of her physical limitations was infinitesimal compared to her vexation over a memory that skated along the fringe—never quite coming into focus. Focus. She saw an image of a beautiful woman behind the lens of a camera. The image was so clear, with the exception of her face. *How is it even possible to have such a vivid, waking fantasy?*

"Who are you, Mandie?" Gail mumbled as she stared at the note. Her index finger traced the letters of the name and she sighed.

✝

Mandie had forgotten all about the rolls of film when she arrived back home to a fishing museum. She gasped at how quickly her father had turned her modern condo into the next location for that show about hoarders. A quick call to a storage facility saved her father's life. He moved the gear when Mandie struggled to navigate around the condo in the wheelchair.

She was rapidly tiring of takeout food; her father was a terrible cook. Mandie decided to try her hand at making a simple meal. Tossing a few chicken breasts on the grill couldn't be too difficult. Mandie grunted in frustration when she couldn't find her tongs. She remembered her father had absconded another kitchen drawer for his partial lures and junk-drawer items.

He'd stuffed the top drawer to the gills. The small blue and green film canisters caught her attention. *What the hell?*

"Dad," Mandie yelled.

"What, pumpkin?"

"I thought you said only one of them was crushed. Geez, what did you do, stuff them inside and slam the drawer?"

"I couldn't figure out why it wasn't closing, so I kept pushing. Both are ruined?" he asked innocently.

"You know very well that both are crushed." She held up the mangled cylinders. "I really wanted to know what was on these rolls. I'll be lucky to salvage any of the pictures. Why didn't you tell me your shove and smush technique affected both canisters? This would have never happened if you hadn't filled up the drawer to make room for your crap. Which, coincidentally, did not work since you took over another drawer anyway."

"Maybe a few pictures survived. Do you want me to take them to the drug store?"

"I guess so. My curiosity is off the charts right about now. I'd forgotten about them. Can you light the grill before you leave? I think I can handle grilling chicken. By the way, where did you shove the tongs?"

Her dad took a step to the right and opened the cabinet at the bottom, where she kept her Tupperware. The tongs sat haphazardly on top of her square containers. "Here you go, pumpkin. They wouldn't fit in the top drawer anymore," he answered while sheepishly looking away.

Mandie narrowed her eyes. She hadn't taken the time to inspect her cabinets since they'd been living off of takeout. "I am giving you twenty-four hours to clean your shit out of my drawers and cabinets, before I go ballistic on you and become the embodiment of Lizzie Borden."

"Where did my sweet, little apple dumpling go?"

"To some intermediate place that allowed me to get in touch with my inner bitch. It should have happened after the hospital fired me, but I guess I needed the accident to grow brass ta tas." Mandie frowned at her use of the word intermediate.

Frank laughed. "Well, you did need to gain confidence. Perhaps you can dial it down just a tad for your old man."

"Sorry, Dad. It's just I don't like being so dependent on anyone. You have to admit, living together stifles both of us, especially in this tiny condo."

"I'll light the grill for you, but be careful. You're still in recovery mode."

"You sound like I checked myself into drug rehab." Mandie's body quivered. "Ew, I'd rather describe it as getting my groove back."

"Okay, honey. I'm going now so I don't hover."

"Good plan."

"Besides, you'll need a breather before your sister comes."

"What?" Mandie's voice increased several decibels.

"Oh, did I forget to tell you? Hope had some vacation time banked and decided she would come to help out for a while."

"Yes, you did 'forget,' you devious old codger. Just what I don't need. Dad, she's going to rearrange all my drawers and organize everything," Mandie moaned.

"Now, you know your sister has the best of intentions. She loves you."

"Where in the world am I going to put her? Have you two figured that out yet?"

"Blow-up bed in the workout room."

"I don't have a blow-up bed."

"I'll pick one up. She's flying in tomorrow."

Mandie pressed her fingers against her temples. "Can you also pick up a six pack of Mike's Hard Lemonade? I'm going to need it."

"Ooh, good idea. I'll pick up some B & B for me."

"I'm sending her to the storage shed to rearrange your crap. I have no doubt her skills will be put to better use there."

"That's not nice." He shook his finger at her.

"Welcome to the new, improved version of your daughter. I don't feel like being nice anymore. Maybe naughty will get me further along in life. So far, they lied; the meek have not inherited the earth. The bitches and bastards have."

"Tough talk, but you don't have it in you to be something you're not."

✝

Gail decided she'd try to work on some half-finished projects. These weren't for clients. She liked dreaming about the wild drawings. Someday she would resurrect one and give serious consideration to building her dream house.

The only redeeming quality to her current home was the view. She looked out the window and smiled at the double rainbow. The colorful display came compliments of the recent Issaquah drizzle. Everyone assumed it rained all the time in Washington, but this wasn't rain. She missed the full out rains of the Midwest. She used to dance outside as the steady stream fell from the heavens in nature's glorious shower.

That sharp corner pricked her mind vexatiously. She was missing something important. Her finger landed again on the note with the spider web of creases. Multicolored rainbows skirted the edges of her memory. *Dammit, why can't I bring that memory into focus?*

Choosing to ignore the rainbows, she picked up her pencil and tried to add to her drawing. Her damned hand wouldn't cooperate. A squiggly line appeared on the rounded outer contour of the dwelling she was trying to create. She knew better. The hand therapist had told her not to try. It was too soon and would only frustrate her. Gail was stubborn. Once she got the cast off, she would be able to move around quite a bit better. Everything took a lot longer to accomplish since the accident, and patience was not a virtue she happened to possess.

Setting the mechanical pencil on the drafting table, she filled her lungs with air and pushed it out. Time to kill a few hours on social media. She could still point and click. Since Gail never participated in the discussions, it was easy to lurk with a mangled dominant hand. She didn't have to type a single word.

The other day, Dale had waltzed into her home to check on her. She was in a particularly foul mood and asked, "What the hell do you want? I don't need a damn nursemaid. What I need is something to occupy my time."

Dale moved another table into her office and laid the laptop within reach of her drafting table. His easy answer to her frustration and boredom was a source of entertainment, social media.

"Thanks," she'd grumbled, sounding a lot like a reluctant, pissy troll.

He'd bowed and backed out of the room without saying one single word.

She was genuinely grateful for the distraction. She'd resurrected her love for books and joined two active book club sites. It was a good solution to her crankiness.

Extending her good arm, Gail managed to pull the laptop forward with her fingertips. Luckily for her, Dale had set the computer on a notepad, and it moved on the table as if the pad had rollers. When the computer was close enough to grab, she picked it up and plopped the device on top of her drawing, hiding her failed attempt. *Damn squiggly line is sticking its tongue out at me.*

Flipping the laptop open, she used her index finger and thumb over the built-in touchpad and activated the prompt for her password. Using the hunt and peck method, she found her way to the first group. The sound of her own laughter felt impossibly loud in her ears, as she became engrossed in the banter among the usual suspects. *Oh, that's an interesting thread.* It never took much to send them down the "sex path," but in this instance, the gutter was unavoidable.

Someone had posted a picture of a hideous couch that was a dead ringer for a repeating pattern of vaginas. The reader challenged the authors to write a scene incorporating the ugly maroon and mauve couch. Already, the comments were causing Gail to nearly pee her pants. After she read the various branches in that thread, she popped over to the other site. A photo caught her attention.

Rainbows. Gail was seeing those damn things everywhere, and now a picture of a rainbow tunnel. Obviously, someone had photoshopped the picture, but the photo stirred an emotion she couldn't quite wrestle to the surface.

She brought her face closer to the screen and tilted her head to the right, then the left. Her eyes squinted to find something that would help with that elusive memory. The post was from M.B. Carter. The woman's periodic posts were always thoughtful. Gail had an acute desire to know more about M.B. Carter. Clicking on her name opened the member's page on the screen. Gail sent a friend request. She had tried to find out more about the mysterious M.B. Carter. Was M.B. a woman? All her settings seemed set to private. M.B. Carter would have to accept her friend request for Gail to learn more.

She absently twirled her pencil on the drafting table, while she waited for a response. Gail had almost given up, when the familiar ding brought her out of her daydream. A private message popped up on her laptop from M.B. Carter. Gail held tightly to her control in a ferocious wind of excitement.

M.B.: *You're that famous architect. I checked your page before responding. Sorry to be so paranoid, but why would you send me a friend request? I'm an out and proud lesbian, and I don't need any bullshit posted on my page. Been there, done that. You couldn't put a single rainbow on your page to give a hint?*

Gail laughed out loud. *Paranoid much?* She frantically searched for how to add that tiny rainbow symbol to the bottom of her profile picture. A number of the book group members used the border on their profiles. In frustration, she popped back over to the book group's page. She typed a desperate post, asking how everyone added the small symbol to their profile. She tapped her swollen fingers on the table until she realized it was causing her a fair amount of discomfort. *Oh, thank you, Jesus. Good old, reliable Erin to the rescue.*

A step-by-step instructional post, complete with screen shots, blinked at Gail. Erin had provided details on how to add the rainbow at the bottom of Gail's profile picture, which was one of her more famous designs. It wasn't easy with her bum hand, but Gail followed the instructions. Soon, her picture sported the telltale rainbow gif. *Take that, Ms. Paranoid.* Instead of tapping on the desk, she used her fingers to create a response to M.B. Carter.

Gail: *Check out my page now.*

Gail knew her response was abrupt, but she wanted to respond before M.B. thought she was some freaky troll.

M.B.: *Hmmm, that's too easy. How do I know you're not trying to appease me?*
Oh, for shit's sake. Gail poked angrily at the keys.

Gail: *Bad accident. One hand. Out and proud too, I assure you. Your picture…it spoke to me.*

Before Gail could censor her creepy-sounding message, M.B. had responded.

M.B.: Okay

Gail smiled at the one-word response. She was eager to check out M.B.'s social media page and only felt mildly like some kind of cyber stalker. M.B. was intriguing, and Gail was bored. Her lurking days were over. If she joined the discussions, there was a chance M.B. would respond to her posts. Gail posted a cute kitten picture on M.B.'s timeline, thanking her for accepting the friend request. *I'm turning into a mushball.* Still, she smiled when the ding notified her of the grinning smiley face in the private message. She was glad she'd clicked *Love* in response to M.B.'s post. The tiny heart icon was brand-new. Anyone could step up their appreciation for posts with the new symbol signifying they *loved* versus *liked* the message.

Quickly flipping to M.B. Carter's page, Gail clicked the *About* link to check her family relationships. Nothing. At least there was no indication she was married. Surely, she would have noted that important piece of information. Same-sex marriage was legal—at least for now. The elusive M.B. had chosen a picture of a cat for her profile and a serene lake for her cover photo. Gail couldn't tell if she was eighteen or eighty. There was no birth date listed. What would her photos reveal?

Bingo. Buried within a collage of distinctive photos was a picture of a stunning blonde standing next to an older man with similar features. *Hmm, older brother or father?*

She clicked back on the *About* link. *Holy shit, she lives in Washington.* Gail's heart beat in double time. She could actually meet this woman. Moses Lake was less than three hours away. Gail admitted to herself that spending the next two hours thoroughly reviewing M.B.'s page was downright creepy. She'd never been that infatuated with a complete stranger before and didn't quite understand what compelled her to essentially stalk the woman.

†

Mandie was grinning, until she heard the keys in the door. Hope had arrived, and every small morsel of peace and quiet was leaving. Reluctantly, Mandie closed her laptop. She'd wanted to learn a little more about Gail Forrester. Her profile pic was one of her more famous designs. Mandie guessed that was because the page was professional and not personal, with the intent to advertise her architectural talents. Not only couldn't she find a studio head shot, she didn't see any casual poses of the woman. Those were the best, pictures that weren't staged. Snapshots captured the essence of a person, when they weren't aware someone was looking into the depths of their soul. *Maybe I'll develop a friendship with the famous woman and learn more about her bad accident. Besides being lesbians, we have that in common.* Mandie wondered how bad Gail's accident was. Could it possibly have been as horrid as her own?

Recovery was slow. Staying behind the lens of a camera gave Mandie joy. She'd captured that rainbow and edited the photo into something similar to the vision that chased her dreams every night since her accident. The multicolored, swirling tunnel of lights kept taunting her while she slept. On a whim, she'd posted the picture to see what kind of reaction it would get. Maybe one of the authors would contact her. Mandie could start a business taking photos for book covers. It seemed like a lot of the covers looked the same and often used similar stock photos. If she gave them a truly unique product, maybe she could make a go of it.

Her curiosity over the mangled rolls of film was at a point of frenzy. She chomped down on her tongue so she wouldn't bite her father's head off when he came home without the prints. *He promised to get them today, after picking up Hope from the airport.* Mandie hadn't remembered taking any photos on her old 35mm camera, but obviously she had at some point. Things weren't adding up. She'd gone on a rampage to find her old camera, but the damn thing wasn't in her condo. That left the storage shed. First order of business for her sister would be to organize the shed and find that old camera.

Mandie mentally prepared for her sister's arrival. For such a tiny thing, Hope was a force to be reckoned with. Hope was a good six inches shorter than Mandie, favoring their mother more than their father.

Hurricane Hope burst into the room. "Oh Mandie, look at you. I am so sorry I couldn't come earlier, but Dad assured me he was taking care of everything. I did come when you first landed in the hospital, but I couldn't stay. I've cleared my schedule now and can spend the next month helping." Hope approached Mandie and offered a careful hug.

Mandie groaned.

"Oh my God, did I hurt you?"

Mandie shook her head. "No, I'm much better. Don't worry. If my body didn't shatter after jumping out of a plane with a faulty parachute, your gentle hug isn't going to kill me."

"That's not funny." Hope poked her shoulder. "What the hell were you thinking?"

"It seemed like the right thing to do after getting fired," Mandie answered drolly.

"You should have sued. They can't fire you for being a lesbian."

"Unfortunately, yes they can. Welcome to the new world order with our current, Make America Great Again president. Being politically correct is no longer in fashion. Didn't you get the memo? Oh wait, you live in a state where it's never been in fashion."

"Can we please not talk politics?"

"You opened that door. Sometimes, Hope, you and your Bible-thumping hubby are so naive regarding that asshole in the White House." Mandie didn't want to get into that old argument again. She'd felt personally wounded after learning Hope and her husband had voted for the president. She tried to expel the bitterness with a cleansing breath. "You're right. I don't want to fight. Dad, did you pick up the photos?"

"Aw crap, I forgot," he answered.

Mandie pushed out a puff of air and rolled her eyes. She moved slowly to reach the keys, lifting them off the table and handing them to her father. "Can you and Hope go to the storage shed and try to find my camera, after picking up the photos? Maybe you can drive to the bistro and get us some food, too."

"I just got here," Hope whined. "Why can't we visit for a little bit?"

"Because I'm hungry and we have squatola in the form of healthy fare in my fridge or cupboards. I haven't trusted Dad's masterpieces. My arteries fill with plaque just listening to him. We've been living on takeout since I awoke and came home. Too bad I didn't wake to a kiss from a beautiful princess. Instead, I saw Dad looming over my bed."

Hope wrinkled her nose. "You know I never liked that bitch, Caroline."

"Is there any woman you'd approve of?"

"That's not fair, Mandie. You know I believe we all sin. I've sinned before. I forgive all sins. You're my sister, and I love you. Love the sinner."

"Do you hear yourself? If I ever find the right woman, I would marry her in a minute. I don't consider that a sin. You keep translating the passages you want to interpret in a way that demonizes gay marriage, and I'll keep reminding you of the book of Ruth." Mandie closed her eyes and began reciting, "'Don't urge me to leave you or to turn back from you. Where you go I will go, and where you stay I will stay. Your people will be my people and your God my God. Where you die I will die, and there I will be buried. May the Lord deal with me, be it ever so severely, if even death separates you and me.'

"You can't possibly believe that was only friendship. Just listen to the passion in those words," Mandie protested.

"I would come to the wedding to support you and help in any way I could."

"But you still believe it is a sin. You would come to the wedding to organize, and dress me in what you believe is appropriate. Sorry, sorry, I'm being a bitch. I know your intent is positive. Can you please go and get some food? I get exponentially grumpier the longer I go without healthy eats."

Mandie's father remained wisely mute. Unless an argument got out of hand, he usually stayed out of the debate between his daughters. Although his personal political views aligned with Mandie's, she knew he loved his younger daughter. Hope usually became defensive whenever Mandie or anyone else challenged her belief system.

"Come on honey, I am a bit hungry myself. Your sister is still having a hard time with her recovery. You shouldn't take her comments to heart. You know she loves you."

"I'm just trying to help," Hope cried out.

"I said I was sorry. I promise, after you come back with food, we can visit."

Her dad slung his arm around Hope's shoulder and led her toward the door. "Asian chicken salad okay with you?" he called over his shoulder.

"Yeah, that would be great, Dad. Please take my credit card."

"I got it. Hey, I forgot to mention the attorney from that skydiving place called again. He said you have fourteen days to decide. He told me he sent the papers next-day. They should be in your mailbox. The ambulance chaser called too. He said he can get you ten times as much. You should listen to him."

"Get my mail and I'll take a look. I'm inclined to take the offer. It's enough to allow me to pursue something I've always wanted to try."

"What's that, pumpkin?"

"Photography. I feel like that's my true calling," Mandie said.

"Can you make any money on that?" her dad asked.

"If I'm any good at it, yeah I can."

"You should, Mandie. I want you to be happy again. I haven't seen you smile in a long time," Hope added.

Mandie nodded at her younger sister. She could hear the honesty in her voice and felt her genuine support. It was a start.

After her father and sister left, Mandie returned to her curiosity over the famous architect. Had Gail learned about her through the story that ran in the *Seattle Times*, "The Amazing Woman Who Survived a Parachute Failure." At first, Mandie had been reluctant and declined the interview. An offer of $20,000 provided extra breathing space while her father stayed at the condo. She didn't want him taking over her bills.

The skydiving company had offered her $1 million in exchange for a release from any further responsibility for future medical issues. She would be set for life, as long as she didn't go on a spending spree. She wasn't about to milk the skydiving company for more than what she considered a very generous offer, one she hadn't pursued at all. Besides, she didn't want to be in the same room as the sleazy ambulance chaser. He oozed slime, and she wanted no part of it. Attorneys. They were all a bunch of cockroaches.

Internet stalking wasn't sleazy though. She typed in Gail Forrester, hoping to get a glimpse of the person behind those amazing natural dwellings popping up all over the Northwest. The rich and famous were scrambling to hire her, but the woman was like a ghost. Mandie could not find one single picture of her and that was frustrating. There was nothing on social media, and she found zip on the Internet. *What the hell? She was the one who friended me first.* Before Mandie could talk herself out of it, she typed a short, private message.

> M.B.: *What kind of accident? Are you okay? Had an unusual one myself a few months ago.*

Mandie was biting the ends of her nails, as she watched the little, typing-in-progress dots shimmer on the screen. The green circle next to Gail's name proved she was still online. That was no guarantee of an immediate response.

> Gail: *Seattle is a terrible city for mass transit in more ways than one. Bus hit me.*
> M.B.: *I'll see your bus accident and raise you one parachute malfunction. Skydiving is as dangerous as everyone says it is.*

Mandie wondered if her response sounded flirtatious. It wasn't her intent to flirt, was it?

> Gail: *Hmmmm. Bat shit crazy comes to mind.*
> M.B.: *Yeah, like that's not something I've heard before…oh, perhaps a thousand times.*

Mandie was surprised to see the words forming themselves as she typed them. This was crazy, having a long-involved conversation with a virtual stranger.

Gail: <grin> *Recovery is hard, talk about another bat shit crazy person, that would be my PT. School of cruel.*
M.B.: *Good one.*
Gail: *U live in Moses Lake, huh. Do u ever come to Seattle?*
M.B.: *Not until I can get around better on my own.*
Gail: *True dat.*

Mandie didn't wish to metaphorically overstay her welcome, so she typed a graceful end to the private messaging.

M.B.: *I'd better let you go. TTYL peace out.*

The thumbs up symbol popped up on the screen and Mandie grinned. She had a cyber pen pal, a new experience she welcomed with wide open arms, legs, and any other body part up for grabs.

†

Mandie must have still been wearing a stupid grin when her sister and father arrived back at the condo. Her sister's disapproving scowl clued her in to the shit pie she was about to receive. Her father had a hard time looking her in the eye. Something big was going on.

"What's with the faces?" Mandie asked. "I don't think I have the physical aptitude to kill anyone yet."

"Um, pumpkin, the drug store people said there were some questionable photos they couldn't print, because of their, uh…policies on nudity and overtly sexual content. Other pictures were completely ruined, so there's only a few they salvaged. He gave me the negatives if you want to develop some of the racier ones yourself."

"What?" Mandie shouted in disbelief. "I don't recall taking any pictures that wouldn't be considered strictly G rated. Gimme them, I need to see what you're talking about." She held her hand out.

Her dad walked over and handed her the photographs. She flipped open the envelope and studied each picture with the laser-like precision of a critical gallery owner. Out of two rolls of film, there were only six clear pictures. Several looked like a six-year-old had chewed on a box of 128 Crayolas and spit them up on the photo paper. The ethereal beauty defied logic. She recognized trees, rocks, and grass, but the colors were all wrong. If shoving rolls of film into a drawer and smashing them was a new technique that created this effect, Mandie thought perhaps she'd give it another go.

After shuffling through the pictures, including the clear landscapes in all the wrong colors, there were three very blurry pictures of two women. It was possible she was one of the women. It was so hard to see any details. Surely, she would remember posing like that with another person. The body language screamed there was more to their relationship than mere friendship. The photo didn't look anything like Caroline. None of this made any sense.

Mandie gasped. A stunning and obviously nude woman had only a sheet draped across her body. A hint of her nipples protruded through the light fabric. The woman's hair was slightly tousled and her cheeks flushed, but it was the look on her face that mesmerized Mandie. The eager anticipation suggested the photographer was getting ready to make love to the woman. To Mandie, it seemed like the camera lens was an extension of the photographer's fingers or tongue.

Mandie didn't know how to develop pictures, but she was damn well going to learn. She would take that settlement and build a dark room if she had to. Her first mission would be to develop those negatives. Then she would find the mysterious woman.

"I think I just met my future wife. Too bad I have absolutely no idea where to look for her," Mandie blurted out.

Her dad frowned. "Pumpkin, are you all right? You're not making sense."

"I know, Dad, I know. Did you get the mail? I'm taking the generous offer." Mandie held her hand up to stave off her father's arguments. "I want to move on. With what I have saved and this settlement, I don't have to find a new job as long as I don't spend like a drunken sailor. It might sound crazy, but I'd like to give photography a try. First order of business, buy that condo upstairs and build a dark room. I'd like to have a separate space for my photography and that seems like as good a spot as any. Besides, I have nowhere to put you and Hope when you visit, so it will be nice to have the extra bedroom."

"You're serious," Hope exclaimed.

"As a heart attack." Mandie grinned.

"God, don't say that. Haven't you had enough bad things happen to you?"

"I think my life is looking up. I can feel it. Something good is on the horizon. I'm going to find her."

Frank and Hope exchanged a look but didn't say anything more, as they laid the food from the bistro on the table.

"Come on, let's eat. Maybe you need food to nourish your brain," Hope remarked.

Mandie chuckled. "Subtle, little sis, subtle. By the way, I am holding you to your promise to be at my wedding, but I'm not going to let you pick out the dress. I'll throw you a bone. You can pick out my shoes, as long as they aren't taller than two inches."

CHAPTER SEVENTEEN

Evelyn was peering at the orb, when she felt a presence behind her. There was no need to turn around. The unmistakable shift in the air marked the presence of Transition Messiah.

"You really took a shine to those two." TM pointed at the globe and placed her hand on Evelyn's shoulder. "Relax, I know what you did. I attempted to undo your meddling, but I guess I have a soft spot as well. I didn't completely obliterate the clues. If they are meant to reconnect, it will happen."

"Did you also know about the camera?"

TM smiled. "Of course I did. Meh, as technology goes, that piece of equipment is the least offensive to me. I quite enjoy the art derived from photography."

"I don't understand. You knew Mandie was taking pictures, and you made sure most of the film was destroyed, but why keep some of the pictures intact? And why not erase Mandie's entire name in that note?"

TM shrugged. "It's an imprecise science, the meddling in human affairs. I enjoyed a few of the pictures and couldn't bring myself to completely destroy that one roll of film. Quite steamy, don't you agree?"

Evelyn laughed. "You're a dirty old woman, but you sure look good for your age." Evelyn folded her hands in front of her waist. "I'm not ever going back, am I?"

TM looked on her kindly. "I would miss you, Evelyn. Even I don't know what the future holds for you. Fate will have its way often enough, but sometimes we have a way of making our own futures. You are special Evelyn, as special as Gail and Mandie but for entirely different reasons. One more day, then you'll know what the universe has in store for you. You may be surprised. Sometimes there's an alternative to returning to earth or moving on. Only the most loyal have that option."

"Do you think it's wrong of me to be scared for tomorrow? I've lived most of my adult life here in Intermediate. I suppose it doesn't matter. I won't remember a thing. Even if I return, it will take forever for my physical body to recover, if that is even possible."

TM kissed her on the cheek. "I'm going to break my own rule. As you've said, you are the longest resident of Intermediate, and your loyalty must be rewarded. You'll understand when you move to the next phase of your existence. Don't be afraid, Evelyn. Everything works out the way it is supposed to. Those are the laws of the universe. Sometimes two souls are meant to blend into one."

✝

Gail was excited to lose her casts. Her therapist had warned her she was still in the middle of her recovery, but she was feeling stronger every day. She was looking forward to moving about more easily and not taking years to compose her private messages to M.B.

She'd held herself back so she wouldn't appear to be a crazy stalker, but they'd been regularly communicating with one another. Gail was delighted when M.B. sent a flurry of messages that opened up a whole new level of intimacy.

M.B.: *I think I shocked my dad and little sister yesterday.*
Gail: *Oh really. Do tell.*
M.B.: *Dad finally took some cannisters of film to the drug store. Apparently, they wouldn't develop all of the negatives. Something about questionable photos.*
Gail: *Questionable? Okay, now you have me on the edge of my seat. How?*
M.B.: *Nudes, I think. But I swear I don't remember taking these pictures. Then there are mysterious ones that look like psychedelic paintings. They are so unusual, maybe I can sell them.*
Gail: *Nudes? Okay color me impressed. I'll bet they're masterpieces.*
M.B.: *I wouldn't say that exactly, but a few have inspired me to consider photography as a vocation. I know it sounds crazy, but with my settlement, I can afford to take risks.*

Gail: *You should. Take risks, I mean. I can tell you have a passion for this art. Passion should never be squashed.*

M.B.: *I'm even thinking about buying the condo above me and turning one of the bedrooms into a darkroom. I could develop the negatives that seemed too risqué for the drug store*

Gail: *Definitely! Go for it and share those naughty pics with me. I need something to keep me entertained while I rehab my hand. Tell me more about the ones you like.*

M.B.: *One is of this woman. I swear, she looks like someone is about to make love to her using the camera. I've never seen anything so...oh, I don't even know how to describe it. I don't understand how I possibly could have forgotten taking the picture. I'm a little worried that my accident has somehow affected my memory. I wish I knew this woman. I told my dad and sister, "I think I've met my future wife."*

Jealousy reared its ugly head. Gail was lucky in life with a successful business but not lucky in love. She didn't want to mark this up as another hard lesson learned, but darn it, she loved talking with M.B. She secretly wished M.B. would never find that elusive woman in the photo. Her curiosity got the better of her.

Gail: *Hmmm, sounds intriguing. Send me the pic so I can judge for myself.*

M.B.: *No. I don't think I should share this one. It seems too private.*

Gail could almost see M.B. blush. She was desperate to meet this woman.

Gail: *Killjoy*

M.B.: *Hey, I gotta go. Talk later?*

Gail: *Absolutely. Anytime. If you won't show me your pictures, at least you can entertain me with your latest shock-Dad-and-Sis stories.*

A smiley emoticon popped up on Gail's screen, marking the end of their longest conversation to date.

Gail could relate to M.B.'s frustration about the photos. She believed M.B. when she said she had no recollection of the woman or her own role as the photographer. Ever since the accident, Gail felt like someone had surgically removed a major chunk of her own memory—precise and unemotional. Gone. Without an ability to fight for it. M.B. had described her feelings exactly and that had cemented their friendship. Both of them felt like the other understood the struggles after their respective accidents.

Gail was researching comas and looking for a support group that aligned with hers and M.B.'s unique experiences. All she could find were support groups that catered to people with traumatic brain injuries. Those groups did not exactly fit their situation. Maybe she would float the idea of starting one on her own or getting one of the OTs she worked with to help organize a group for people with memory issues. Dale thought she was nuts. He hadn't discovered anything wrong with her memory, except client names, but that was a problem before the accident. He'd pointed out she had no problems remembering every single client meeting and what she needed to tweak to meet their needs and desires related to her designs. She had to accede those memories were sharp in her mind. Still, Gail knew there was something important she'd forgotten. She wanted that memory back. It was a compulsion she did not understand.

Dale had come along for the cast removal and leaned over to see what she was doing. "You don't text people. What's captured your attention so thoroughly you feel the need to struggle with typing on that tiny screen?"

Gail balanced her smartphone precariously on her leg, as she typed her message. She placed her hand on top, blocking Dale's view. "None of your business, Nosy Nathan."

"Mmmm, Nathan, now he was a scrumptious specimen of manliness. Come on, tell Uncle Dale who's got you all hot and bothered."

"I am not hot and bothered. It's a friend who had a similar experience. That's all."

"Is she a lesbian?"

"You don't even know the person is a she. It could be a man."

Dale snorted. "Not with that lovesick expression on your face, deary."

"Gail Forrester," the nurse called out.

"Lucky dog, you were just saved by the bell. Don't get too comfy, because we're talking about this after you lose your plaster," Dale said.

The buzzing sound from the saw made Gail cringe. The prospect of losing the casts and moving to soft support had her giddy with excitement. She flexed her fingers. Although they were a little stiff, she didn't feel pain. She was anxious to tell M.B. she wasn't a lopsided gimp anymore. Before Dale could stick his nose in her affairs again, she pulled out her phone and sent a quick, private message.

> Gail: *I'm free from the weight of the world, okay maybe not the weight of the world, but those blasted casts are off. I can use all my fingers again.*
> M.B.: *Now that sounds intriguing and how would you like to use those fingers?*
> Gail smiled. Definitely a flirtatious remark.
> Gail: *Are you offering to help with my rehab?*
> M.B.: *LMAO. My evil sis is calling. TTYL*

The smile melted from Gail's face like wax. Every time they ventured into suggestive territory, even when M.B. started it, she backed off and made an excuse for why she had to go. Gail decided she would find a way to meet the Stunning Swede, even if she had to court a new client who happened to live in Moses Lake. She could offer to make the three-hour trip and meet with the client, then somehow track down M.B.

Stunning Swede? That nickname is oddly familiar. Frankly, Gail was surprised by her use of the nickname. It wasn't like she didn't see M.B.'s name blinking at her several times a day. Every time she logged on, Gail saw M.B.'s name and smiled. The private message awaiting her response brightened her day. She wasn't sure why she'd never asked for M.B.'s first name. Perhaps she was afraid she would forget and have to scroll back several times to remember. That would offend her new friend.

Gail shoved her smartphone back in her pocket. She exited the room several pounds lighter but with a burning need for something she couldn't quite put her finger on.

†

Evelyn felt the soft caress on her hand and heard the quiet sobs. When she opened her eyes, she saw the top of a thick mop of chestnut hair with reddish highlights. Who was this woman holding her hand and whimpering by her bedside? She tried to remove the cobwebs from her brain to consider who would have stuck by her all these years.

"Hello," Evelyn croaked.

The head popped up, and watery hazel eyes opened wide. "Lyn, oh Lordy. Hang on. Nurse, nurse, she's awake," the woman yelled. She reached to press the call button. A quick kiss on her lips from the woman, and Evelyn was more confused than ever.

"Who…" Evelyn started to say.

The hazel eyes lost their initial spark of joy and another tear formed. "Shhh, it's all going to be okay." She kissed Evelyn's forehead.

The nurse bustled in, and the flurry of activity was almost too much for Evelyn. She had one thought and pushed out the words. "Mirror, I need a mirror."

"Oh, baby, you're not deformed, just a nasty bump on your head," the chestnut woman said. She rummaged in her purse and produced a compact and held it in front of Evelyn. "See, not a single mark on your beautiful face."

Evelyn blinked her eyes and looked into the mirror. She estimated the woman in the mirror looking back at her was approximately forty years old. If she looked closely, she could find gray strands in her ash-blonde hair. Although her face was pale, it was not unpleasant to look at. By most people's standards, it was an attractive face. None of her features were too small or too large to overpower the others and seemed to blend well for an overall agreeable effect. She rather liked the light gray eyes that stared back at her. When she looked down at her body, she was dizzy with joy. This woman took care of herself. While the body wasn't ripped, it was fit.

"Thank you," Evelyn whispered to TM. From the look in the eyes of the woman who hovered over her bed, at least one person on earth loved her; even if everyone else from her previous life was absent. Evelyn wondered what had happened to her old body. Did they decide to let her go? Evelyn didn't know if she would try to find out or just accept the gift of a new life.

When the physician strode into the room, Evelyn feigned exhaustion to dodge the inevitable questions. She would try to find out as much as possible about her new life before answering, so she wouldn't cause unnecessary pain to the woman.

"Tired." Evelyn closed her eyes.

"It's okay that she sleeps after waking, right? What's important is that she opened her eyes and said a few words. If things are fuzzy or she lost her memory, will she get it back?" The woman's voice quivered.

"We'll do some thorough testing, but don't alarm yourself about any confusion at first. That's to be expected. Yes, it's a great sign she woke up," the physician answered. Evelyn hoped they would continue to talk, and she could glean more information about her rebirth.

She was still playing possum a few hours later, when another voice registered in the room. Evelyn learned she was a successful gallery owner and married to the chestnut-haired woman, whose name was Eve. *Oh, TM, you are a crafty old bird, with a twisted sense of humor.*

Transition Messiah said two souls were sometimes meant to blend into one. She had not returned Evelyn to earth as a new soul. Instead, Evelyn inhabited the body of an old soul. *Do parts of that soul remain? What happened to my previous vessel? Did they decide to pull the plug and let it go?* Evelyn surmised that must have happened, otherwise, TM would have returned her to that sixty-five-year-old body. A body in its sunset years was hardly worth returning to, but this body had plenty of time left on earth.

A plan formed in her mind to get the two star-crossed lovers together. She knew that was her reason for returning. This was not the original plan. *What kind of grief is Transition Messiah getting from Creator? This plan has TM's Amazonian fingerprints all over it.*

CHAPTER EIGHTEEN

"Are you out of your damn mind? Why in the world would you want to drive three hours for a pitiful job we'll barely break even on? The time and energy you've put into that design compared to what you quoted is a friggin' travesty. You didn't even consult me. I'm your partner." Dale stood with his hands on his hips. His right side jutted out to create an asymmetrical pose, a perfect exclamation point to his rant.

"Consider this my version of philanthropy. I've made plenty of money for both of us after you pawed through my designs and played salesman while I was indisposed. I have my reasons." Gail leaned back in her chair.

She regretted giving Dale a key to her place. Lately he'd been barging in to "check on her." His unannounced visits were wearing on her. They interrupted her peace and tranquility, not to mention her well-guarded privacy.

"Does this have anything to do with the mysterious person you keep texting?"

"I told you, I'm not texting anyone." Gail only felt slightly bad about the half-truth. Technically, private messages were not texts. "I'm going to Moses Lake. I promise I will be back for the big meeting with Pretentious Pair."

"The Goldsmiths," Dale shouted. "Might I add their name is spot on, they practically shit gold and have offered to triple your standard fee for a quick turnaround. Promise me you won't do anything to screw that up."

"I promise." Gail sighed. "When is it enough, Dale? When will you have enough money? I'll lose my joy in creating these designs if it becomes all about the money. If my passion goes, you won't like the consequences."

"Fine, do what you need to do, but can't we intersperse good paying clients into your passion? Please, pretty please?" Dale batted his lashes.

"Don't worry, I'll continue to draw and keep you in the standard to which you've become accustomed. I know how much you would hate to go back to polyester."

"I've never worn polyester," Dale huffed.

Gail grinned. "Gotcha."

"Artists," Dale grumbled.

"This artist keeps you in natural fibers. Just remember that."

Dale kissed her cheek. "Do you want me to go with you? Oh, road trip! Maybe there will be some manly farmer looking for a good time."

"No," Gail blurted too quickly.

Dale narrowed his eyes. "You've something up your sleeve."

"Leave it."

"All right, but when you're ready to fess up to your new lady love, Uncle Dale will be right here to put her through the paces. If she's a Des clone, I'll scratch her eyes out and feed them to the wolves before you have a chance to fall for her."

Gail sighed. "Hmmm, and you wonder why I don't tell you everything."

"Aha, there is someone."

Gail held out her hand. "I want my keys back."

Dale's lips pursed together in a pout that would give a three-year-old a run for their money. It looked plain silly on a grown man. "Don't be like that, Gail, you know I love you."

"Not enough to stay out of my business."

"But we're partners. That means I'm required to be all up in your business." Dale twirled his index finger and pointed up.

Gail rolled her eyes. "Not my personal life. That's hands off. Do we need to have the talk again about boundaries?"

"No, but when you are ready to share this person, I get first dibs at checking them out."

Gail tapped her pencil on the table. "Who else would I introduce anyone to? It's not like I have a life outside of the business. You're my only friend who has interrogation rights."

"Good. I'm glad that's settled. Now can I keep the keys? I get worried something will happen, and I feel an acute need to keep tabs on you."

"You just don't want the gravy train to stop."

"Do you really feel that way?" Dale's face adopted a pained expression.

"No, God, I'm sorry. I'm frustrated. I feel like there's something important I'm missing. If I don't uncover the mystery, I'll never find it. Besides, I'm still irritated about that bloody note."

"Yeah, literally. You know the blood…"

"I get it. I wish there was a way to remove the blood and see the last name." Gail looked up at the ceiling, hoping the answer would materialize in the textured plaster.

"Don't you know any cops who could, oh, I don't know, send it to some crime lab or something?"

"No, the only cop I came across was about to give me a speeding ticket. Although I detected a note of flirtation in her voice and a veiled invitation to meet up at her favorite watering hole."

"You should do it. Go find this cop and chat her up. Maybe she'll help you." Dale leaned against the drafting table.

"Oh sure, let's play that out…Hey, fancy meeting you here. By the way, I'm looking for this woman…"

"Okay, I get it. You lesbians can be such a jealous bunch. I suppose if she's interested in you, she won't want to help you find another woman."

"Are you done harassing me? I have work to do. If you're a good boy, I'll let you come with me to Moses Lake."

Dale clapped his hands together. "Oh, goody, goody. When will we leave?"

"Next Monday. Now march your ass back out of my hair."

Dale wiggled his fingers and pivoted to leave. "Toodles my golden goose."

Gail smiled. She enjoyed working with Dale. He kept her on track and provided entertainment on occasion. She didn't like the realization that, besides Dale, she hadn't connected with too many people. Her work had all but consumed her for the past four years. She vowed to obtain more balance in her life. Maybe M.B. would be a friend who would help her with that.

†

The locks disengaged after two quick beeps from the shiny, royal-blue car. Eve hadn't even pulled the keys out of her purse. Evelyn schooled her expression, hoping she wouldn't reveal her astonishment at the new technology. She folded herself into the compact vehicle and was surprised when Eve pressed a button on the dash to start the car. That was new. She observed some of the advances when she hovered over the orb to watch her version of a soap opera. This new hybrid vehicle was unfamiliar to her.

She understood how those fake fortune tellers worked now. All she had to do was remain relatively quiet, while Eve revealed bits and pieces of their life. *Lyn. I must remember my name is Lyn now.* Eve prattled on about various things, bringing her up to speed. Lyn recognized the chatter as nervousness. Eve needed to fill the void of Lyn's silence with something other than quiet discomfort. The revelations were helpful. A few well-placed questions, and off Eve went with detailed explanations. Eve was a kind soul. Lyn could tell that right away. She understood why the soul who had occupied her new body had married Eve. Lyn could feel herself warming to the idea of spending the rest of her life with this woman.

184

Lyn turned her face to Eve. "I'm sorry I worried you."

Eve swiped a tear away. "Oh Lyn, I was so distraught when you didn't respond. Next time, will you please listen when I suggest we can call someone to take care of it? I know you think you're Miss Handywoman, but…"

Lyn tossed out a small response, hoping she would collect more information. "It seemed like something so simple to do."

"Your improvisation gets you in trouble every time. What were you thinking, putting a chair on top of the counter, while lifting that fan to attach it to the ceiling? I picked the damn thing up. It weighs a ton. No wonder you slipped and fell. I heard the crack of your head against the granite counter all the way in the bedroom." Eve shuddered. "I'll never forget that awful sound. It will haunt me for the rest of my life."

Lyn laid her hand on top of Eve's. "I'm fine. Maybe my head will be a little scrambled for a while, and certain details will be fuzzy, but I remember the most important thing."

"What's that?" Eve asked.

"That you're the love of my life, and I'm lucky to have you." As the words spilled from Lyn's lips, she realized the statement was true. Remnants of the previous soul remained embedded into the fabric of her own soul. The two souls were inexplicably intertwined. Blended souls, like Transition Messiah had said before returning her to earth.

Eve squeezed Lyn's hand, and a brilliant smile flashed across her face. "I'm not feeling very inspired to paint right now. Besides, I'm in between projects. I plan on spoiling you rotten."

So, Eve is a painter. Is that how we met? She was sure she would learn their story soon enough, if she relaxed and let fate take its course. Lyn wondered if Transition Messiah was having a laugh in Intermediate.

"How about if I make a special dinner for us? You don't have to worry about the gallery. Tori is handling everything. She says we can hold off on securing an artist for the photography exhibition. The sculptor doesn't mind having the extra visibility. More time to sell her wares," Eve continued.

"No, no, I want to work on that as soon as we get home. I might be a little slow with how to proceed. Maybe Tori can help me. Perhaps she can walk through what she's finished already with the exhibition. Was anyone secured?"

"I don't know. You'll have to ask Tori. Will you at least wait until tomorrow before you jump back in with both feet?"

"I will." Lyn brought Eve's hand to her lips and sealed her promise with a kiss.

Each day, flashes of Lyn's memories surfaced. The soul that was Evelyn would tease out those minute pieces and make this new life her own. She hoped the tiny sprinkling of Evelyn's personality on top would be a welcome addition.

†

Mandie's eyes were riveted to the seemingly innocuous post on her favorite social media site. Lately she'd spent more time in the reading groups, especially after connecting with Gail. These groups had more interesting discussions than the photography groups.

Tori Fielding had shared a link. Mandie second guessed whether she should respond. She didn't have a whole lot to offer. There were old wildlife photos her friends had raved about. Then there were those scenes she had captured when she'd gone to Africa. The women going about their business in colorful garb made a stark contrast to the arid backdrop of the seasonal drought, and had caught the eyes of more than a few of her colleagues. Art was supposed to bring emotion to the surface, and these pictures certainly had.

> *I know this is primarily a book site, but I thought I would share this link. There may be some budding artists out there who are waiting for the opportunity to display their photography. We are a lesbian owned and operated gallery, looking for lesbian photographers who wish to showcase their work in an upcoming exhibition. Send me a private message if you're interested.*

Before all reasoning returned, Mandie sent a friend request to Tori Fielding and waited for her acceptance. The first step was the easiest one. Further action would become incrementally more difficult. Step two, sending the private message to request more information. Step three, following through on whatever submission guidelines Tori laid out.

Mandie hadn't built that dark room yet, but she had looked at the negatives. From what she could see in the basic shapes, and the fact that the drug store refused to develop them, there were some very erotic pictures. She wished she could remember taking them. Until she had the settlement funds in hand, she was hesitant to put in an offer on the condo above. She hoped no one would beat her to the punch, but so far, she didn't have anything to worry about.

She held that captivating photo the drugstore had printed and fleetingly considered submitting a print. There was no doubt a lesbian audience would appreciate the not-so-subtle raw sensuality. The photo seemed too private to share. Maybe she would submit this one as a teaser. On the infinitesimal chance they accepted her work, she wouldn't include it in a public exhibition. She'd already scanned the picture into her computer. Using her index finger, she traced the outline of the woman. *Who are you?*

A ping from her computer brought Mandie out of her private musing. She noted the acceptance from Tori Fielding. *Okay, step two, here we go.*

> M.B.: *I saw your post and would like more information on how to submit.*

Mandie sat back and stared at what she'd written. Her finger hovered over the *Enter* key. She almost felt like an invisible force was taunting her.

"Whatcha doing?" Hope asked.

Mandie jumped in her chair. "Shit, you scared me."

Hope scratched the back of her head and blinked her eyes as she yawned. "Did you make coffee?" Hope was easily distracted. The first question went unanswered, after Mandie failed to respond other than noting her surprise that Hope was awake. Since Hope often tinkered around until the wee hours, she normally didn't wake until later in the day. Their father had already left for his morning stroll.

Making coffee didn't take a lot of strength or effort, so Mandie had insisted this was something she could do in the morning. She pointed to the counter where the French press sat all alone, surrounded by nothing. "You'll need to nuke it. I made that several hours ago."

"Thanks," Hope mumbled.

Another ping from her computer brought Mandie's eyes back to the screen.

Tori: *Send three digital photos that best represent your work to* torifielding@hotmessmail.net

Mandie immediately clicked into her photo directory and selected a wildlife photo, an African woman with her child, and the altered photo of the rainbow. She clicked and unclicked the photo with the mysterious woman multiple times. When she finally uploaded the photos, she didn't realize until too late that she'd added the woman with the bed sheet seductively wrapped around her. *Oh well, too late now.*

Her email program allowed for retrieval of an errant email. Unfortunately, Mandie could never remember the steps. Who could figure out how to accomplish that before the timer had passed the point of no return? She clicked on the digital version of the photo and relaxed in her chair.

"Who's that?" Hope pointed to the picture in question.

Mandie jumped, startled when her sister snuck up behind her as she zoomed in on the woman's face. "I wish I knew."

CHAPTER NINETEEN

Lyn could not have asked for a better reset to her life. It was like TM or Creator had made Eve specifically for her. The love she exhibited toward Lyn seemed to flow out of every pore, like a sprinkler offering precious water to tiny shoots. Lyn needed the life sustaining substance, a perfect companion to the rays of sunshine from Eve's smiles.

"Are you sure you're up to a meeting with Tori?" Eve asked.

Lyn grabbed Eve's hand and pulled her to the sofa, where she was relaxing with a refreshing glass of fresh-squeezed lemonade. She never remembered tasting anything as good in her previous life. "I'm fine. It was good to speak with her and hear she has a few prospects to share with me."

"That's wonderful. I'm glad you want to give local talent a voice, well, local as in Washington State."

"That's an interesting way to put it. I suppose all of the arts let our voices speak, whether in the written word, a song, a movie, or the fine arts, including photographs. A little piece of ourselves always makes its way into the art, huh?"

Eve's musical laughter filled the air. "I do believe you fell in love with my paintings before you fell in love with me. I maintain there was more than a little piece of me in every one of them, and that's what drew you." She brought their clasped hands to her mouth and kissed one of Lyn's knuckles.

"Maybe you placed yourself on a premeditated path to win my heart by painting those specifically for me. A gallery owner would be defenseless against your ubiquitous ways."

"Guilty as charged. You were the most eligible lesbian in Seattle and irresistible to an artist in so many ways."

"I've no doubt you would have burst into the art scene as a new, bright and shining star without me. I'm glad I found you first."

The doorbell rang. Lyn was anxious to fulfill the task she was sure Transition Messiah had sent her back to earth to perform. She smiled to think the woman she'd believed was untouchable, was a die-hard romantic at heart.

Tori Fielding gusted into the house, her loose clothing fluttering about. Elegant was the one word Lyn would use to describe the tall woman with skin the color of dark chocolate.

"Girl, since when did that brain of yours fail to reach the top floor? That's what all those scrumptious butch gals are for. They fix and install everything for me, while I watch their muscles flex. And don't give me that 'I'm married' shit. When you get to be a certain age, you've earned the right to look. Besides, it strokes their little egos when I ogle them," Tori chastised.

"And what does Patricia think of your little answer to home repairs?" Eve asked.

"Oh honey, she makes the popcorn and plops down right next to me. Let me tell you something else. She isn't shy about making lewd comments."

"I already got the lecture from Eve, so there's no need to continue to chastise me. No more home repairs. I promise." Lyn stroked Eve's cheek and kissed her.

"You two are so damn sickening with all that sweetness after being together so long. You know what Patricia said this morning?"

"I'm afraid to ask." Eve chuckled.

"You should redo your hair, hon. It's looking kinda ratty today. As if." Tori tossed her head and her braids clinked together.

"But you redid them, didn't you?" Eve smiled.

"That's beside the point. She shouldn't have mentioned it. I would have decided to have them redone without her snide observation."

"How'd you get in and have your hair done already? It's barely noon," Eve asked.

Lyn decided to remain quiet, hoping to learn more about Tori.

"I have connections. So…enough about my hair. Let me show you what I've got so far. I know it's hard to envision on this tiny tablet, but it'll help us narrow the field. I have my favorites, but I want you to weigh in. Who knew the wide casting of my net would catch an unexpected little fishy?"

"What do you mean?" Lyn asked.

"I belong to a few lesfic reading groups. I especially like the ones where they give suggestions on erotica. Anyway, I tossed a post on a popular site and got a bite from someone who provided four very different photos. If I didn't know better, I would suspect each photo came from a different artist. Not many people can do that. I guess her signature could be the variance in style. She sent a wildlife photo, a woman and child, and this surreal rainbow—that's the best way to describe it. I don't think she meant to add the last one, but I'm sure glad she did. Wow! I wanted to jump into the photo and continue seducing the woman. It's that powerful."

"Sounds interesting. Who's the artist?" Lyn asked.

"Someone named M.B. Carter."

Lyn smiled. Now all she would have to do is get Gail to attend the exhibit. She was sure that, with Tori's enthusiasm, they would select Mandie as their artist to showcase in the gallery.

"She sounds promising. Do you have others to look at?" Lyn wanted to give the appearance of fairness.

"Of course." Tori sat next to Lyn and pulled her tablet from her enormous shoulder bag. Pressing the icon to open the photos folder, Tori showed Lyn the various submissions.

"So, out of these ten artists, how many do you want to narrow it down to?"

"Three is always a good number. If all three are willing to meet with us and show off their portfolios, we can have a decision two weeks from now. Then we'll get the ball rolling."

"What are your recommendations for the three finalists?" Lyn asked.

"Well, based on my earlier comments, I'm sure you've already guessed that I'd like to include this M.B. Carter woman. At least I hope it's a woman. You never can tell, you know. There are a lot of pervs who pretend to be lesbians and hang out in the various social media sites. I guess we'll find out."

"And your other two choices?"

Tori swiped the screen with her finger. "This one." She continued to scroll through the pictures until she came to her final choice. "And this woman."

"Agreed. Can you set up the meetings for us?"

"Sure thing, partner, on one condition."

"What's that?"

"You let me arrange for the next handywoman to fix whatever is broken in your house. Mmm, mmm, mmm. I know just the person, and I'll supervise her for you."

Lyn shook her head. She liked her business partner. A lot. "You are incorrigible."

†

Gail pushed the button on the side of the passenger seat to recline, as Dale pulled onto I-90. The faint hum of the motor along with the movement of the car started to lull her to sleep. Just like a crying baby, shove her in the car and, in no time, she's snoozing in the front seat. Her eyelids drooped before the upturn in pounding music startled her awake.

"Rap, Dale? Can't you turn that shit down?"

"Nope, not if I'm forced to drive to that Podunk town, way on the other side of the mountains in the middle of the desert. You need to stay awake and keep me company."

Gail reluctantly pushed forward the button to move the seat up. If she had to remain awake, she needed to get uncomfortable.

"Fine. I suppose that's a fair compromise."

"So, have you contacted whomever you're stalking?"

"I am not stalking her."

"Aha, I knew it. Stalking, texting, sexting, all the same."

"I told you I am not texting anyone and certainly not engaging in sexting. That's just, uh…."

"Don't knock it 'til you try it. God, you're already an old fogey, and you've barely turned forty."

"I can be adventuresome, and I like trying new things. I just prefer face-to-face interactions. I get to touch after looking," Gail argued. "Sharing provocative photos through a tiny screen doesn't do it for me. Maybe if I were on my way to their place, but you shouldn't text or sext and drive, you know."

"You're not driving now." Dale glanced at Gail and smirked.

"I'm not sexting anyone. Just drop it."

"Did you at least let her know you'd be in her neck of the woods?"

Gail folded her arms across her chest. "No."

"Do you mean to tell me we are driving three hours in the vague hope you'll run into a woman you insist you aren't stalking?"

"I guess, when you put it that way, it sounds a little crazy."

"You think?"

"I was going to send a private message later, in case she had time to meet and have a drink or something."

Dale laughed. "You're pathetic. You know, you used to be more confident. Where'd that go?"

"Just drive. I plan on playing it by ear. Spontaneity is a good thing."

When Dale turned back to concentrate on the road, Gail pulled out her smartphone and popped into her social media site. She supposed a short, private message telling M.B. she'd be in Moses Lake wouldn't register as stalking. She'd let the message dangle. If M.B. suggested getting together, it was definitely not stalking.

> Gail: *Hey you. Would you believe I'm going to be in Moses Lake in a few hours? I'm meeting with a client.*

When Gail didn't hear back from M.B., she slumped in her seat and pouted, refusing to answer Dale's questions with more than a one or two-word response.

The ping brought her out of her foul mood an hour later, then shoved her right back in.

"Crap."

"Trouble in paradise? I'm guessing your stalkee did not want to hook up today."

"Shut it." Gail looked again at the screen and smiled. She smirked at Dale and typed a new response.

"Why do I think you mentioned me, and not in a good way? Don't you dare say anything mean about me to your new girlfriend," Dale said.

"She's not…oh forget it. Think whatever you want to think."

Gail toyed with convincing Dale to stay the night. She could nonchalantly share with M.B. that they had decided to remain overnight in Moses Lake. Maybe it would be possible to meet for breakfast. Yeah, that was a good idea. She'd do that—after she sweet talked Dale into her plan, without exposing her unusual interest in a woman she'd never met in person.

"Sorry for being testy with you. I guess getting back into the swing of work has been harder than I thought. To be honest, your assumption about this particular job not being lucrative irritated me more than I should have allowed it to. I hope you'll keep an open mind." Gail wanted to prepare the soil for when she would seed the notion of staying in Moses Lake for the evening.

Dale glanced over and narrowed his eyes. "Fine, I'll keep an open mind, because I know something else is whirring around in your calculating brain."

†

Mandie couldn't believe her luck. Tori Fielding had responded so quickly to her submission and asked if she could bring her portfolio to the gallery. Mandie didn't have a portfolio. She hadn't even framed any of her pictures. *What was I thinking? I'm not a professional.*

Of all people to come to her rescue, her younger sister encouraged Mandie to let her fingers do the walking. She'd found a company online that could produce professional prints in a hurry. She'd selected the best of her negatives and digital files, and sent them next-day to the company. She now had her makeshift portfolio. She was ready to make the trek to Seattle only three days from Tori's request.

Mandie was on her way to Seattle when she heard the ping. She guessed the text was from Gail but resisted all temptation to read the message while driving. With her luck, that tiny distraction would lead to another accident. Maybe this time, it would be fatal.

Her smartphone beckoned like an alien tractor beam. A person was powerless to resist. After a full hour of self-torture, she pulled into the rest stop and pressed the button to satisfy her need. *Son of a bitch! Just my luck.* Gail would be in Moses Lake, and she was on her way to Seattle. It figured. Mandie wanted to meet Gail but was hesitant to suggest anything. Now the perfect opportunity to propose getting together was zooming out the window.

They were like two ships passing in the night. *That is a stupid analogy*, she groused. An image of star-crossed lovers made its way into her head, before her logical side reminded her, she didn't know this person. She'd formed an online friendship with Gail and seemed to connect to her in so many ways. It was an astonishing realization that since that first private message, she communicated more with Gail than she did with her father or sister. She'd wake up to a daily morning message and always went to bed with a final goodnight from Gail.

One of them would need to get off their ass and make a face-to-face meeting possible. *Oh right. Gail just did, and I had to go gallivanting off to Seattle.* Mandie decided the next move was hers. Even though she was hating the drive into Seattle, she would make the drive again. Maybe Tori Fielding would give her the perfect excuse.

> M.B.: *Darnit. I'm on my way to Seattle right now to meet with this gallery.*
> Gail: *Okay, maybe someday we'll get to meet. Hey, you aren't texting and driving, are you?*
> M.B.: *No, are you?*
> Gail: *LOL—No. My annoying partner, Dale, is.*
> M.B.: *Wish me luck. If I get this gig, then I'll have to travel more to Seattle. We could finally meet.*

Gail: *I'm sending every positive thought out to the universe. I'd like that. Now get back on the road so you aren't late.*
M.B.: *Bossy much?*
Gail: *LOL. Good luck!*

Mandie didn't care one bit if she sold any of her photos; she wanted an excuse to return to Seattle. Maybe her luck was turning around and she'd get her happily ever after with a meaningful career and someone to share her life with. It was never too late for that. As her mother always said, when one door closes, a window opens. *A window to love. I like that idea.*

†

The trendy Capitol Hill area in Seattle was the mecca for lesbians and every other letter in the alphabet. The term fluid sexuality popped into Mandie's head, and she wasn't sure why. That label seemed to fit and be all-inclusive. She chuckled to herself, as she thought of all the controversy over labels. She could see the incredible irony of insisting on terms such as nonbinary, questioning, or queer, when the new generation was not into labels. In what universe would those names not be considered labels? She didn't want to be mean or anything, but she agreed with some of the lesbians who insisted the L was disappearing or becoming so washed out. It was difficult to find the kinds of books that appealed to her.

Finding a parking space was, as usual, a total pain in the ass. Mandie circled the block six times, before she spied the blinking taillight. She caught the eyes of the driver in the car approaching from the other direction. She knew he was thinking of making a U-turn to nab this cherry spot. *Over my dead body*. She glared at him, hoping he would get the message. She'd gotten there first, and he'd better move along. He grinned and waved as he passed. *Gay man*. She knew she was stereotyping. In her experience, a gay man was more likely to accede a parking space than a white, testosterone-filled, straight guy who oozed privilege.

Mandie was still at least four blocks away from the gallery, but the walk would do her good. With each mile traveled, her anxiety had grown. She was now at the flushed neck, shaking hands stage. *Deep breaths, deep breaths.*

Before reaching for the door she looked at the building nestled between a cafe and novelties shop. She liked what she saw. The gallery had a charm with the red bricks and large glass windows, offering the casual observer a glimpse into the treasures inside. Mandie paused, as she took in the prominently featured sculpture of one woman offering comfort to another who was weeping. The emotion of the piece hit her squarely in the chest. Mandie wanted to purchase it without even knowing the price. It was far greater than she should consider—at least until she received the settlement from the skydiving company.

Feigning more confidence than she possessed, she yanked open the door and walked inside. The soft lighting calmed her nerves. The illumination showcased approximately twenty sculptures, artistically arranged to pull the potential consumer further into the artist's world. All of the pieces were of women in various stages of dress and represented a whole range of emotions. Mandie saw compassion, sensuality, eroticism, love, success, joy, disappointment, jealousy, anger, disgust, and so much more.

The art was beyond amazing. More than anything she'd ever wanted before in her life, she needed to become a part of this gallery.

"Hello. Are you M.B.?" a tall, striking woman asked.

Mandie switched the brown leather, newly purchased case to her left hand, then offered her right in greeting. "Yes, I'm Mandie. Are you Ms. Fielding?"

A beautiful smile appeared. "Yes, I'm Tori. You're a little early. Lyn should be here any moment." She took Mandie's hand in both of hers and squeezed. "I'm very excited to see the actual prints. They were so different."

Mandie coughed. "Um…yeah I didn't know how long it would take to get to Seattle, so I gave myself four hours."

A bell tinkled, and she turned her head to see another woman enter, whom she assumed was the other gallery owner, Lyn. While Lyn was not as striking as Tori, all of her features came together for a pleasant, overall effect. She was an attractive, middle-aged woman, who wore her age well. The slow smile on her face put Mandie at ease.

"Hello there. Welcome to our gallery. I'm Lyn." She ignored Mandie's hand and hugged her. "I know we'll get to the hugging stage, so I've decided to forgo the interim greeting ritual."

"And you call me a dirty, old woman," Tori quipped.

"Don't mind her. She's just pissed she didn't think to hug you first."

Mandie laughed. In less than five minutes, the gallery owners had set Mandie at ease.

"Come." Lyn gestured to the right. "We have a small conference room in the back. I'm anxious to see your portfolio. Oh, and Tori, she doesn't need your help. Guiding her to the room with your hand on the small of her back will give her the wrong impression." Lyn laughed.

"Funny, Lyn. You know I draw the line at inappropriate touching. There is something intimate about placing your hand on the small of someone's back. My wife told me, when I did that on our first date, it cemented her decision to join me for an after-dinner cocktail. And then…" She wiggled her eyebrows.

"In case you didn't realize, we practice this routine. It always works to put artists at ease," Lyn said.

"Thanks. It worked." Mandie sat in one of the plush, lavender, conference room chairs. She tried to keep her hands from shaking, as they rested on top of her case.

Once all three women had seated themselves, Tori took charge. "Okay, Mandie, let's see what you've got there."

Mandie unzipped her case and pushed it over to Lyn and Tori. They flipped through each photo, making small, mmmm sounds. Mandie wondered if that was a good sign or bad.

Lyn clapped her hands together when they reached the end. "Extraordinary. I hadn't envisioned anything less after Tori showed me the digital photos."

"Brava. I agree. We have one more person to see today, but" —Tori cupped her hand and whispered— "I doubt very much she will hold a candle to your art. This reminds me of the varied emotions our current sculptor elicits. Most artists have a narrow focus or style, but that is not what we're looking for here."

"How long will you remain in Seattle?" Lyn asked.

"Um…I hadn't given that much thought. I was going to turn around and go back today."

"Why don't we pay for you to stay at the Silver Cloud tonight? We can meet tomorrow to give a final decision and go over the contract. If that is the ultimate outcome. After all, you traveled quite a distance to meet with us. It's only fair we offer accommodations for the evening. Do you need to head back tonight?"

"No, I don't. That's very generous of you and I accept. Can you tell me how much that sculpture in the display window is?"

"Three thousand, and that, my dear, is a steal," Tori answered with a smile.

"I'll take it," Mandie declared. She thought it was reasonable. Considering the windfall coming from the settlements and what she already had saved in her retirement accounts, she believed it wouldn't be a problem. In a flash of sudden appreciation for her situation, Mandie realized she could message Gail to let her know she'd be spending the night. Maybe the two of them could meet for breakfast. Gail had made the first overture. Surely this wouldn't seem odd to her. She nodded to herself as the brilliance of her plan formulated. *I'll message her tonight after I'm settled in at the hotel and know more about my potential future with the gallery.* She hoped she could share the good news with her new friend.

"I'll make the hotel arrangements, while you sell her that sculpture." Lyn grinned. "Oh, and don't make dinner plans. We can all have dinner together after we grovel to our wives and apologize for having a late dinner meeting again. The cafe next door has an eclectic menu and the food is quite tasty. I'll get us a reservation for six thirty. Will that work for you?"

"Yes. That would be lovely," Mandie answered. "I can meet you back here at the restaurant, if you can point me in the direction of the hotel."

"It's down the road, walking distance from our gallery, but you'll want to drive there. They offer better parking options," Tori advised.

CHAPTER TWENTY

Since the clients were a pleasant surprise to Dale, he was ripe for convincing him to stay the night. He was in a good mood when he realized Podunk (Moses Lake) had very rich residents who could pay well for their designs. When he drove up to their current house on the lake, his eyes grew wide. Gail grinned. They'd walked out with a fat check to retain their architectural services, and the trip became worth every mile they'd driven.

Gail smirked at Dale, as she settled in the passenger's seat. "You may now kiss my feet in appreciation."

"Okay, so I made a hasty judgment. I promise not to do that again. Why didn't you tell me these people have more money than God?"

"Because the best teachings come in the form of actual experiences."

Dale turned his wrist and glanced at his watch. "So, we can head back and catch something to eat along the way, or try to find something edible to eat in town."

"Geez, apparently it takes more than one brick slammed against your head for you to learn. Careful, Dale, your pretentiousness is showing again."

He slammed his hand across his mouth. "Oh my God, I can't believe I'm about to say this. You're right. I am an arrogant prick sometimes."

"Sometimes?" Gail raised her eyebrow.

"Okay, most of the time."

"I was thinking we could grab something to eat and check out the town. You know, stay the night. I need to get a feel for the place, so I can create a better design for them."

Dale narrowed his eyes. "You've got something up your sleeve, and I have a feeling it has everything to do with your message mate."

"Do not."

"Prove it. Give me your phone." He put his hand out and smirked.

"I will do no such thing." Gail shoved her phone in her back pocket and took two steps away from Dale's outstretched hands.

"Fine, but if I see you texting while we're, 'checking out the town,' then I'll know you lied. Besides, you know I'm going to meet her eventually. I don't have a change of clothes for tomorrow, and neither do you."

"We'll go shopping. That's your favorite pastime anyway."

"I get to pick out your outfit for tomorrow."

"That works for me." Gail grinned.

Dale caught her eyes and set his laser-like glare on her. "You gave up way too easy on everything. Hey, no trips to the washroom either, unless you hand me your phone."

Gail held out her palms. "Seriously, I'm not planning to message or text anyone while I get a better feel for Moses Lake. I simply admit you have better taste in clothes than I do."

Gail had it all worked out. She'd get Dale drunk. While he nursed a hangover, she would make arrangements to meet M.B. for breakfast. All she needed was a few minutes in the hotel room to set things up. Dale would want to drop off the bags from shopping before dinner. That would give her plenty of time to message M.B. from her own room.

†

Mandie found the hotel. Because she liked to leave her options open, she had packed a small overnight bag. She'd read that I-90 was shutting down for a couple of hours to do blasting, as they continued with their major road repairs at the pass. She was thankful she didn't have to commute over the pass every day. It seemed like they were always working on the highway around the mountains. Every year, they threatened to make studded tires illegal, but they never did. Instead, the Department of Transportation was perpetually fixing the road. That was the primary reason for packing the bag. Besides, when she'd made the plans to travel to Seattle, she'd wanted to give herself plenty of time to spend with Gail, in case they connected. Now that Tori and Lyn had suggested she stay the night—on their dime—she had enough time to stroll around and check out the area. She debated whether to send a message to Gail before dinner or after. She wondered if Gail was still meeting with her clients in Moses Lake. Not wanting to interrupt her meeting, she decided to wait and send a message after dinner with Tori and Lyn. She could give Gail an update and toss out a suggestion to meet for breakfast at the same time.

Capitol Hill was very different from Moses Lake. Same-sex couples strolled down the sidewalks hand in hand, not bothering to hide a single thing. She longed for the freedom to do that. Feeling free to hold Caroline's hand hadn't been an option for her, even if she was willing to endure the stares or random, rude comments. Caroline had established the rules long ago. There would be no public displays of affection—period. Mandie wondered if Gail felt like she could show her love without restraint. She wasn't even sure if Gail had a partner. She'd never mentioned one, and none of the articles about her revealed her relationship status. Other than enjoying their back and forth messaging over the last several weeks, she didn't know a lot about the talented architect. Gail didn't even know her first name. Mandie had only put her initials on her social media page. Maybe they could change that when they met in person. That brought a smile to Mandie's face.

She found herself in front of a tattoo parlor. She briefly entertained the idea of venturing outside of her comfort zone, again. She'd never considered putting ink on her body, but the thought of it was more appealing to her now. A tiny tattoo on her ankle would be tasteful, yet adventurous. Before she chickened out, she pulled open the door. A bell tinkled, announcing her presence.

A young woman greeted her. Not only were both arms covered with ink sleeves, but her face showcased more metal than Mandie wore in both ears. Somehow, Mandie thought it suited her, and she smiled at the young woman. Her head was bobbing to 80s music, and her long, asymmetrical bangs flopped around to the beat. The hairstyle fit too. Mandie liked the angular lines created by her partially shaved head. Her multicolored bangs reminded Mandie of a rainbow.

"Hey. You looking to get some ink?"

"Yeah, I am. I'd like a small rainbow on my ankle," Mandie answered.

"Cool. Good choice. Do you want anything at either end of the rainbow?"

"Nope. Just the rainbow, please. Wait. I'd kinda like the rainbow to look like this." Mandie pulled out her smartphone and scrolled to the photo she had submitted, the rainbow manipulated to look like a tunnel.

The young woman peered over her shoulder. "Oh, that's wicked. Okay, I can do that. Take a seat, and I'll get everything ready." She pointed to one of the chairs, and Mandie settled in. She took a deep breath, preparing for the pain that was on the horizon. She'd survived jumping from a plane with a faulty parachute. *Bring it on.*

The buzzing of the needle wasn't able to drown out the ping from her phone. Although Mandie wanted to take a peek, she was in the middle of getting her tattoo and not willing to take a chance that any movement would mess up the art. The phone sat innocently on the table, just out of reach. She craned her neck, hoping to catch a glimpse. Too far. She couldn't read anything, and the message quickly disappeared.

Two hours later, Mandie decided this would be the last time she ever decided to be so extemporaneous—unless she plied herself with copious amounts of alcohol. She would forever call the tattoo artist's trade tool, the needle of Lucifer.

Gathering her bag and phone, Mandie retrieved her credit card and handed it to the woman. She'd almost forgotten about the message, but was reminded when she stuffed her phone in her bag. After she paid up, she would check her phone. She glanced at the clock on the wall. If she didn't get a move on, she'd be late for her dinner meeting. Mandie hated being late.

The cafe was only two blocks away, and Mandie pushed her body to its limits, as she hurried down the sidewalk in a half jog and power walk. She was still recovering from her accident and not quite at full capacity. She chuckled to herself. She probably looked like a disjointed cross between a penguin and a chicken. Mandie didn't care as long as she got there on time.

†

"Pinky's Shop of Fashion and Maurices! Those are our choices?" Dale complained. "Don't even get me started on my choices. Do I look like a North 40 or Walmart kind of guy?"

"Don't be so dramatic. You only have to wear it for one day. Maybe you can use the Carhartt pants or Wrangler jeans as a Halloween costume. Pick out a nice plaid shirt to go with." Gail smirked.

"Funny. I do not look good in plaid. If I have to buy Wrangler's, so do you." Dale pouted.

"I hate Wrangler's, they make my butt look big and flat. I'm strictly a Levi's gal. Can we please just go to Maurices for my outfit?" Gail needed to send M.B. a message, hence

210

she needed to try on various outfits in the dressing room of a women's boutique. She'd decided not to wait until they checked in at the hotel, because she was anxious to arrange the meeting.

"Fine, but you're going to owe me. I'm making you buy me a nice fitted shirt when I get to go to a real store in Seattle. Trust me, it will cost you more than both our outfits combined, and by the way, all the purchases and dinner are on you today."

Gail smiled. "No problem. I'll gladly buy your clothes." She snickered.

Dale selected a pair of slim-fit Wrangler jeans and a solid-black, long-sleeved Carhartt work shirt. At the counter, Gail picked out a bolo tie and an enormous silver belt buckle, and offered them to Dale. "I will scratch your eyes out with my bare hands if you don't stop right now," he threatened.

"But they complete the—" Gail giggled at his glare and ran toward Maurices.

With a pair of fashionable, skinny jeans and bright-colored tunic that complimented her Mediterranean complexion, Gail walked into the small dressing room and retrieved her phone.

> Gail: *Hey you. It turns out we'll be spending the night in Moses Lake, rather than traveling back tonight. How about breakfast tomorrow? I hear the bistro is a good place to go. I'll buy, because I know we'll be celebrating your success with your photos.*

She took her time trying on the clothes and called out to Dale to get her the bigger size, even though the jeans fit perfectly. Fifteen minutes later, she gave up on hearing from M.B. She hung the jeans and tunic over her arm. Grabbing a pair of underwear from one of the bins, she headed to the counter.

"You look like you lost your best friend. That can't be the case, because I'm right here." Dale's eyebrows shot up with his epiphany. "You sent a message to your lady love, didn't you? And, because you haven't heard from her, you're all sad again."

Gail pulled a credit card from her wallet and handed it to the shop attendant. "I'm starved. You're seeing a look of malnourishment on my face, that's all."

"Whatever. When are you going to trust me with the truth?"

"You're a terrible gossip; I'd never trust you with my deep, dark secrets."

"Now that really hurts. You know I'm the only person you confide in. I'll wait you out. Eventually, you'll come running to Uncle Dale when you have something to share."

The smile slipped from Gail's face. "I don't want to get my hopes up. Have you ever had the feeling you're supposed to be with someone before you've even met them? Like something great is around the corner."

Dale touched her arm. "Whatever is meant to be, will happen, hon. Trust in that. So, are you ready to tell me what the hell has been going on in Gail's world?"

Gail sighed. "I'll tell you over dinner and cocktails. Lots of cocktails."

CHAPTER TWENTY-ONE

Tori and Lyn were sitting at a small, round table in the corner of the cafe and waved when Mandie opened the door. Their broad smiles put her at ease as she approached the table.

She pulled out the chair and sat carefully, still feeling the tingle of her new tattoo. When her ankle brushed against a table leg, she winced.

"You okay? Let's put you out of your misery right now. We've selected your photos for our next exhibit," Tori blurted out.

Lyn chuckled. "Tori seems to have a lack of restraint when sharing good news but makes me give the bad news to the other artists."

Mandie liked the sound of that—artist. She was officially an artist now. "Oh, that's not why I pulled the face. I've just gotten a tattoo and it's still tender. Bumping into the table did not help."

"Oooh, let me see. I love ink on women," Tori exclaimed. "I presume it's in a location that isn't too private."

Mandie lifted her foot for both women to inspect.

"Mmmm, nicely done. Did the tat artist use your photo?"

Mandie nodded. "She did."

"How appropriate. Now you have a permanent symbol of your first exhibit, and perhaps this might come to mean something more for you," Lyn noted.

Mandie caught Lyn's eyes and wondered at the knowing look but chose not to respond. "So, I shouldn't admit this, but I have no idea where to go from here. Do I sign a contract? How does this work?"

Lyn patted her hand. "We have a contract to give you. I assure you; we are very reputable and treat our artists fairly, but feel free to have your attorney look it over."

"Okay. That's a good idea."

"Great. Then we don't have to spend the whole time going over the contract. We can get to know one another and enjoy dinner," Tori said. "Are you partnered, my dear?"

Mandie blushed. "No. I lost my job and fell from the sky, landing in the hospital for a little over a month. She dumped me. I don't think she wanted an unemployed girlfriend with a disability."

"Wow, there is so much in those two sentences. I don't even know where to start prying," Tori exclaimed.

Lyn laughed. "Then don't—pry that is."

Mandie waved her arm in the air. "Don't worry, I'm over it. I even met an online pal who had a similar circumstance. We've sort of bonded over our calamities. She's a famous architect, whose work I've admired for some time now. Speaking of which, I was running late and she may have messaged me. Do you mind if I check? I don't want her to think I'm ignoring her."

"You go right ahead." Lyn shot her that knowing smile again. Mandie should have felt creeped out, but for some strange reason she didn't mind.

"Ugh." The universe was conspiring against them. Perhaps meeting Gail was not in the cards. Then why did she feel this acute need to connect with the mysterious woman? Surely for some other reason than to compare notes on their different experiences after their accidents.

"Bad news?" Lyn asked.

"Sort of. The stars don't seem to want to align. Ironically, she'll be in Moses Lake until tomorrow, and I'm here in Seattle where her office is located. I suppose we could try to connect at a rest stop tomorrow, if she can time things correctly. That seems kinda tacky. Maybe I'll suggest she come to my exhibition opening. At least then I'll have a mechanism for putting my best foot forward," Mandie tittered.

"That sounds perfect. Maybe she'll bring her influential friends," Tori responded.

Mandie glanced back at the message and thumbed a response.

> M.B.: *Sorry. I was getting a tat. At dinner now with the gallery owners. Guess who is going to have an exhibition. Unfortunately, I won't be back to Moses Lake until later tomorrow.*
>
> Gail: *Congrats! I knew you'd be their choice. I'm disappointed, but I want an invite to your big opening. Is that what you call it? A tat?*

M.B.: *I'll show you when we meet. I'll send the gold-plated invite to your office. Gotta go. Schmoozing right now with the gallery owners.*
Gail: *TTYL Celebrating with some alcohol right now in your honor. So proud of you.*

The last message caused such jubilation, Mandie was grinning from ear to ear. Besides her parents, no one had ever said they were proud of her. She supposed that said something about her choice in partners. In the future, she would need to change that. Never again would she select someone like Caroline, who criticized her daily on her life choices. *I deserve to be with a lover who adores me.*

"Will you two be connecting after all?" Lyn asked.

Mandie shook her head. "No, not today, but I believe she'll come to the exhibition opening."

A slow smile formed on Lyn's lips. "I look forward to meeting the person who seems to bring such joy to your world. I find that either extreme happiness or sorrow unleashes the best in artists, though I prefer happiness. Sorrow or pain can result in depressing works of art. The piece you purchased today is an exception. That sculpture generates a feeling of compassion and hope for things to get better, as the title, *This Too Shall Pass*, suggests."

"I agree. That's how the piece spoke to me. I feel like I'm on the verge of everything getting better, after a whole load of shit was dumped on me," Mandie answered.

"Tell us more about you and this woman who seems to have captured your interest. I adore learning about our artists and their potential loves." Tori leaned forward and her eyes twinkled.

"That's because you're nosy and like to live vicariously through others. You love hearing about that initial spark of a new love," Lyn interjected.

"Whoa, back that love train up. We're merely computer pals. I don't even know the term for that. We can't call ourselves pen pals. There's no pen involved. Has this new world of technology given messaging friends a name yet?"

Lyn's brow furrowed. "I don't know what you'd call that type of correspondence. I am woefully behind the times."

"The younger generation has numerous terms such as e-pal, netpal, e-friend, keypal, or cyberpal," Tori offered.

"How do you know all that slang?" Lyn asked.

"Hey, I keep up. I'm hip to the new generation, you know." Tori pointed at Lyn.

Lyn laughed. "The fact that you use the term hip makes you as much a fuddy-duddy as the rest of us."

Mandie laughed. She had such a great time, sharing dinner with the gallery owners. She knew their friendship would last beyond the exhibition. She relished making new friends that were not part of Caroline's circle.

†

Gail was sipping her wine, when she felt the buzz in her pocket. Her need to keep the frequent messaging with M.B. on the down-low took a back seat to her excitement about the possibility of meeting the woman she'd taken an instant liking to. When she read the message, she groaned. Unfortunately, Dale was watching her.

He raised his eyebrow. "Bad news from your lady love."

"Shhh." Gail typed a response. She needed to remain upbeat and encouraging. At least M.B. would have her

217

exhibition in Seattle. Gail would move heaven and earth to be there. She wasn't about to let anything, even a client meeting, get in the way of attending that event. She was determined to be there for her new friend. Excitement bubbled up, as she realized she would finally get to meet the elusive M.B.

Dale sat back in his chair. Gail thought he was waiting rather patiently for her to finish. When she looked up, he asked, "Well?"

"I'm going to meet her, just not tomorrow. I had planned to get you drunk, then sneak out for breakfast while you were nursing your granddaddy of a headache."

"Devious. I almost respect you for that. Do I get to meet her as well?"

"Maybe. Her photos will be in an exhibition at a gallery on Capitol Hill."

"Oh goody." Dale clapped his hands together. "I love exhibitions. Which gallery?"

Gail frowned. "I don't know."

"Well you'd better find out."

"She said she would send an invitation to our office. I guess should get more details from her—just in case."

"Just in case what?"

"Well, with our luck, the invitation will get lost in the mail and never arrive. The universe seems to be conspiring to keep us from meeting."

"What exactly do you know about this person?"

Gail smiled. "She's funny and sweet. She's an amazing photographer, and we have this weird connection because of our accidents. Both of us were injured and dancing precariously on the edge between life and death for a month.

Not only that, but the accidents and the stint in la-la land, happened at exactly the same time. How freaky is that?"

"Wow! Maybe you met somewhere in the great beyond and are destined to be together. Oh, that is so romantic."

Gail smacked Dale. "You big mush ball. You know stuff like that is only in the movies. I don't believe in any heaven, hell, or whatever intermediate place there is where people hang out until their future is determined."

"That's because you have no imagination."

"Excuse me? I've been pegged as the most imaginative architect of my generation. At least that's what the magazine said about me."

"Sure, you're a genius at work, but your love life lacks any imagination. Let Uncle Dale help with that." He clapped his hands again. "Oh yes, I can help you woo this woman."

"I don't need your help." Gail pouted. "I've done quite all right on my own."

"Uh, Des?"

"A tiny mistake."

"Hmmm, what about Angie, Lucy, Hallie, and what's her name before that? I don't even know who came before her. Let's face it, you've had a string of failed relationships."

"Well aren't you the man with the biggest stone sitting inside that glass enclosure? I could design a better house for you that doesn't include all that breakable material."

Dale waggled his finger. "Uh, uh, uh. First, we weren't talking about me. Second, I don't want a Steady Eddy yet. When I do, you can be sure I'll be able to keep him. You've been ready to settle for some time now. Unfortunately, you either pick the wrong gal, or you push them away when you become absorbed in a new design. Another artist may relate to you. This new one sounds promising. How old is she?"

"I don't know."

"You don't know. God, she could be eighty and butt ugly."

"She's not eighty. Looks aren't everything, you know."

"Maybe, but you at least have to want to see them naked. If there isn't a physical attraction, then all the intellectual chemistry in the world isn't going to cut it."

"For you, maybe, but I'd like to think I'm not that shallow."

"Oh, please. I've met all your past girlfriends. Not one of them was a dog."

"Well, that's why none of them worked out. A pretty package but no substance."

"Perhaps, but why can't you have both? You have it all." He waved his hand over her body. "Smokin' hot outer layer and an appealing inner core."

"Besides, if she's the tall blonde in the picture on her social media page, she's stunning. Anyway, we're both getting ahead of ourselves. There hasn't been a single mention of interest besides meeting and continuing our friendship."

"Yet." Dale grinned. "You're enamored with her. Admit it."

"Fine, I am intrigued. I suppose I'll know right off when we meet if there is any chemistry, but I like having this friendship as a base. It's nice. Different, but nice."

"Here's to new friendships. Cheers." Dale lifted his lemon drop martini and clinked his glass with Gail's.

CHAPTER TWENTY-TWO

The easiest step in the process toward her first exhibition was passing the contract by an attorney. The labor lawyer Mandie had worked with at the hospital recommended one to her. The woman reviewed the contract and didn't see any issues at all. Instead, she remarked on how generous the offer was for a brand-new artist. That was all Mandie needed to hear. The contract was signed, dated, and mailed back by next-day air. The gallery was handling everything. They would arrange for food, marketing, invitations, and preparation of the final prints for show. In exchange for all that, the gallery took twenty-five percent of the profits. The arrangement was a no-hassle deal for Mandie. That was exactly the right game plan for someone who didn't have the foggiest idea how these things worked.

Lyn called, personally, to tell Mandie the date was set for the following month. This was far enough away to give them plenty of time to set everything in motion, select the final photos, and prepare the prints for the show. Mandie was almost afraid to believe no snags would occur. It was all going along so swimmingly…

"That will be perfect. I'll rummage around and find something to replace the one I don't want shown. I'd feel funny about displaying the photo of the woman with only a bedsheet wrapped around her obviously naked body. I can't do that without knowing who the model was who sat for me." Mandie began pacing as she talked. A nervous feeling rumbled around in her stomach.

"Mandie, that is the one that caught our eyes and the one that will snare prospective buyers. Unfortunately, this is not up for debate. While you are the artist, we know what sells."

"I'm afraid I don't know the identity of the woman. What if I don't have her permission? Isn't that some kind of violation? It seems too personal. Too raw. She's revealing far more than I believe she intended to share to the world."

"Yes, yes, that's the point. From the way she looks in the picture, I'd say she was definitely posing voluntarily. It wasn't like you were at some public event where cameras were not allowed. Without that picture as the centerpiece to the exhibit, it would not be the same. You've already signed the contract, which gives the gallery complete control over which photos are displayed." Lyn's matter-of-fact declaration left no room for any wiggle room. The photo was in, and Mandie couldn't do a thing about it.

Bile threatened to erupt, and Mandie barely kept her uneasiness at bay as she squeaked out a mild, "Okay." All that newly found confidence withered away. Mandie breathed deeply and made a final plea. "But, can you at least place it somewhere less spotlighty?"

"I can hear how important this request is to you, and I am not unwilling to compromise. We have a semiprivate room in the back, with exceptional lighting. We'll add your rainbow to that room as well."

Mandie's stomach settled. "Thank you." With that, the conversation ended and her fate was sealed.

Mandie hadn't built that dark room, and the other prints remained undeveloped. All she knew was the photos violated the drug store's policy. She suspected the woman in the one photo would be front and center in all the others.

Mandie tried not to let her frustration get the better of her regarding the massive hole in her memory. Caroline never messed with her camera. Obviously, Mandie had taken those photos. The woman staring back at her aroused such a strong reaction. Mandie had to know her—intimately, if one went by the expression on her face. Mandie couldn't imagine herself cheating on Caroline, but she didn't have a better explanation. That did not set well with her. No wonder she'd blocked this person from her memory. She probably felt guilt and shame over her choices.

She didn't believe the photos came from the photography class she'd taken several years ago. She vaguely remembered the session when the instructor had arranged for models to sit for the amateur photographers. She would have remembered this model.

Mandie's father and sister had moved out after she insisted, she didn't need their help anymore. She had to admit Hope had impeccable taste in clothing. They'd agreed to a quick shopping trip in Spokane, to select an outfit for the exhibit opening. However, acknowledging Hope's expertise did not stop her from complaining to Gail after the long day of shopping. Gail had lamented about her own personal shopper, her partner, Dale. He also had better taste in women's clothing, and she'd enlisted his talents to select her own outfit for the upcoming event.

✝

Nerves took over Mandie's body as though she were possessed by the devil himself. She plopped down on her couch.

> M.B.: *Please talk me out of eating a whole tub of chocolate-chip cookie dough ice cream.*
> Gail: *Why would I do that? LOL*

Mandie settled in for a long chat with Gail. They'd decided not to take things to a different level through any of the video programs available. They wanted the experience of their first good look at one another to be in person at the opening. That seemed more fitting to both women.

> M.B.: *Because I'll be sick all night long, and my drive to Seattle will be miserable.*
> Gail: *Oh right. Tell me again why you're coming to Seattle. LOL*
> M.B.: *Funny. If that is your way to settle my nerves, it's not working. You'll be there, won't you?*
> Gail: *Be where? LOL. Sorry, just kidding. Of course I'll be there. I've forced myself not to drive by the gallery. No sneaky glimpses before*

the main event. I want the full effect of your brilliance.

M.B.: <Groan> I'm afraid I won't live up to those inflated expectations.

Gail: Yes, you will. Have a glass of wine instead of the ice cream. It's a much better choice for anesthetizing nerves.

M.B.: Not if I only have one.

Gail: Then don't stop at one, but definitely stop at two—or three at the most. Wine hangovers are worse than ice cream hangovers.

M.B.: I can't decide if I am more nervous about the exhibition or meeting you.

Gail: I won't dictate how you should feel, but I can match your nerves and raise you to a state near panic.

M.B.: Oh no, neither one of us should panic, should we? I mean it's not like our parents have conspired to arrange a marriage.

Mandie wasn't sure what possessed her to write that. They hadn't talked about anything more than a possible friendship.

Gail: LMAO, now that would be quite the twist…an arranged lesbian marriage.

M.B.: I am looking forward to meeting you. Is that okay to say?

Mandie pushed things along just a little further on the off chance there would be a spark when they met face to face.

She knew she felt something during their frequent messaging sessions.

> Gail: *Very okay and ditto. Listen, I know we're friends and all, but can we leave the door open a crack just in case?*

Mandie jumped from her chair and danced around the room. When she heard the second ping, she hurried back to her laptop.

> Gail: *Sorry, ignore what I just typed, the fingers get me in trouble all the time. My mouth does it when I'm face to face, so be warned.*
> M.B.: *No apology necessary. Consider the door cracked or a window wide open. When I got canned, I thought that a door closed, but a window or two would open for me and they have.*
> Gail: *I'd better say goodnight then and end on that happy note. I'll wait to make a complete fool of myself in person, tomorrow. Sweet dreams.*
> M.B.: *You too.*

Mandie was smiling, as she walked to her refrigerator and retrieved an open bottle of wine. She poured herself a generous glass of Riesling and sipped the sweet and fruity wine before retiring for the night. The morning would come soon enough, and then, show time.

†

The realization that they'd exchanged messages every single night since the epic fail to meet up, hit Gail full on. She'd panicked at the slight delay in response time after what she called her "toe dipping" message. She sent a quick follow-up. Maybe M.B. wasn't on the same page as her. The ultimate reply sent her floating to her bedroom, dreaming about their first meeting. Finally, she would meet M.B. She knew they would hit it off in person as much as they had through cyberspace.

Gail had threatened to slice off Dale's man parts if he scheduled any clients for Friday afternoon. He'd grabbed his crotch and winced. With her afternoon free, she could buy fresh flowers and select an appropriate gift to celebrate M.B.'s success. She'd hesitated to ask Dale for a suggestion. If an idea didn't surface soon, she might have to get advice from the smug bastard. *Maybe something with a rainbow.* Capitol Hill was the LGBTQ mecca of Seattle. She was confident she'd find something with a rainbow.

Gail frowned. *M.B.* That would be the first thing she would ask when she met her cyberpal. *What does M.B. stand for?*

That night Gail dreamed about a tall blonde woman taking her hand and leading her into a rainbow tunnel. Gail was smiling and looking at the woman like she was the most important person in her world.

In a flash, everything disappeared. Gail was looking around in a fog of white, calling, "Mandie, where are you?"

"I'm here, Gail, come find me on the other side," a woman's voice broke the eerie silence.

"I can't. I'm not allowed. You promised to find me," Gail pleaded.

"I can't find the clues. We both have to try."

Gail walked on and came across an Amazon of a woman. She had to be at least seven feet tall. The woman was smiling but wagging her finger at Gail.

Next to the Amazon, a gray-haired woman smiled at Gail. "Don't worry, Gail, she's a softy under all that bluster. It will all work out the way it's meant to. I'll be there to help."

"They'll have to pass one more test," the Amazon remarked.

"I have faith," Gray Hair answered.

Gail's eyes popped open. She tried to remember the details of the dream, but they were already dissipating. The only thing that remained clear was the name, Mandie. The same name as in the bloody note. Gail smiled and reached for the worn paper on her nightstand. *Is M.B. Mandie? Could Lake be Moses Lake? Wishful thinking.* Gross as it was, the bloody note traveled everywhere with her. She couldn't seem to let go of whatever thread held her to some unknown destiny.

†

Lyn woke the next morning with the dream fresh in her mind. She'd known all along Transition Messiah was pulling most of the strings. Lyn was a willing puppet if it meant the two women would come together. She hated insisting that Mandie include the photo of Gail. It was so private. Yet, that was the price TM demanded to allow Evelyn to retain her own memories, start a new life, and assist the two souls. This was the test that would determine their fate. How Gail reacted and ultimately processed seeing herself hanging in the gallery would set the stage for their future.

228

Today was the day. *Were the other fluids hovering around the orb watching the events unfold?* She guessed a few of the more unsavory sorts were taking bets, and she wondered about the odds. She supposed she shouldn't be too harsh on those who still had a lot of time to kill in Intermediate. Anything to pass the time. She'd been tempted quite a few times herself and had capitulated to watching the orb for entertainment.

Her wife turned on her side and caressed Lyn's arm. "You seemed restless last night. I've never seen you stressed about an opening before. What's going on?"

Lyn leaned in to kiss her wife. "Just a feeling that something either special or disastrous is going to happen today, and I'm not sure which."

"That sounds ominous. I'm sure it will be the former. We've already had our major calamity for the year. I refuse to consider going through another nail-biting experience."

"Oh, don't worry, hon, this precognition is aimed at someone else."

"Not that I want any misfortune to fall on another person, but that makes me feel slightly more at ease." Eve chuckled. "You seem to be fond of your new artist. Is this about her?"

Lyn nodded.

"Hmmm. Should I be jealous?" Eve grinned. "I know how irresistible artists are to you."

"Don't be absurd. I have it on good authority we are a match made in heaven, or maybe pseudo heaven."

"Pseudo heaven? That's an interesting term."

Lyn grinned. "I don't think we know what happens to us in the great beyond. Having a near-death experience opened my horizons to the many possibilities."

Eve frowned. "Someday, you'll have to tell me more about that. Right now, I'm still too rattled by your accident to want to explore the topic." She pushed aside the covers and swung her feet to the floor. "I'll make you some coffee and breakfast. What time shall I show up for the opening?"

"You don't need to come early. Don't you remember how frantic I get right before the doors open? I like fooling you into thinking I've turned into a perpetually unflappable professional. You can come at three, or arrive fashionably late if you get in a groove with your new painting."

"No, if I start painting, I won't pay attention to the time, and I never miss an opening. I'll putter around in my garden until it's time to get ready, then I can be there right on time. Besides, you always seem to find something for me to do at the last minute."

"I do. What would I do without you?"

"We don't have to find out, because I'm not letting you go. I'll follow you into the depths of hell if that's what it takes."

"Don't worry. Neither of us are destined for hell."

"I suppose you have that on good authority."

"I do, indeed. Your wife has incredible pull with a powerful person." Lyn chuckled.

"Good to know I chose well."

"As did I." Technically, Transition Messiah made that choice, but Lyn was not complaining one bit. She couldn't have selected a better partner for herself and believed she was duly rewarded for her loyal service in Intermediate.

CHAPTER TWENTY-THREE

Mandie decided to ignore Lyn and Tori's advice and left early enough to arrive at the gallery before noon. Both gallery owners warned her that right before an opening was a frenzied time. They preferred not to have their artists caught up in the madness, which would only intensify their nervousness. Mandie knew she'd go stir crazy waiting in her condo. All alone, she'd be tempted to message Gail, who was probably busy working since she'd taken the whole afternoon off to attend the exhibit. Mandie would be forced to concentrate on driving, rather than ruminating over whether anyone would like her work. Or, think it was a pile of steaming poo. In reality, only one person's opinion mattered—Gail's.

With her coffee in hand, she walked out the door and slid into the driver's seat. Setting the mug in the cup holder of the middle console, she sucked in a large amount of air and breathed out. The sun was shining. Even though she wore her sunglasses, she pulled down the visor, then pushed the button to start her car. Mandie was on her way. She turned on the public radio station and listened to the news for distraction. Depressing. She connected her smartphone to the car stereo via Bluetooth and switched to her playlist.

Like Pavlov's dog, she couldn't resist peeking in response to the unexpected ping. She smiled when she read the short message.

> Gail: *You're on your way, aren't you? What a little rebel you are...Oh, and don't text and drive. See u later.*

A loud blast of a car horn brought Mandie's eyes back up to the road. She jerked the wheel to return to her lane. *Damn, I need to stop reading messages while I drive.*

After crossing the bridge over the Columbia River in Vantage, Mandie glanced at the signs warning about elk or deer crossings. Although she hadn't ever seen one on the highway, she knew this was a dangerous section. The road passed through Wanapum Recreation Area. Weary travelers did not heed the warnings, resulting in devastating consequences. She'd read somewhere over 1,000 accidents resulted in injuries and a couple of fatalities in Washington every year. Those numbers seemed high.

Mandie slammed on her brakes. Her car fishtailed, narrowly missing another vehicle on her left and the guardrail on her right. Gripping the wheel, she wrestled the car back in control. Her heart was pounding in her chest. When she loosened her grip, her hands were shaking. She'd missed the solitary buck who'd jumped the fence at the highway's edge. She was a believer.

Two narrow misses in one morning. *What final catastrophe is in store for me?* Things always happened in threes. So many possibilities for number three. The ominous cloud hovered for the remainder of her journey. She kept poking at it, wondering what would happen next. *Would the exhibition be an epic fail? Would Gail turn out to be a complete let down? Was I supposed to die in the skydiving accident, and today is the day the reaper will make things right?*

Mandie breathed a sigh of relief when she found a parking space not too far away from the gallery, and her car was stationary. Of course, Gail was hit by a bus. Just being parked didn't necessarily mean she was out of danger. Mandie shook her head. *Okay, now I'm being paranoid.*

Grabbing her purse, she wobbled a little as she made her way to her final destination. She needed to focus on walking in the damn heels. The shoes Hope had found to go with the new outfit were not only uncomfortable, they made it hard for Mandie not to stumble and land flat on her ass. She absently adjusted her clothing and wondered if anyone ever died from walking in three-inch heels. Looking hot in her new outfit took a back seat to those morose thoughts.

She paused before knocking on the locked door. When Mandie spied the chaos inside the gallery, she regretted her decision to come early. Tori unlocked the door and waved her in.

"Good, you can settle an argument. I think this photo should hang here and bullhead over there, insists it goes better on the opposite wall." Tori pointed at the rainbow print.

"Oh…um…" Mandie cocked her head to the side. "I'm not sure how to answer. I might kill my new career before it has a chance to start if I take sides."

Lyn laughed. "A diplomat. See, this is why we said you should arrive later. Now you've gone and done it, because we will insist on an opinion. You are the artist."

"But I've never done this before. I don't know the first thing about where each piece should hang. Isn't that your area of expertise?" Mandie asked. "Besides, I thought you were going to hang it in the back with…um…the controversial photo."

Tori threw up her hands in exasperation. "There's no way this ethereal rainbow belongs with the very definition of raw sensuality. I can't believe Lyn agreed to that just to appease you. The two photos are completely different. We do this every single time. It's a miracle we've survived our partnership for so many years. This dance occurs at every opening. Selection of artists is the easy part. We agree on that ninety-nine percent of the time. How to showcase the art is a whole other kettle of fish."

"Speaking of fish, I'm starved. Can we hold off on World War III while we grab something to eat? That may douse the fire. Everyone's crabby when they're hungry," Lyn answered.

"Now that is the first good idea you've had today." Tori smiled.

Lyn glared. "You're buying for making that mean comment."

"I'll buy," Mandie piped up.

Tori threaded her arm through Mandie's. "Oh, I like this girl. A preemptive strike. She's decided to butter us up so that when she weighs in, we'll go easy on her. Sorry, my little buttercup, you won't escape one of us becoming incensed with your choice."

"Don't mind her. She's kidding. Over the years, we've found that the artist knows best. Trust me, you will not be the first to ignore our advice. They always come early to settle these little disputes, don't they Tori?" Lyn threw her head back and laughed.

"Yes, they do. Thank goddess artists are neurotic freaks who must be in the muck of things, especially for their first show. Your wife was on the doorstep before we even opened the gallery. That's when you fell madly in love with her. She looked like a naughty puppy sitting there—all apologetic about ignoring our advice to come a half an hour early and not a minute before."

Lyn nodded. "True, true, she was so damn adorable."

"Speaking of adorable. Is your friend coming today? You were quite fetching yourself when you answered her messages at dinner." Tori grinned.

Mandie could feel the joy oozing out her pores and she smiled. "She is. I got a message from her this morning." Her stomach grumbled. "I haven't had anything to eat yet—I was too nervous—and the coffee is definitely taking its toll on my empty stomach. Can we go somewhere close? These heels are killing me."

Tori looked at Mandie's feet. "Hmmm, they go quite well with your outfit. Is the cafe next door okay again?"

"Sure. Thanks. Yes, my sister picked them out but forgot that I don't wear heels. I think she was born in them."

"They take practice," Tori answered.

Mandie was glad for the distraction of having lunch. After they finished, she would be able to concentrate on maneuvering the dangerous territory of where each photo should hang. The only thing she was adamant about was a more private and subdued placement of one particular photo. The sheet draped over the mysterious woman only enhanced that raw sensuality Tori loved.

†

Gail was twirling a mechanical pencil in her hand and dazing off into space, when Dale entered her office. She glanced in his direction and knew he was about to ask something that would irritate her.

"What do you want, Dale?"

"The Goldsmiths want to meet today to go over a few minor changes in the design. I know you said no meetings for the afternoon, but these clients are important. Can't you be a little late for the opening? It lasts several hours."

"Nope."

"Come on, please," Dale begged.

"No, I am not showing up late."

"We could lose them."

"So?"

"How about if I try to arrange for one? That should give you plenty of time to make it to the opening by three. I don't understand why you said no afternoon meetings."

Gail sighed. "Fine. I had you clear my calendar, because I knew you would try to do this. I needed the empty space to offer as a compromise, but if they can't meet at one, don't schedule because I won't show up. I hope you're happy now that I don't have time to pick up flowers and a gift. Oh, and one more thing. I'm leaving at two no matter what. I'll walk out midsentence if the meeting goes one second past two. Are we clear?"

"Yes, your Majesty." Dale bowed.

"Get out before I change my mind."

Gail was lamenting the loss of the shopping time. She had decided on a rainbow camera strap. She almost asked Dale to shop for her but somehow that felt more inappropriate than going to the exhibit empty-handed. He'd mentioned he wasn't able to make the opening, because he'd scored a date with some dreamy guy he'd been working on for months. As Dale was leaving, Gail's phone pinged.

M.B.: *Thanks for the message earlier. I'm not texting and driving, but I did peek when you sent the message. I almost crashed into a truck. Near miss number two was a deer in the road. I'm considering how to avoid the third impending disaster. Any chance you can come early to settle a dispute regarding where to place the photos?*

Gail: *No way. You're on your own with that. Besides, I just agreed to a late breaking one o'clock meeting. I will leave by two, even if I have to be rude to the clients.*

M.B.: *Don't do that. I know you'll be here. It doesn't have to be right at three.*

Gail: *But I want to be rude to these pretentious prissypants.*

M.B.: *Pretentious prissypants…LOL…that's a new one.*

Gail: *Better than pretentious pricks.*

M.B.: *Oh, I don't know, sometimes a bit of profanity is the perfect way to purge the system.*

Gail: *A girl after my own heart…so glad you won't be offended when I let a string of curse words flow in an instant of weakness...I have my moments.*

M.B.: *Hmmm...not touching that.*

Gail: *LOL...I'll be there on time. I promised, and I never break a promise to a beautiful woman.*

M.B.: *How do you know I'm beautiful? I could be 1,000 pounds with facial hair and warts. Would that matter? Could we still be friends?*

Gail: *I saw a pic on your social media page...Stunning Swede. The pic was blurry, but I could tell...and of course, we could be friends, no matter what you look like. I, of course, expect the same from you...you'll be my friend no matter what, right?*

M.B.: *I think I already am...too late for you to yank that away from me.*

Gail: *I am looking forward to finally meeting you in person, but even a good friend would not jump into the melee of temperamental artists deciding where to hang your photos.*

M.B.: *Chickenshit!*

Gail: *Uh huh...good luck with that, my friend. Hey gotta run, Dale is giving me his prune face.*

M.B.: *TTYL...in person.*

✝

Don't panic. Mandie turned her wrist to glance at her watch for the tenth time. The doors to the gallery had opened five minutes ago. A crowd of mostly women came pouring inside. Her face hurt from smiling at all the prospective buyers. Being the center of attention was not her cup of tea.

Her nervousness at that moment had less to do with meeting new people than it did with something profoundly more disappointing. She hadn't yet met the one woman she was searching for. None of the women who shook her hand were named Gail.

Lyn patted her arm. "Don't worry, dear, she'll be here. We've only just opened the doors. There is a power couple I would like you to meet. If either one enjoys your work, your future career is a lock."

Mandie plastered on a smile, as she let Lyn lead her to a stunning couple. Although the tall, honey-blonde woman gave her the once over, Mandie sensed the blatant cruise was more out of habit than anything else. Her gaze returned to the woman standing close to her. The softness and admiration for the dark-haired woman by her side was unmistakable. These two women were in love. Mandie offered her hand in greeting.

"Hi, I'm Mandie, the photographer for this little shindig."

The blonde shook her hand. "Lara Beck, and this is my lover, soon to be wife, Dillon Sanders."

Mandie's mouth hung open, as she realized Seattle's power couple and two of the richest women in the country were standing in front of her. Photos didn't do either of them justice.

"Oh…um…it's…uh an honor to meet you both."

"You've done it again, hon," Dillon said.

"Done what?" Lara answered.

"Rendered someone speechless." Dillon threw her head back and laughed.

"I feel confident it was you who rendered the lovely Mandie speechless." Lara turned her penetrant gaze back to Mandie. "I'd like to purchase the piece in the far back room and any others in the series, if you have more. I suspect there is quite a story behind that photo."

"I don't know if there are others, I haven't gotten around to developing the rest of the film. The canister was damaged and the drug store…uh…declined to develop the other prints."

A salacious grin formed on Lara's beautiful face. "Now that sounds far too tempting not to explore. I'll buy a photo lab and personally see to the development of those negatives, as long as I have first crack at the pictures."

Mandie could feel the color drain from her face. "I'd better develop them myself and take a peek before I offer them up for sale." Intuitively, she knew they were for her eyes only. She wasn't sure when that insight had come to her, but there was not a doubt in her mind those pictures would never be a part of any future show. She'd never sell them to anyone.

"I'll have the piece wrapped up and shipped after the show concludes. Would that be all right?" Lyn asked.

"Yes, absolutely. I wouldn't want anyone deprived of viewing that glorious photo, depicting a kind of raw sensuality I don't believe I've ever seen before."

As Mandie was speaking with Lara and Dillon, she felt an odd sensation. Not wanting to be rude to the power couple, she resisted the urge to turn around. She sensed someone waiting to approach. They hesitated and moved on. Mandie could still detect the crisp citrus scent as it passed. Gail was here. She inherently recognized that fact as surely as she knew the events that were about to unfold would mold her destiny. Before she extricated herself from the conversation and turned around, a loud gasp rose above the din of conversation in the gallery.

Mandie stumbled on her heels, as she attempted to run toward the noise. Tumbling to the ground, she kicked off the offending footwear and attempted to rise. She looked up into chocolate-brown eyes with equal parts anger, sadness, and confusion. The mysterious woman in her photo was standing in front of her, and one word came to Mandie's mind. Betrayal.

"Gail?"

"I don't understand. Why am I up on that wall, practically naked, exposed for everyone to gawk at? How could you do this? Humiliate me? Where…"

"I don't know. I can't remember," Mandie cried in anguish. *Walking hand in hand in a multicolored forest.* Mandie grabbed her head. A jolt of pain accompanied the waking dream.

"Mandie? Are you all right?" Lyn hurried to her side.

†

Gail loved living near a progressive city like Seattle, but on days like today, she cursed the social consciousness Seattle was famous for. She hadn't planned on being stuck in traffic for nearly an hour because of the massive demonstration in the center of town. If she'd remembered, she would have taken the long way and made it to the gallery in plenty of time to meet M.B. before the show started.

The only parking space was eight blocks away. Gail slammed her car door shut, then hurried to shove her credit card into the parking meter. After attaching the receipt to the passenger's side window, closest to the curb, she ran the entire eight blocks. She tried to catch her breath before entering the gallery. She glanced at her watch and sighed. *Only ten minutes late. Not too awful.*

Gail spotted M.B. right away but wasn't sure whether to interrupt her conversation to introduce herself. She might have to time her introduction. The lovely M.B. was more than likely going to be a very popular woman today. Gail strolled around the gallery and checked out M.B.'s work, so she would have something intelligent to say about the photos. Leaning in to look more closely at the rainbow tunnel that had caught her eye on social media, she saw the tiny signature in the corner. *Bingo.* Her first name was Mandie. Was that a coincidence? Mandie from Moses Lake, that was too weird. Gail stuck her hand in her pocket and fingered the rumpled note.

Mandie's talent was more than technical skill; each photo revealed a subtle essence that had the power to evoke emotions. Sadness. Jubilation. Hope. Despair. Each photo brought those feelings to the surface, teased them out whether the onlooker wanted them to or not. Gail kept sauntering through the gallery. In the farthest room, at the back of the gallery, a print was spotlighted with such care that the subject almost came to life. Gail gasped.

Blinking, she stared at…herself. A myriad of emotions flowed over Gail. She was drowning, and all she could do was gasp for breath. A commotion behind her startled her from the pain of betrayal. She turned to meet the eyes of her tormentor.

A quick exchange of harsh words left Mandie holding her head in obvious agony. Something loosened in Gail's pit of anger and despair. She touched Mandie's arm.

The spark between them generated a vision in Gail's mind. She and Mandie were dancing the tango. She felt a wave of arousal. Her gaze met pain-filled pools of blue. The anger dissipated, but confusion remained.

"I know you. I don't know how, but we…" Gail began.

Mandie blinked. A tear was set free and traveled down her cheek. "I'm sorry. I didn't know it was you."

Gail swiped the tear away with her thumb. "I know. I believed you when you told me about the picture and said you couldn't remember. Are you okay?"

"I think I've got the mother of all migraines. It's like my memories are trying to punch through."

"Let them, then we can make sense of…" Gail pointed to the photo.

"Come, dear. Let's take a little break for a few minutes. I'll get you some water." A woman whom Gail presumed was one of the gallery owners took Mandie's arm and led her to the private office in the back. An attractive woman extricated herself from a couple standing in front of the photo of the African woman and child. The woman helping Mandie said, "No, you go back and mingle with the potential buyers and settle my wife. She'll be worried. I'll get Mandie and…"

Gail followed Mandie and the woman in charge. "Gail," she offered.

"Yes, of course, Gail. I'm Lyn, one of the gallery owners, and that is Tori, my business partner." Lyn pointed to the attractive woman and said, "We'll be out shortly."

The business partner nodded and walked toward a group of women gathered in front of a wildlife photo. She took the arm of a chestnut-haired woman, whom Gail suspected was the gallery owner's wife, and whispered in her ear.

✝

243

Lyn wondered if Transition Messiah was satisfied with the final test results. Gail had rejected her anger and sense of betrayal. Her instinctive feelings for Mandie had apparently overcome the initial outrage at seeing herself flayed open in front of the world. The ultimate insult for such a deeply private individual. Love won out.

It couldn't hurt if Lyn led them in a certain direction. Could a suggestion of what might have happened cause any harm? Perhaps the two souls did not need all the finer details in the grand scheme of things. Wasn't that the reason TM had sent her back to earth?

Gail was looking at Lyn closely. "Why do I have this feeling I know you too? No offense, but for some reason, I'm thinking I gave you a nickname. It doesn't match you at all."

"Oh. Do tell?" Lyn grinned.

Gail looked down and mumbled, "Gray Hair."

Lyn laughed. "Mandie tells me that both of you had serious accidents, so did I. Do you suppose it's possible there is an in-between place where we met?"

"Seriously." Mandie was stunned. "You think that's the explanation for something I can't even begin to fathom?"

Gail's head popped up. "We danced the tango together, and it was…oh my God, hot."

"I should have never sent in that picture. I knew it was too personal," Mandie said.

"Nonsense. If you believe in fate, everything that has happened was destined to occur," Lyn insisted.

"Please, tell me you haven't sold my naked self to anyone."

"You're not naked in that picture." Mandie looked away.

"Lara Beck is interested," Lyn added.

"Lara Beck!" Gail exclaimed. "That's who you were speaking with when I came in. I should have recognized her. Figures. She's a letch. She probably made an indecent proposition along with her interest in my naked ass." Gail narrowed her eyes. "Well, did she?"

"No…um…she offered to have the other photos developed…" Mandie answered.

"Other photos?" Gail asked.

"Yeah, there were negatives not ruined in the jump. The drugstore wouldn't develop some of the prints."

"Oh, this keeps getting better and better. Please tell me you didn't agree."

"No, of course not. I told her I would have to develop them myself before agreeing to sell them to anyone—in case they weren't appropriate…"

"Gail, Lara Beck is not the kind of woman that Mandie should cross. While I can understand your reluctance to have yourself exposed, letting Lara have this one photo will guarantee Mandie's future."

"It's not for sale anymore." Mandie stood. "Take it down. Take it down right now."

Gail touched Mandie's hand and coaxed her back to the chair. She intertwined their fingers. "No, I give my permission for you to sell it to her, but only one. Don't make any other copies, please."

"I would never…" Mandie smiled. "What about one for my personal pleasure? I have just the place for it—right above my bed."

"Who goes into your bedroom?"

"I'll only allow one person into my bed or bedroom." Mandie looked at the clasped hands and then hopefully at Gail.

"This is crazy. You know that, right?" Gail grinned.

"Ah, sanity is overrated. Life is way too short to second guess intense emotions screaming to be set free. I almost died. You almost died. Isn't that enough of a message from the beyond to wake us from our dreary lives?"

"Not that you need my permission or anything, but I've never in this life or Intermediate life seen two souls more suited for one another," Lyn declared.

"Intermediate life," Gail and Mandie said in unison.

"Rings a bell, doesn't it?"

"Who are you, our guardian angel, or something?" Gail asked.

Lyn shrugged. "Well, I am something. Perhaps you'd prefer Gray Hair."

"Nah, it doesn't fit. I'll have to think of another nickname."

Lyn didn't think her meddling was needed anymore, but perhaps these two would remain in her life until she passed to the other side. When she was ready for that final journey, she hoped she would bypass Intermediate. She wasn't interested in going back, even if it meant seeing Transition Messiah again.

Gail and Mandie had both offered to sacrifice their own self-interests. That was most likely the final indication they were meant for one another. Both were willing to take a huge leap of faith, because it felt right.

†

Eve was so sexy sitting up in bed with her cheater spectacles perched on the end of her nose, reading on her tablet. She looked up and smiled at Lyn who was pulling back the covers and grinning like a fool.

"What are you grinning about? That was quite the bombshell today at the gallery. I still can't believe those two walked out together, seemingly in love. And they can't remember meeting before today?"

"Who's to say? Messiahs work in mysterious ways. Many religions believe in destined souls, reincarnation, or some other ways that true love can rise above the din of confusion."

"You're such a matchmaker. I don't know what you did when you pulled those two into the office, but it worked. I must admit, they had a certain glow about them. They seemed to fit. A match made in heaven."

"Not heaven, dear, but close enough."

"Why do I get the impression there is far more to this love story than you're revealing?"

"What will I have to surprise you with in our old age, if I don't leave a few confessions hidden? Someday, I'm going to tell you a story. Today is not that day. I will leave you to your reading the twists and turns in those books you favor. Just remember, life is truly stranger than fiction."

"Of that I have no doubt." Eve cocked her head to the side. "You know, ever since your accident, you are much more philosophical. I like it."

"I'm glad for that. I do love you, Eve. That love increases each day I unravel those little pearls about our life together."

Eve furrowed her brow. "I suppose that's good, because I don't think my love for you will ever stop expanding. You, my dear, are a habit I will never tire of."

One old soul and one repurposed soul joined in a passionate kiss.

CHAPTER TWENTY-FOUR

It had only been a few weeks, but Gail was itching to broach the topic of one of them moving closer to the other. They'd talked about somehow knowing this was right, but neither wanted to be the cliché. They were dating. The three-hour drive was inconvenient but workable. They'd done the unthinkable and held off on intimacy.

Mandie signed them up for dancing lessons. She wanted to learn to tango. Gail had laughed at first. When Mandie pouted and insisted she was serious, Gail agreed to the plan. The lessons were in Seattle, so that ensured Mandie would make the three-hour trek regularly. A big bonus.

Since Mandie didn't need to worry about keeping a regular work schedule, the Wednesday night classes could turn into long weekends for the couple. Gail thought she was smooth when she offhandedly suggested Mandie stay with her.

"Well, duh, why do you think I selected the Wednesday night class? A long weekend was the idea. I was going to invite myself to stay with you if you didn't come to the same conclusion. Good thing you have a razor-sharp mind," Mandie said. Gail outright laughed.

†

"Our first lesson is tonight. I swear to God, Dale, if you schedule any late meetings you will not survive to see another day." Dale backed away with his hands raised in surrender. Gail wanted to have an early dinner before the lesson. She hadn't expected Mandie to show up early—at the office. Gail hadn't allowed Dale to meet Mandie yet. When she heard them in the outer office, she cringed.

"Mmmm, well I must admit you're a lot finer than Gail described. No wonder she wanted to keep you all to herself, even though she knows this penis don't swing that way."

Mandie chuckled. "You must be the famed, Dale. It's good to meet you. Sometimes Gail doesn't speak unkindly about you."

"Oh, my, she got herself an honest one this time."

"Don't worry, it's common knowledge that people only give grief and tease the people they love. Otherwise, she'd ignore you and not even bother."

"Nice recovery. I need to thank you, because she is slightly less cranky since you arrived on the scene. I do hope she's getting some."

Gail catapulted from her chair and ran out of her office. "Don't you dare respond to that. He's like a heat-seeking missile once he gets onto a topic. He'll ferret out every single

249

detail of our love life. It's not our fault you squandered your opportunity to corner her at the exhibition."

"Oh, love life." Dale waved his hand in the air. "I don't give two shits about your love life. I want all the nitty, gritty details on your sex life."

Gail grabbed Mandie's hand. "We'd better head out now. We have dinner reservations we shouldn't be late for. You know how unpredictable Seattle traffic can be."

"Tootles, ladies. We'll have to get together for dinner one evening, so I can get to know this scrumptious creature," Dale called out as Gail tugged on Mandie's hand and led her away.

"That would be fun. I'll be here until Sunday afternoon. Maybe Thursday or Friday night," Mandie suggested.

"Don't encourage him. It only brings out his wildly inappropriate side," Gail gritted out under her breath.

"It's best to get all the questions out and determine which ones we'll answer and which are strictly out of bounds," Mandie replied.

Gail sighed. "Fine, tomorrow night. You only get one shot, then I'm shutting down the Spanish Inquisition."

"One night is all I ever need," Dale called out, as the door slammed shut and Gail and Mandie ran for the elevator.

†

The dance studio had the typical shining wood floors. She'd contacted the dance instructor to ask whether they should bring special shoes. Mandie wondered why they didn't have to wear gym shoes like when she was in high school. The school officials were always so particular about the floors in the gymnasium. The dance instructor had said they could wear whatever was comfortable but to bring a cloth to clean the bottoms before entering the studio.

Considering her performance at the gallery with the three-inch heels, Mandie decided that, no matter how sexy her legs looked in heels, she was not going to subject herself to the discomfort again. Gail had sweetly informed her she'd look sexy in a pair of motorcycle boots and to wear whatever was comfortable. Mandie compromised with a two-inch heel she thought went well with her tailored pants.

Mandie and Gail had advanced to video chatting on the nights they were not able to spend together. Gail went into greater detail about her vision of the two of them dancing the tango. That same night, Mandie had a vivid dream with similar images to what Gail had described. Her dream went further. Mandie was holding a camera, while Gail posed for her. Vivid sex dreams were rare for Mandie. This topped any she could possibly think of. She'd suggested the dance lessons the very next day.

After the instructor walked them through the basics, the music began. Gail and Mandie attempted to replicate the steps the dance instructor demonstrated. The two women were giggling as they began.

"Okay, this is a lot harder than it looks. I don't recall being such a klutz in my dream." Mandie took a tentative step to the right, throwing Gail off balance when she missed the beat by a half a second.

"Um, yeah, you were a lot smoother in my vision, too," Gail admitted.

"Well, I am nothing if not determined. If we have to take lessons for the rest of our lives, I'm going to become proficient at the tango."

"That's the spirit. By the way, you never told me the rest of your dream."

Mandie felt her face flush. "Um…"

"That good, huh?"

"Well, it involved my camera and you in some very interesting poses."

Gail stopped abruptly. She took a step away and released Mandie's hand, gazing at her intently. "You know, we haven't developed those other negatives yet. I'd rather not have anyone else but you and I see them. Um…do you think someday, uh…we might consider living together?"

"Wow! I'm trying to connect the two topics. That's quite a jump from photos to cohabiting."

"Forget I said anything."

Mandie chuckled. "No, no, I want to connect the dots, but I suppose I'd better answer your question first. Yes, I see us living together, someday, in one of your brilliantly designed houses. I haven't figured out where that might be, but I suppose it makes a lot more sense for me to travel in your direction. Any gallery exhibitions will more likely be in Seattle than Moses Lake."

"I was thinking that whatever house I design will have to include a state-of-the-art dark room, but I'm not sure I want to wait that long to see the rest of the photos."

Mandie frowned. "Now, that is quite the conundrum. I need a dark room to develop the photos, but we are a long way from that dream coming to fruition."

"Isn't there a college or something that offers photography classes and access to dark rooms? I'm surprised you haven't thought of that yet, considering you were quick to sign us up for tango lessons."

"Ladies, is there a problem?" the instructor asked.

Mandie grabbed Gail's hand and started to follow the steps they'd been taught. Their movements were jerky, and they stepped on each other's toes. "You're right. I'm going on the Internet tonight to find a class. Maybe I was hesitant to face some mystical thing I couldn't quite understand, but it doesn't matter now."

"Why doesn't it matter?"

"Because, I know" —Mandie stopped dancing again and touched her heart— "in here that this is right. We are right. No matter how risqué those pictures are, I won't reduce them to something tawdry and meaningless. Is it okay to say I've fallen in love with you?"

"Very okay," Gail answered. "I love you too."

"Ladies, do you need me to demonstrate the steps again?"

Mandie giggled. "We are terrible students, aren't we?" she whispered.

"Hopefully, you'll be a better student when you take that photography class."

"I promise to be the very best apprentice. I'll keep on developing those negatives until the pictures are crisp and clear. I can't wait to see them." Mandie wiggled her eyebrows.

"Letch. I thought you said they weren't tawdry."

"Not tawdry, but I'll bet they're sizzling hot." Mandie grinned and pulled Gail tight against her. This time, she hit her rhythm.

†

Gail hurried to Capitol Hill, where she planned on meeting Mandie for dinner. Mandie wanted to check out the

Capitol Hill arts workshop that offered classes on using a dark room. She'd also mentioned needing to visit with Tori and Lyn. Gail was so proud of her. Mandie's photos had sold well. Lyn and Tori were interested in creating a limited number of prints for prospective buyers who had indicated a fascination with Mandie's work. She'd messaged Gail earlier in the day to say they were already talking about arranging another exhibition in six months. They wanted to discuss the details for a new showing.

A few minutes alone with Mandie. That's all Gail needed, before Interrogator Dale showed. He'd been bouncing around the office with entirely too much energy. Dale only agreed to give her a little space after she threatened to show up late for an important client meeting. That strategy always worked. She used it sparingly, in case he called her bluff. In this instance, she needed to prepare Mandie for what was about to occur.

Gail jogged down the sidewalk to Purple Cafe & Wine Bar. She frequented the restaurant, which had great food. The close proximity to the office made it a favorite hangout for her and Dale. After opening the door, she glanced around the room and found Mandie's brilliant smile. She rushed to the table and placed a quick kiss on her lips.

"Hello, gorgeous, forget the food. You look good enough to eat." Gail pulled out a chair and sat.

"Where's Dale?"

"I engineered a reprieve of about thirty minutes."

Mandie laughed. "What did you threaten him with?"

"The only thing that works, a possible loss of clients. How was your day? Did you have fun?"

Mandie's dazzling smile returned. "I found the perfect place to develop those prints and signed up for classes. I might have to stay with you again, while I attend the course and learn about dark room techniques. Can I commute into Seattle with you?"

"Of course, and I won't argue if you bring me lunch again on any day you're hanging out in the city." Gail grinned.

"Hmmm, I guess you like me assuming the role of love slave."

"Well, it appears as though I've been your sex slave in another life, so it's a fair trade. Where are you hiding the negatives?"

Mandie blushed. "I carry them around with me, since I learned they might dance along the edge of social acceptability."

"Oh, my. I'm dating a kinky girl." Gail smiled.

Mandie wagged her finger at Gail and leaned forward. "So, level with me. How much digging is Dale planning on today? He really has no filter, does he?"

"Afraid not, but I believe his intentions are marginally pure. Well…as pure as Dale is capable of."

"It's a good thing we don't have too many details to offer on why we have such a connection. Lyn knows more than she's saying, but I couldn't wrangle anything more from her. I tried. I pushed for additional information, but she was tight-lipped. She threw away a few comments that we found our way to one another and there isn't a need to understand anything further."

"Have you had any more dreams?" Gail asked.

"I keep seeing us in this weird, multicolored world, dancing the tango and…uh…making love after a very hot photo session."

"Me too. Do you think it's possible that somehow, we met on a different plane or whatever you call it, while we were both in a coma? It's not like I've lost any other memories. I'm positive I would have remembered meeting you. Plus, there's my bloody note with your name Mandie and the word Lake on it, and those photos you can't remember taking."

"Bloody note?" Mandie asked.

Gail pulled the note from her pocket and smoothed it out for Mandie to see. "I've been carrying this around since the accident. Somehow, I knew it was important. I know it's kind of gross with all the blood on it, but I couldn't bring myself to throw it out. Only three words are visible. It's far too much of a coincidence for this Mandie to be someone other than you, especially since you live in Moses Lake."

"I guess it doesn't matter in the long run. Now that I've connected or reconnected with you, I'm not letting go. Is solving the mystery behind our intense chemistry that important to you?" Mandie asked.

"No, I guess not. I like the idea of some intermediate place and learning more about our time there through our dreams. It's so romantic. Don't you think?" Gail folded the note and put it back in her pocket.

"I do. One of the other reasons I love you—you're a mushy romantic. I was thinking we should wait to, you know, take this to the next level. Just because we've confessed our love doesn't mean we have to jump into bed. Maybe we could become more proficient at the tango?"

"I like that idea." Gail smiled. "It sort of balances the crazy out. On the one hand, we jump into a relationship with the vaguest notion we've met on another plane, but we bring back the sanity by slowing down the physical aspect.

Besides, anticipation is good, isn't it? My feelings won't change one bit if we wait. I suspect they will only grow— probably to a fervent level."

"I do love you, especially now that you're on the same page about not jumping into bed. Been there, done that before. It didn't work out all that well."

"I suppose it seems rather odd. If our dreams are accurate, we didn't wait before. Do you think that other place speeds up time or something?" Gail asked.

"I don't know. Perhaps we didn't have a whole lot of time, so our experiences were condensed or something—like cramming several years into thirty days. We have our whole lives ahead of us now and don't need to rush." Mandie grabbed Gail's hand and kissed it.

"Oooh, what did I miss? You two had a moment, didn't you? Tell Uncle Dale all about it."

Gail rolled her eyes. "Just remember, when he asks questions that are over the line, do what I do."

"What's that?" Mandie asked.

"Threaten to slice off his man parts." Gail grinned.

Dale's hands covered his crotch, and he pursed his lips in a frown. "You're mean. Now, stop picking on Uncle Dale and dish. I want to know how you two met."

Gail glanced at Mandie and she nodded. "Don't judge, but we're not exactly sure. We think we may have met when we were both in a coma."

"Shut the front door. That's so, oh I don't know, unbelievable."

"We're both having the same dream. Remember that note I had you recover at the hospital? Mandie's name is on it and the word Lake. The final clue is that picture of me that

Mandie took—way too many coincidences. Don't you think?"

"Well…I suppose when you put it like that, it's possible. Oh, it's so romantic, like a match made in heaven or something."

"I don't think we went to heaven—more like a holding zone—some in-between or intermediate place, I think," Mandie added.

"So, did you two have sex there?" Dale grinned.

"Don't answer that." Gail glared.

CHAPTER TWENTY-FIVE

For the first time in many months, perhaps even years, Gail was enjoying her time away from the office. She wasn't about to make the same mistakes with Mandie that she had with other girlfriends. Mandie deserved her undivided attention.

Although the plan for Saturday wasn't anything out of the ordinary, she was looking forward to walking along the path in the forest near her house. She hadn't taken the time to explore the area around her home, even though people bragged about the beauty.

They were having coffee, when Gail suggested they take a hike to Poo Poo Point, a scenic part of Tiger Mountain State Forest. Mandie started to giggle and they laughed for nearly five minutes.

"You're pulling my leg, I've never heard of this trail," Mandie said.

"Honest, it's called Poo Poo Point. The name came from the steam whistle sounds during the early logging days."

"Wouldn't that make it Choo Choo Point?" Mandie asked.

"Apparently not. I swear it's supposed to be spectacular. I'll throw in a picnic lunch if that'll make the difference."

Mandie set down her coffee and brushed her fingers down Gail's face before kissing her. "You had me at spectacular. I believe you, and I haven't been on a hike slash picnic in eons. I miss being outside, taking leisurely strolls, kayaking, or riding my bike. Can we make a pact we'll never be too old to enjoy the great outdoors?"

"We can. My job requires me to spend way too much time inside at a drafting table. At least your new profession lends itself to traveling outside or around the world." Gail sighed. "You'll make sure I don't get too pasty, won't you?"

"I will. Now come on, let's get this show on the road. I can't wait to see all the colors. I'm taking my camera."

"Is it okay if we stop at PCC to get our picnic lunch?"

"What? You're not going to prepare it yourself with your loving hands?"

"Not if you want to live to see another day. Cooking is not my strong suit, buying is."

Mandie laughed. "Okay, I can already tell that I'm going to have to be the one to take over the domestic duties."

"I can clean. Does that count? I don't even mind doing toilets."

"Perfect. I hate cleaning toilets."

†

Gail stuffed the food, a checkered cloth, and sparkling cider in her backpack. Mandie offered to carry half of their lunch, but Gail insisted. Just because she wasn't a giant didn't mean she couldn't handle carrying their bounty up the trail. Mandie made a heartfelt plea about starting off their relationship on an even plane, especially with the small things. Gail had to agree.

As they walked hand in hand on the trail, Mandie had to concentrate on slowing her long stride. She sensed Gail might be a little sensitive about her height.

The colors surrounding the two women as they walked among the fall leaves reminded Mandie of her dreams. Vivid color was such a big part of photography, and Mandie never tired of how nature created that ethereal beauty. Although she missed the vibrancy and odd combinations of color that made their way into her nightly visions, the fall colors came close.

"These colors are so beautiful, but not as stunning as what I see in my dreams," Gail remarked.

Mandie stopped in the middle of the trail and looked at Gail. "Tell me about your dream. Describe the colors, because I think we're having the same dream again."

"We were walking hand in hand, kinda like we are today. The trees, rocks, sky, everything was a rainbow of colors, but they were all wrong."

"Or all right." Mandie chuckled. "Maybe it's all wrong here, and wherever we were, was the correct way."

"That's a novel idea, but somehow I get the impression we engineered it that way. Maybe I was bored or you were bored, and we needed variety." Gail hopped up on a rock and took Mandie's face in her hands as she kissed her. "Now this is what I call being on the same plane."

"Works for me. Hey, this looks like a good spot. By the way, there was something oddly familiar about the way you kissed me." Mandie dropped her pack and unraveled the blanket she'd rolled up and attached to her bag.

"Hmmm, it does seem familiar, doesn't it? Yeah, this is a great spot." Gail unloaded the food and checkered cloth, laying out a beautiful spread for them to enjoy.

After they'd had their fill of curry chicken salad, cheese and apples, and a scrumptious couscous, Mandie folded her arms behind her head and laid back on the blanket. The fall sun warmed them. She'd taken off her light jacket, leaving a thin shirt as her only protection against the cool breeze and Gail's increasingly intimate touch. She felt Gail trace something on her stomach.

"What are you doing?" Mandie asked as her arousal rose.

"I'm drafting a very special house."

Mandie laughed. "I guess it's hard for you to go from sixty to zero. I thought you wanted to be a total slug over the weekend."

"Baby steps. Besides going on a hike is not a couch potato activity. I have to get this design out of my head before I lose it. Ah yes, that's perfect."

"How do you know it's perfect, the lines are invisible?" Mandie asked.

"I have a great imagination. In my head, not only do I see the whole plan, but I can envision it on your naked body."

Mandie sucked in an enormous breath. "Stop. Stop, or I won't be able to live up to our agreement to wait."

The fingers stopped their movement, and Mandie felt Gail's soft lips on her own. "Thank you for this day. I needed this. It feels so decadent to relax on the weekends." Gail laid back and nestled her body next to Mandie, connecting hip to hip as she reached for Mandie's hand and their fingers wove together. "I could fall asleep in the sun and take a nap right now."

"Let's do it. I love naps. They shouldn't be reserved for small children," Mandie said.

"Okay. You are going to be so good for me."

"And you for me."

"You know when I first realized I was falling in love with you?" Gail asked.

"No, when?"

"When I sent you that message telling you to get back on the road so you wouldn't be late for your meeting in Seattle. I remembered back to your first message, chastising me for not having a rainbow gif on my page. I thought to myself how we were already acting like an old married couple, and we hadn't even met yet." Gail released Mandie's hand and turned to face her.

Propping her head on her hand, Mandie rolled to her side. "I fell in love with you when I saw the picture of you with that sheet draped over your body. Remember when I messaged you about telling my dad I'd just met my future wife. I was only half kidding. I figured that whoever the mysterious woman was in that picture, if she was gazing at me like that, I'd found my soul mate. No one's ever looked at me like that, with such desire and anticipation." Mandie paused. "I was conflicted, though, because I also started falling for my cyberpal. When you said my picture spoke to you, I was halfway down that highway of love. Good thing sexy photo woman and my netpal were one and the same."

"I didn't know for sure if you were the stunning blonde in the photo on your social media page, but I assumed it was you. That reinforced my obsession. I hate admitting that, because it sounds so shallow. You at least described an expression versus my physical appearance."

"Oh, don't be too impressed. That sultry look was only part of the reason I wanted to find you. You are so beautiful; I can barely breathe around you." The small distance was too great. Mandie closed the space between them, kissing Gail as if it were the last day they had together.

Panting, they broke apart, and Gail lamented, "The no sex until we finish class rule is going to kill us."

"It'll be worth it."

CHAPTER TWENTY-SIX

The last day of dance class arrived. Without the women conspiring to coordinate their outfits, both wore their slinkiest, most form fitting dresses. Their unspoken idea was to recreate the experience each woman saw in her dreams. Gail didn't want to drive back to her home after the class. She'd arranged for a room at the Silver Cloud, which wasn't far from the dance studio. The challenge would be keeping her hands off Mandie until they slammed shut the hotel room door, closing the rest of the world off from the two of them and their passion for one another. Three months. That's how long they had waited for this moment.

Earlier in the day, Mandie had rushed into Gail's office, breathless. She clutched photos in her hand. When Dale's keen eyes landed on the prints, Mandie held them against her chest.

"Sorry, Dale, these are definitely not for your eyes," Mandie exclaimed.

"Well this is a happy surprise. Did you bring me lunch too?" Gail asked. "Run along Dale, nothing to see here."

"Aw you two are such killjoys," Dale answered.

Mandie was still trying to catch her breath. "No, babe, I'm sorry. I was too excited. After jumping off the bus, I ran the whole way to your office to show you."

"Dale, stop lurking and go get us all some food. We're not going to show you the pictures. If you're a good boy, we might tell you more about the theory we have on their origins. Just so you know, it's an outrageous notion, but we don't have another explanation," Gail offered.

"Promise you'll tell me. You've been leaving out details for the past three months." Dale pouted.

"We promise," Mandie answered.

"Turkey sandwiches from the deli okay with you both?" Dale asked.

Mandie and Gail nodded, and Dale left in a flourish.

"You're all flushed. These must be exceptional," Gail said.

"Oh. My. God. You have no idea. We definitely knew each other on a different plane or in a different life—really well, and more intimately than our current situation."

"We both agreed to waiting until tonight—after our last dance lesson." Gail looked into Mandie's eyes, seeking any indication of regret.

"I know, I know, but wait until you see these pictures. I'm not sure why the drugstore didn't develop the last photo that survived my father's brutal shove in the junk drawer. It's a photo of the two of us arm in arm, and we're fully clothed. I'm wearing the shorts I had on when I went skydiving. We look like we're in love. As for the other photos, if I was the photographer—and I sure hope that's the case—I was undeniably making love to you with my camera. I've never seen anything more…I don't even have words to describe how utterly amazing these pictures are." Mandie handed the photos to Gail.

The photo of them fully clothed was on top. Gail's heart stopped beating for a second. She saw herself looking at Mandie with an almost aching expression of love mixed with determination. Mandie turned toward her, and Gail recognized the same look of adoration as in the photo. Mandie was right. They were, beyond doubt, something special to one another. The next pictures brought forward distant memories of her feelings of excitement and arousal at what was to come next. They also brought a fair amount of embarrassment at being so stripped of any pretense or guard.

"I'm…uh…so exposed and so…"

"The raw emotion comes through, doesn't it?"

Gail flipped back to the first picture of the two of them. "I'm wearing the slacks I had on the day I was hit by the bus. That can't be a coincidence."

"No, I don't suspect it is."

"Do you have your camera with you?" Gail asked.

"I do."

"Will you make love to me with your camera tonight?"

Mandie took the photos from Gail and set them face down on the table in the outer waiting room. She gathered Gail in her arms, and Gail felt the love and yearning behind the kiss. The softness evolved into a spark of passion. Gail knew this was a small precursor to their special night.

After they broke apart, Mandie whispered, "Oh, you know I will."

"How in the world am I going to work after that kiss and my obsessive thoughts about tonight?"

"Take the afternoon off and come play with me."

"You are such a temptress but no. That would be far worse, because I wouldn't want to wait. I'd probably turn into some prehistoric humanoid, claiming her mate as she drags her into the temporary lair."

Mandie laughed. "That's not exactly the picture I have in my mind." Mandie collected the prints from the table. "I'd better not leave these lying around. I wish you had a safe or something I could put them into."

Gail held out her hand. "Here, let me put them in one of my canisters and tape them up. I'll put your name on it in big black marker, so I don't mix them up with any of my other designs. Can you imagine me sitting with a client and pulling them out?"

Mandie roared with laughter. "As funny as that is to picture you showing your bare ass to clients, I'd better take those with me and lock them in your car for safekeeping until we can tuck them away in your house. My mission this afternoon will be searching for a fireproof safe where these pictures and the negatives can be stored without the threat of them falling in the wrong hands."

Mandie handed the pictures to Gail who walked into her office. She rolled the photos into a canister. After drawing Mandie's name in large block print on the outside, she set them on her desk. "Don't forget to take this with you after we have lunch. I don't want Dale poking around and finding them."

"Oh, heavens no, you would never hear the end of it."

"End of what?" Dale blew into the office, holding a large white bag.

"Never mind, nosy," Gail answered.

Dale's eyes landed on the canister. "Is Mandie a new client?" He grinned.

"Keep your paws off this canister. I swear, if you so much as put a pinky on this, I'm going to—"

"I know, I know. Give me a sex change. Now, let's have lunch, while you tell Uncle Dale the real story of how you two met. Remember, you promised."

†

The music began and Gail and Mandie were immediately lost in each other's worlds. Mandie raised their hands together and spun Gail around. She pulled her close using their clasped hands that rested against Gail's stomach. She moved ever so slightly behind Gail, forcing her to rock with her, before she used her free hand to stroke Gail's left shoulder. As she breathed warm air against her neck, she let her lips slide across her skin. Mandie's left hand moved down Gail's shoulder, then across her breast to a quivering stomach. She used the tips of her fingers and palm of her hand to brush over Gail's behind. She repositioned herself face to face with Gail. She clasped her right hand with Gail's left, as her other hand moved to the small of Gail's back. She brought their bodies abruptly together again. Pushing out their intertwined hands, Mandie found the rhythm of the music and began the first steps of the dance they'd been practicing for months. She blocked out every other stimulus except the beautiful woman in her arms. After the music stopped and the dance was finished, she brought her lips to Gail's and kissed her with unbridled passion.

Clapping startled the two lovers. "I believe you two are the best students I've ever had. Brava. That was indescribable."

"No offense, but we're going to cut our session short tonight and…" Mandie said.

The dance instructor smiled. "It's been a pleasure teaching such eager students. You ladies have fun tonight. The tango is the ultimate dance of passion, and none of that is lacking between the two of you. Oh, to be young again."

Mandie grabbed Gail's hand and giggled, as they ran out of the dance studio.

†

"You know, with a few minor differences, I feel like this is the ultimate déjà vu. We're in our own twilight zone." Gail was standing in front of the bed waiting for direction.

Mandie lifted the camera to her eye, twisted the dial, and pressed the shutter. The sound, as Mandie depressed the shutter in rapid succession, stirred an instant reaction in Gail. She struggled to maintain her composure. Gail observed Mandie in slow motion, lifting the camera strap over her head and setting the camera on the desk. Her movements were deliberate, as she stepped into Gail's space and reached around to the back of her dress. Mandie gently tugged the zipper down.

The caress against Gail's shoulders of the slinky black dress sent shivers up and down her spine. Her swollen anticipation was almost too much to endure. Gail licked her lips. The brush of Mandie's fingers made their way down her chest and unclasped her lacy black bra. Gail reached around and returned the favor, by slowly unzipping Mandie's dress.

She pushed the silky fabric down, and it fell to the floor. Mandie stepped out of the dress wearing only her underwear.

"Stay just like that when you take the pictures," Gail breathlessly requested.

Gail's near undoing came when Mandie used that same feather-light touch to remove the matching lace underwear. She took Gail's hand and led her to the side of the bed. She pushed the covers down, then gathered all of the pillows to one side of the bed. She positioned Gail against the soft pillows.

With a gentle stroke, Mandie lifted Gail's arm above her head and arranged her in repose against the headboard. Mandie nodded her approval. "Just like that. Let me capture this moment."

Gail was laid bare, without a stitch of clothing. Mandie's appreciation was evident in the intensity of her appraisal. Gail kept her posture open and willing. She wondered if Mandie saw the same smoldering look she'd seen in the original photos.

The click of the shutter sent Gail into overdrive again. She wanted to touch herself. When she'd looked at the pictures, it was clear that she'd been pleasuring herself in front of the photographer. She wanted to again.

Mandie lowered her camera. The look in her eyes was full of love and passion. "Yes, you can touch yourself."

Gail instinctively knew Mandie had, once again, caught on camera the exact moment of her climax. She'd heard the click of the shutter. Crying out Mandie's name, she ached to have Mandie join her on the bed and feel her mouth and hands as they roamed all over her body.

With all her senses on high alert, she heard Mandie set the camera on the dresser. She felt a slight breeze, as Mandie neared the bed. Finally, they were skin to skin, exploring every inch of each other's bodies.

Gail found the small rainbow tattoo on Mandie's ankle and traced the outline with her fingertips. "I like this. It feels like a permanent reminder of something we don't quite remember. Maybe I should get a matching tat. This rainbow would suit me better than tattooing your name across my breast."

Mandie laughed. "I know. That's exactly what I thought, but I'm wounded you don't want to inscribe my name on your body."

After several hours of lovemaking, Gail said, "I think I'd like to take a photography class. Is there any chance I can use your camera after I learn a few tricks?"

Mandie rolled to her side and caressed Gail's face. "Lifelong learning is a good thing. Yes, of course you can use my camera."

"I'd like to make love to you like you did with me. You have no idea how completely out of the universe that feels."

Mandie smiled. "I might have an inkling, but from another vantage point. For some reason, I have the urge to set up a timer and make sure we capture both of us on film at precisely the right moment. Thank God for remote devices."

"Lifelong learning, huh? So, dance and photography classes, those were a nice beginning. Ever wondered what all the fuss is with tantric sex?" Gail asked.

"I'm sure there's a class we can take. If one doesn't exist in Seattle, I'll bet we can fly somewhere and find a workshop or two."

"I'm game. I'm going to enjoy all this learning we're about to embark on. Can I talk to you about something else?" Gail wasn't sure if this was the right time, but she decided there was no time like the present. Life could slip away in an instant. "You didn't open the canister, did you?"

Mandie quirked her eyebrow. "No, why?"

Gail slipped from the bed and walked to the chair where Mandie had set the canister. She pulled open one end and removed her design. Unrolling the large sheet of paper, she laid it on the bed in front of Mandie. "This is a special house design I drafted. The idea began formulating right after I awoke from my coma. Do you see the curves? Does it remind you of something?"

"Yes. I've seen this in my dreams."

"I want to build this house for us."

"Is this your way to ask me if I'll move in with you?"

"Yes, and the promise of even more in the future. I won't ask you to marry me right now, but consider this design a big diamond ring."

"I accept."

Gail moved to Mandie and climbed into the bed, then gathered her in her arms. They kissed with enthusiasm. "I have a piece of land that's kind of in the boonies but close to Seattle." Gail shifted on the bed. "We can look around Moses Lake as well," she added.

"No way. Your office is in Seattle. There is not one single thing tying me to Moses Lake. I love you for offering, but I'm more than happy to move west. We can keep the condo for when we want to get sun after feeling the drizzle too many days in a row.

"I hope you weren't lying when you said you love cats. We're a package deal, you know—Xena, Gabrielle, and me. They don't much like when I leave them to the cat sitter during my long weekends. I'm feeling guilty for rescuing them from Caroline, then leaving them so often."

"I love cats and have been meaning to adopt a kitten. Now I have a ready-made family and a vacation condo. Good plan. I love you," Gail stated.

"I love you too. I told you I would find you again. Destiny will always prevail."

"I'm glad you finally believe that. Yes, it will. We had a little help from some unlikely sources." The image of a tall Amazonian woman flashed in Gail's head, and she smiled.

"I may have been nuts when I jumped out of an airplane," Mandie acknowledged, "but when a door closed, I jumped through a window. A window to love."

ABOUT THE AUTHOR

Annette is an award-winning author, published by Affinity Rainbow Publications, who lives in the beautiful Pacific Northwest with her wife and their five furry kids. With sixteen published novels and one Goldie Award for her fourth novel, Locked Inside, she finally feels like a real author. Annette is as much a reader as a writer and is always looking for the next lesfic novel to queue up. She came up with the One Fan at a Time tagline, because it rolled off the tongue much better than One Reader at a Time. After pondering who she was at her core, it was all about connecting to each reader on a personal level. Annette would be the first to admit she doesn't do well with the masses. If someone picks up her book and it touches them, she believes she has achieved what she wants with her writing by reaching each reader. It is who she is at her core.

Drop her a line, she loves to hear from readers
annettemori0859@gmail.com.

Sign up for her mailing list
Check out her blog: Everyday Occurrences
Visit the Affinity Rainbow Publications website for her
books and many other outstanding authors:
https://www.affinityebooks.com

OTHER AFFINITY BOOKS

<u>Free Spirit</u> by Erica Lawson
Priory McAllister has fought off boardroom sharks, handled high-pressure jobs, and thought she'd seen it all. She found her dream home and couldn't wait to move in. Unknown to Priory, two ghosts…Rhee and a mischievous Dylan…have inhabited the house since 1935. They have no intention of leaving. Jacey Ryder, Priory's long-suffering secretary, gets to play referee between her boss and a bossy ghost, as each side try to lay claim to the house. What can she do when an unstoppable force, (her boss) meets an immovable object, (the ghost) besides hope for a peaceful solution? They are like two peas in a pod—two *angry, stubborn* peas in a pod.

<u>Addicted to You</u> by Erin O'Reilly
Elin Prescot's dream to be a top fashion designer is finally within her reach—then Marissa Banks enters her life. Snared by her first taste of passion, Elin is consumed by desire for more. Her life spirals out of control until she meets Doctor Aimee Sullivan, who understands all too well what Elin is going through. Can Elin let Aimee into her heart? Or will her addiction keep her enthralled with Marissa? This story

explores first love, intense passion, manipulation of emotions, and the gentleness of real love and true romance.

<u>At Last</u> by JM Dragon
A perfume company in trouble, leading to a town in peril. Old Loves. Unrequited Loves. New passions. Can the reclusive Gene Desrosiers save her family company and the people she cares for, even though some are not aware of it yet? Will an ultimate sacrifice win the day, or will Grady end up a ghost town of unfulfilled lives? This love story will warm your heart.

<u>Deuce</u> by Jen Silver
When Jay Reid was in her twenties, she had it all. A professional tennis career, Charlotte, the love of her life and a new baby. Charlotte's research vessel, *RV Caspian*, was lost at sea, leaving Jay to raise their child alone. Rescued by a local fisherman, with no memory of her life before, she lives on the Faroe Islands as Katrin Nielsen. Seeing a beached seal one day triggers her memory. Twenty-three years is a long time. Is the love they once shared strong enough to be rekindled or have too many years passed eroding all hope of a happy ever after?

<u>After Dark</u> by Samantha Hicks
Can a love that starts out in terror be real or last? Meredith Ashcroft disappears on her way to a client meeting. Five months later, art gallery manager Stephanie Edwards is also held and tortured by the same sadistic man. Thrown together trying to overcome their shared ordeal, they find themselves falling in love. Is it true love or just an attachment to each other born out of fear for their lives?

<u>The Book Witch</u> by Annette Mori
What if someone had the power to bring characters from a book to life…should they be allowed to glimpse reality? Imara is that person, a book witch who is convinced of her superiority, especially over book magicians. Join award-winning author, Annette Mori, and the gang from Asset Management, The Organization, and the colorful women in The Book Addict to bring you this delightful, magical romance.

<u>Calling Home</u> by Jen Silver
Sarah Frost, director of the Frost Foundation makes her home at a writers' retreat—The Lodge on the Lake. Galen Thomas, who is taking a break from her vet's practice goes to the island to fill the post of handy person. A revelation of events from forty years earlier, threatens what they now call home. Will the lives and loves of Sarah, Berry, and Galen survive the disturbing past legacy?

<u>Reach of the Heron</u> by Angela Koenig
After an automobile accident takes the lives of her parents and nearly her own, Arkadia O'Malley faces a painful recovery. She also seeks custody of her younger sister, Rini, and contends with Irish law. Arkadia's efforts to reunite with her sister are aided by powerful women from this reality as well as from Elsewhere. Will they find her in time to save her?

<u>From Wind and Water</u> by Laura Kovack
Surrounded by the Lands of Earth, Fire, Water and Wind is the Seventh Kingdom. All but Earth have rulers. A new

enemy threatens all Lands and it is imperative to find the last ruler of Earth. Morgayne, ruler in Land of Water and Ventus, ruler of Land of Wind, form a tentative relationship in this quest. Will they allow or deny their feelings in this fantasy adventure?

The Book Addict by Annette Mori
This is a captivating story of Tanya, a young woman whose life is without any friends or lovers. When she meets Elle, the alluring owner of the new bookstore. Tanya is immediately infatuated with the mysterious woman. Maybe, the books won't be the only thing enchanted if Elle allows the magic of love to enter her heart.

Colors of Rage by Nanisi Barrett D'Arnuk
Dr. Kailyn DeKendran, head of the Acoustic Research Department, and her sister Jayanta, are drawn into a fray of unrest. When Kailyn disappears, family and friends band together to find her. Time is running out, and the riots are getting more violent. Will they find Kailyn before it is too late to put an end to the madness that has overtaken them?

Naomi's Soul by Renee MacKenzie
This is the second book in the Karst Series and picks up where Kai's Heart left off. Everyone is still struggling to find the balance between reconciliation and guarding. Warrior Naomi Adams is on a routine mission for the Peace Movement when a devastating earthquake strikes her contingent. She will need to dig deep to find the strength to move past what has split up her party.

My Starlight by Loryn Stone

If only we could have met sooner…
Orly Kochav likes nerdy things including beautiful girls. When she meets Danielle Cohen, the rising attraction to her threatens to make Orly question every choice she's about to make.

<u>True North</u> by Ali Spooner
Cam's story continues as the Gator Girlz business thrives under her leadership. Will self-doubt jeopardize her relationship with Luce? Will a devastating injury to Sandy end her career as a gator hunter or open a door to love? Join the St. Angelo family for a third adventure to find out more about life, loving, and family in Bayou Country.

<u>The Dream Catcher</u> by Annette Mori
What if all your dreams — the good ones and the nightmares—came to life in the real world? Heaven is a Dream Weaver, and that is her reality. She meets the alluring Maya and the powerful Dream Catching sisters. Time is running out for Heaven. Who she can trust? Can the lovely Dream Catcher Maya protect her or is Heaven truly on her own?

<u>Gator Girlz</u> by Ali Spooner
In the sequel to Diamond Dreams, Cam St. Angelo finished her freshman year on a high. Her softball career is on path and everything seems to fall in place for Cam and Tab as the new school year and softball season take off. All too soon, unfortunate events at the home front force Cam to leave college and her softball dreams behind. As always, it's family first.

eBooks, Print, Free eBooks

Visit our website for more publications available online.

www.affinityrainbowpublications.com

Published by Affinity Rainbow Publications
A Division of Affinity eBook Press NZ LTD
Canterbury, New Zealand

Registered Company 2517228